THIS TIME MIGHT BE DIFFERENT

Stories of Maine

OTHER TITLES FROM ISLANDPORT PRESS

Closer All the Time by Jim Nichols

How to Cook a Moose by Kate Christensen

Settling Twice by Deborah Joy Corey

Straw Man by Gerry Boyle

THIS TIME MIGHT BE DIFFERENT

Stories of Maine

ELAINE FORD

With a Foreword by Wesley McNair

Islandport Press
PO Box 10
Yarmouth, Maine 04096
www.islandportpress.com
books@islandportpress.com

First Islandport Press edition published March 2018.

ISBN: 978-1-944762-44-5
Library of Congress Control Number: 2017952156
Printed in the USA by Bookmasters

Dean Lunt, Publisher
Cover and book design by Teresa Lagrange, Islandport Press

Once more,
for Arthur

Je pense que oui

OTHER BOOKS BY ELAINE FORD

The American Wife

Life Designs

Monkey Bay

Ivory Bright

Missed Connections

The Playhouse

TABLE OF CONTENTS

FOREWORD

In today's literary scene, the recently departed Elaine Ford was an anomaly. She never attended a writers' conference with the intention of networking for her career. She didn't promote herself on Facebook, or send out email blasts when she published a book, or tweet her followers about her latest literary achievement. She simply wrote. In the process she created several notable novels and some of the best short fiction that this state, known for its writers, ever produced.

Maine is at the center of the stories in this book, and she knows its town life and nature intimately. She takes us inside the state's factories, churches, grocery and hardware stores, and apartment houses. We enter the homes of the poor and the beach houses of affluent summer visitors, discovering what the inhabitants eat for dinner, and how they talk to each other as they eat it. She shows us mud season in early spring, and what the mud looks like after a late snow falls on it. And when a Down East native gives a woman from away a tour of the seashore, Ford knows just how to describe the crabs, crumb-of-breads, and dog-whelk barnacles they encounter.

But her most impressive achievement by far is her characters. Like all exceptional writers of fiction, Ford understands that everything depends on the people she creates and the choices they make. Women are central among the choosers—girls who decide between empty home lives with family elders and moving in with dubious suitors, or disappointed women in middle age offered a second chance with old lovers who've reappeared. Sometimes the crucial choices of her characters have been made before the story starts, as in the darkly comic "Elwood's Last Job," where a mentally challenged man discovers in a laundromat a group of town women who once mocked him in childhood, then robs them, duct-taping their ankles, wrists, and offending mouths. Other times, Ford brings a central figure right up to the edge of a life-changing decision and ends the story, as in "Millennium Fever," asking us to imagine what choice Carlene will make as we consider her conflicting motives.

On her website, Elaine Ford explains that she is drawn to characters who are "marginalized by class, ethnicity, physical appearance, or geographical location." At the root of her inspiration is a raw belief in the democratic ideal of individual worth and equality that this country was founded on, and has so often betrayed. Grim as the circumstances of her characters may sometimes be, there is a kind of solace that gradually emerges as one reads her work—a sense that here is someone who understands and cares about their plight. Others, including many of her fellow writers, may have turned away from them, but for her, they matter.

Ford is such a good writer that she makes us pay attention to them, too. Starting a story by Elaine Ford is like falling into a trance. Her plots are not applied from the outside, but rise from the inside out, as we experience the urgency of a central character's feeling and thought. The words of her dialogue are both natural and precisely right for the characters who speak them. Ford links descriptions of setting and the mood of her stories with the hand of a master. And her images have the surprise and compression of poetry.

That poetry comes to mind when one reads Ford is no accident. She loved it so much that she often committed poems to memory. Once when I asked her in an email why poetry was important to her, she answered: "Oh, that's easy. It's the attention to nuance and detail, rhythms of speech, devotion to the accuracy of language. For me a good poem is nothing but a short story told with extreme concision." Talking of poetry, she seemed to speak also of her own work.

How fitting it is that Islandport Press has brought out this collection—not only because of the press's importance as a publisher of Maine writers, but because Elaine Ford was so deeply committed to Maine in her fiction, writing stories about this place, and in the end, about all human places.

Wesley McNair

THE DEPTH OF WINTER

OVER A DEAFENING, pounding roar the buzzer sounded. Like a great beast brought down with a single bullet, the machinery halted, and the last few rings tinkled from the trough into the drum. Kori let the muscles in her shoulders go slack. "Gawd," Freda said, yanking her earphone out, "thought that buzzer would never go off." Kori followed her to the honeycomb of cubbies by the coat rack, where they grabbed their mugs. Everybody headed for the stairs, gumboots thumping on riserless steps.

The only good thing you could say about the break room was that it had windows, unlike the welding room downstairs. If you wanted, you could look out on the icy bay, the cannery, the fishing boats moored in the harbor, the boulders on the shore. Kori liked to watch the sea birds. Her favorites were the crook-necked shag, black devils that drove the fishermen crazy because they gobbled up the fry. So deftly they pumped their wings low over the water and dove into it. Yet how awkward they looked perched on the boulders, their wings outstretched to dry like they were pinned to a line by their elbows. You didn't see shag at this time of year, though. Kori didn't know where they went.

On the hot plate the kettle hissed and spat. Freda carried it to the picnic table and filled their mugs, which contained instant coffee or teabags. Gladys spread the county newspaper on the oilcloth and turned to the obituary page, Freda ragging her about how everybody Gladys knew was under a gravestone or about to be, and Gladys saying the deceased were better off than some, spared having to listen to a load of nattering. Freda, the elbow of her sweater out, looked into her rumpled paper bag as if expecting a surprise, found a peanut butter sandwich and a banana. On the opposite bench frail old Miriam opened her lunch box and took out a hard-boiled egg, tapped the shell against the box. Everything the same as every lunch break since Kori graduated from high school and started working here.

Kori took her mug and stood at a window. Below in the freight yard boxcars inched along a siding. The guys who worked in the yard would pack the boxcars full of crates of metal rings, thousands and thousands of rings, and send them jerking out of town, out of Maine, their wheels screeching on the rails. By next Christmas the rings would have boughs of spruce or balsam wired to them, and they'd be nailed to doors all across the country.

"Aren't you going to eat, girl?" Freda called from the picnic table.

But Kori didn't feel very hungry. The sandwich her mother packed would gag her, the filling too thick, the bread too dry. She'd make do with coffee.

Later, after work, Kori went into Henegan's Variety to cash her paycheck. She had a little time to kill before Freda would be through in the Pick 'n' Pay and honking for her outside, so she wandered back to the table of marked-down seasonal merchandise: plastic mistletoe, strings of tree lights half ripped out of their packages. She thought the cut-glass oil lamps would be kind of pretty if you dusted them off. Not real crystal, of course.

Though gardens and fields lay frozen under a foot of snow, this year's seeds were already in stock. Kori twirled the flower rack and admired the color-splashed packets, tempting new hybrids of cosmos, zinnia, marigold. She imagined the field behind her mother's vegetable garden filled with flowers of every variety and color—shell pink, crimson, creamy white, butter yellow. Kori would be able to wade into them and gather them by the armload.

Metal struck metal. Across the aisle, in the hardware section, a guy was plunking handfuls of common nails into the scale pan. He wiped his hand on the seat of his jeans and took one of the paper sacks by the nail barrels. A good-looking guy. Dirty-blond hair that curled on the collar of his jacket, lighter stubble on his cheek. She didn't know his name but she'd seen him before, hanging out with some other guys, lobstermen. He stuffed the nails into the sack and then, as he was turning toward the register, looked straight at her. Kori felt prickling in her armpits. After a moment he said, "You're Emma Eade's kid, aren't you?"

Without answering she returned the packet of cosmos seeds to the rack and moved the other way, into a thicket of rubber hip waders and sneakers, boxes stacked tipsily in the aisle. "Don't tell me Emma taught you not to talk to strangers," he called after her, and then she heard a croaking sort of laugh.

~

Grab wire with left hand, fit ends into clamp, jam foot on pedal, *hiss*, with right hand drop ring into trough, with left hand grab another . . .

The top of Kori's head was too hot under the heater that dangled treacherously on chains suspended from the ceiling. She imagined her hair smoldering and then bursting into flame. At the same time her feet on the concrete floor felt like blocks of ice. The smell of singed metal burned in her nostrils. Her back was killing her. Every bone in her body vibrated to the yammer of the machinery, and her nerves twanged at the same shrill pitch as the rings spinning into the drum at the end of the line. Thank God it was almost quitting time. Maybe she'd get a Walkman to plug up her ears like Freda had. Or maybe she'd just stop by the front office and tell Mr. Stinnett, "I quit."

It wasn't much of a job, though people told her she ought to be glad to have it, considering how scarce jobs were in town. She guessed she'd been hired mostly because of her looks—she'd heard Vernal Stinnett had a weakness for pretty girls—but at least the old man didn't bother her. And it was steady, regular, a paycheck you could count on every Friday afternoon. Not like waitressing at the Brass Lantern, where you'd most likely be laid off during the winter months, or cramming sardines into tins at the cannery, where you'd only have work if they brought in a catch. Or worse yet raking blueberries in August and brushing in the fall and making wreaths at home to sell to Vernal Stinnett, scramble scramble scramble, the way her mother always had, no steady man bringing home the bacon.

She remembered that guy's crack: *Don't tell me Emma taught you not to talk to strangers.* Emma would do well to take her own advice, he meant. Well, he could go to hell, Kori didn't care what he thought.

At the sound of the buzzer the machine shuddered and quit, and no more unwelded rings came slithering out of its mouth. The women bunched around the time clock and retrieved their coats from the row of hooks. "Who wants a ride today?" Freda asked. "You, kid?" Kori shook her head, but old Miriam went out with her, even though she didn't have far to go.

Outside the galvanized-iron building Kori found a dusting of new snow, gritty like cornmeal, scattered on top of the ice in the factory yard. Dusk was gathering and a mean wind whipped off the bay. Kori hurried past the shut bakery, Phil's Video and Redemption Center, the gas station. Across the road, beyond the church, the Brass Lantern was blasting an aroma of hot grease into the frigid air. She wondered who'd be inside, lingering over coffee and cigarettes, maybe, or a beer. For a second she pictured herself sitting in a booth with a crowd, her parka unzipped, her long coppery hair bright against the vinyl upholstery. She might be smiling at a joke her friend Britt or one of the guys had made. Music would be playing on the jukebox, bittersweet keening after a lost love. Smoke would encircle them.

But she didn't cross the road. Instead, she turned the corner onto Bridge Street. There Kori paused a moment and watched the river current moving recklessly toward the bay, tide going out and pulling the river water with it. She shivered and cursed herself for not hitching a ride with Freda, wondered why she hadn't, except for some reason she hadn't been in the mood to be stuffed between the two women in the cab of Freda's pickup.

On the far side of the bridge the road became Route 1A. It followed the river for a while, and then struck out on its own. If you went straight you'd get to Freda's place, on the River Road a mile or so beyond the fork, up on a rise. An old house painted white, with a sign out front that said *Small Engine Repair.* Freda's brother did the repairing.

At the fork Kori stayed on 1A. The road wandered in a northeasterly direction across some marshy land, which gave way to rock-strewn blueberry fields—everything under snow. One or two vehicles trundled by as Kori walked the shoulder of the road, past a farmhouse with sheds, more fields, a trailer. By now night had truly fallen. She came to a cluster of ramshackle houses and trailers and junked cars at the Finney place and then a stretch of woods.

Here was higher ground, but you couldn't see any lights ahead—or behind you, either, if you turned to look—no dwellings within a quarter of a mile. In the woods Kori heard a bird call, an owl maybe. Then a pickup slowed and pulled to a stop on the shoulder. Some gravel flew up from under the truck's tires, peppering her leg like buckshot, and a man leaned over to the passenger side. He rolled down the window. "Give you a lift?"

She saw it was the guy from Henegan's. "No, thanks."

"Sure? Cold out there."

"I'm fine." She started walking again before he revved the engine and pulled back onto the road. For a while she watched his taillights, like a pair of glowing red eyes, and then they disappeared.

The road dipped down to a stream, frozen over and buried under layered crusts of snow at this time of year, and then up again. Nearly home now, a quarter of a mile to the strip of land they farmed on the right side of the road, corn stalks sticking out of the snow, and the big old farmhouse with the falling-down barn attached to the far side.

In the mudroom Kori unlaced her boots and left them on the floor next to her mother's, hung her coat on a peg. The kitchen was warm compared to the outside. Wood wet with snow hissed in the stove. Emma stood at the sink peeling potatoes. Her hair, once wheat-colored but now threaded through with gray, was twisted into what looked like a mouse nest at the crown of her head. Stray tendrils curled around her face and on her neck. She half turned to smile at Kori and said, "How'd it go today?"

"Okay," Kori answered. She took cutlery, bent and mismatched, out of a drawer and set places on the table. Stew tonight. She could tell without even looking in the kettle. A few stringy pieces of beef in a gravy thick with lima beans and corn they'd grown and canned themselves, chunks of potato. Nourishing, but heavy and bland, always gristly knots in the meat. She had no taste for it.

"Tired?" Emma asked.

Sure, she was tired. She didn't have the strength in her arms that her mother had, or a broad back, or thick muscular legs traced with blue veins like Emma's. She could feel Emma's watchful, worried eyes on her, and she lifted a shoulder, as if she could flick off her mother's glance like a bothersome insect. The room seemed suffocatingly hot now, so hot her eyes watered. At the window Kori peered beyond her own reflection, out onto the snow-covered field, and pressed her forehead against the icy glass.

Her mother set plates of stew on the table and scraped her chair back. "More snow tonight, they're saying on the radio." Kori nodded, and sat, and put a forkful of meat and beans in her mouth. She chewed slowly, focusing on the dried goldenrod, now colorless and brittle, that Emma had arranged in an earthenware crock last fall. The limas were mealy as candle wax, and the meat had a rank aftertaste. "Every winter seems longer," Emma went on. "This time of year is the worst." She sliced a piece of bread and spread apple butter on it. "No wonder people take to bashing each other."

Kori looked at her mother, then down at her plate. More than once she'd seen her mother with bruises on her neck or shoulder after hearing sounds, thuds and intakes of breath, in the night. Emma had never talked about it. Nobody was ever around in the morning. "You could take up crafts," Kori said after a while. "Sell them on the stand, to the summer people."

"I've seen what they sell to the summer people. I wouldn't waste my time on that kind of rubbish."

"It was only an idea."

"Your food's getting cold." Emma sighed, her hand resting on her big breast, her fingers spread across the flowered cotton material. Kori watched her mother's hand rise up and down as she breathed. "You don't eat enough. That's the reason you're so peaked."

Pee-kid, a word Kori had heard since childhood, a label she hated.

"Ma, don't start."

Emma frowned and got up to stoke the wood stove. Kori looked out the window and saw that it had begun to snow again.

⁓

Saturday night Britt picked Kori up in her Pinto, and they drove the forty miles to the movie house in Millettsville, the county seat. A light snow was falling. The tinny little car skittered on the road, its wipers whacking and its radio playing staticky pop music. Britt puffed on one cigarette after another and talked about her boyfriend, a guy from their class who'd joined the merchant marine. Most of their classmates were gone now, off in the service or moved south to find work. Britt bagged groceries in the Pick 'n' Pay, a job she loathed. The stingy old goat of a manager was forever breathing down Britt's neck and giving her a hard time.

The movie house stank of perfumed bug spray and stale popcorn; your shoes stuck to the floor because of all the spilled drinks. Still, Kori always felt a quiver of excitement when she pushed through the door, anticipating the new world she'd be invited to enter. Kori and Britt chose seats near the back. Before the lights went down Kori noticed that guy who'd talked to her in Henegan's, ambling down the aisle with a couple of rough-looking characters. She turned toward Britt and started to say something, hoping he wouldn't see her, but before she'd got two words out he'd swung into the seat next to hers and was staring at her. Crystals of melting snow glistened on the shoulder of his jacket. Could be beer she smelled on his breath.

Kori dropped her eyes and Britt said, "Did you want something?"

"Just to say hello."

"Well, hello and goodbye," Britt said.

For a moment he continued to look at Kori, not saying anything. She picked at a small hole in her mitten. Then he got up from the seat, letting it bang so hard Kori could feel the impact jolt her spine. "Enjoy the show," he said over his shoulder.

"You know him?" Britt asked.

"No," Kori said.

"He's one of those Duggans that have camps down on Coffins Neck."

Coffins Neck? That's why he was driving in that direction the night he stopped to give her a ride. "Oh," Kori said. "In the bog."

"Pete, I think his name is. He seemed to think he knows you."

"Well, he doesn't."

The lights dimmed, and the previews of coming attractions came on. Over the soundtrack Kori could just hear Britt say, "Duggans are nothing but trouble."

~

Monday after work he was there waiting for her, in a black pickup with scars from past collisions and scabs of touch-up paint over rust. Since Freda was watching her, and Miriam right behind her, Kori decided not to argue there in the parking lot. He leaned over to open the passenger door, and she climbed into the cab. "Are you following me, or what?" she asked.

"It's cold out. Shut the door."

She slammed it and said, "I don't want you following me." They watched Freda and Miriam get into Freda's truck and pull out of the lot, and then Gladys roared past in her old heap. Kori yanked on the door handle, but the latch didn't open. Stiff or frozen, maybe. She never should have closed the door. What was she thinking?

"I just saw a doe," he said. "On Bridge Street."

Kori half turned to look at him.

"I was heading onto the bridge and she came loping down the middle of the road right toward me. I thought sure she was going to get her hooves caught in the grate on the bridge. Would have been a shame." He glanced at the shotgun in the rack behind them. "Sure wouldn't have wanted to have to shoot that poor old doe. Out of season, too."

"I bet."

"Just before she got to the bridge, she scrambled down the rocks to the riverbank and vanished into thin air."

"You must have dreamed it. I never saw a deer in town."

"Swear to God." His eyes seemed very dark, the color of tar or blackstrap molasses. A touch of stubble on his cheek. "I'm heading up 1A, " he said. "I'll give you a lift home."

"How'd you know where I live?"

"Bought a dozen ears of corn off your stand, more than once. Don't you remember?"

Maybe she did, kind of. Across the street she could see the lights on inside the Pick 'n' Pay. Pete started the engine and rammed the truck into gear. "Wait," she said, but he didn't. The truck lurched out of the lot.

Kori wondered if Britt was inside at the checkout counter. She wondered what Britt would think if she knew what was happening.

On the bridge Pete let the truck idle and told Kori to look down. Maybe she'd spot the doe. All she saw was the black river channel spurting into the bay, and great slabs of seaweed-encrusted ice piled against the banks, and sea smoke rising from the bay in billows. But she thought the doe might be there, invisible, disguised somehow. She couldn't say she wasn't.

He drove up along the river and then swerved right onto 1A. Dusk already, too cloudy for stars. The marsh seemed dark and secretive, hidden under snow.

"How long you been working at Stinnett's?" he asked.

"Half a year, about."

"What's it like?"

"Not so bad. Kind of boring."

He switched on the radio, but could find nothing but static—a nest of hornets—and switched it off again.

Behind them in the open truck bed she could hear various kinds of gear rattling. They passed the Finney place and then the spot by the woods where she'd said no to a lift. Now here she was in the truck and hurtling along at some speed, although a thin layer of new snow was slick on the road. He turned on his wipers but didn't slow down, even as the road sloped down toward the stream, and she felt the truck lose traction for a second. Only one of his hands on the wheel. "Careful," she wanted to say, but didn't.

At the top of the rise she said, "Slow down. The house is coming up on the right."

"You don't really want to go home yet, do you?"

She had a momentary image of the overheated and stuffy kitchen, of Emma's broad-beamed body at the stove. "What else do you suggest?" she asked, a little surprised at the way her own voice sounded in her ears. Wise, like Britt. He didn't say anything. She listened to the wipers crash back and forth and looked at the falling snow, tiny swirling black flecks in the headlights. On the right the snow-covered garden slid past, and then the old house—lights on in the kitchen—and then the tumbling-down barn. Kori felt the truck accelerate, and once in a while it briefly slipped onto the shoulder of the road. She was scared, yet at the same time she was enjoying it, in a way, the wildness.

They passed the town boundary sign and in another hundred yards the truck abruptly turned to the right, brakes screeching, onto an unmarked road. The truck bounced along from pothole to pothole, the loose gear in back slamming violently into the sides of the truck. A couple of times her head hit the roof of the cab. She couldn't imagine how he could see where he was going. He must know every twist and turn in the road, every rut and pothole, by heart.

Without slowing the truck dived into an even narrower road, room enough for one vehicle only. Branches crashed into the cab on either side. Abruptly they reached a clearing, and in the headlights she caught a quick glimpse of a trailer. The truck jounced to a stop. Sudden silence, except for a dog barking inside the trailer.

"Don't worry," he said. "He won't attack unless I give the word."

Pete got out of the truck and came around to help her down from the cab. For a moment his grip was tight on her mittened hand, and then he let her go and turned toward the trailer. She followed, fitting her boots into the tracks he'd made, thinking she must be out of her mind. He went up the steps and opened the door. She heard a thrashing sound, and then saw he'd got the dog by the collar, a big black dog that snarled in spite of the choke chain. "Easy, boy," he said.

Inside the trailer was a smell of dog, and something salty or fishy, and a whiff of propane. He switched a light on, but the room remained dim. She saw pots piled by a sink, some clothes and other gear hanging from nails on the wall: a wetsuit, a diving mask. The dog had slunk under a couch. He gnawed on his tail, keeping an eye on her.

Pete turned up the gas heater, and it began to take the edge off the damp and chill inside the trailer. "Sit down," he told her. Since the dog was under the couch, she took a chair at the little folding table, which had some old mildewy-smelling magazines on it. She pulled off her mittens and her cap, and unzipped her parka. He hadn't taken off his boots so she didn't, either. They were beginning to drip onto the dirty floor. Almost idly she wondered what was going to happen. She felt the situation was out of her hands entirely.

He got a couple of cans of beer out of the refrigerator and put them on the table. Then he brought a cookie tin from the makeshift counter by the sink and pried it open. Inside was a round cake of some kind. "Want some?" he asked.

She hesitated, and he said, "It's good. I made it."

He cut off a wedge and laid it sideways on a plate. Tentatively she broke off a small piece of cake and put it in her mouth. It was moist—almost soggy—and buttery, and sweet, and it had some kind of seed in it, poppy seed maybe. She ate her whole slice and then let him put more on her plate, and she finished that, as well. He popped open his beer and she opened hers, too, although ordinarily she didn't much like beer. The delicious sweet cake had made her thirsty.

After she took a drink from the can she looked at the wetsuit. "You dive for urchins?"

Yeah, he told her, that's what he did.

"Isn't it dangerous? People drown diving for urchins."

"Only stupid people."

In a sort of built-in scabbard on the leg of the wetsuit, she saw the handle and part of the blade of a steel knife. "What's the knife for?"

"Fighting off giant man-killing lobsters."

"Are you kidding?"

"What do you think?"

"I wouldn't like it, so far down under the water."

"Why not?

"Not being able to breathe."

"You can breathe fine, as long as there's air in the tank."

She shook her head. "The darkness down there. The pressure of the water, I'd hate that."

"Maybe you wouldn't if you tried it." He put down his beer can and gazed at her so long she felt her face go hot. The dog under the couch moved restlessly, his collar rattling on the floor. She licked butter from her lips. Finally he reached across the table and touched her copper-colored hair. "Pretty," he said. Then, "Time to take you home. Your old lady must be wondering what happened to you."

~

At the end of break when Kori was heading out of the john, she found old Miriam waiting for her by the door. "You *will* be careful, dear," she said, her thin hand fluttering on the sleeve of Kori's sweater, "won't you?" Her breath smelled of Polident or something like that.

"Careful? What do you mean?"

But Miriam didn't explain, just picked her work gloves out of her cubby and went to her place on the line. Not that Kori was dying to hear any more.

It was crazy. First Emma with her inquisition—*Why are you so late getting home? Whose truck was that you got out of?*—and then her bruised silence, and now old Miriam's cryptic warning, when Kori hadn't even done anything yet.

~

Sunday morning the temperature was 22 degrees when Kori set out. She left Emma sleeping in her bed and didn't stop to eat breakfast.

Very little traffic on 1A. A spotted cat whipped across the road and disappeared in the ditch. It had snowed lightly in the night. On the fields blueberry bristles sprouted out of the fresh snow.

After she passed the town limits sign she began to look for the road. A hundred paces—past a fieldstone wall, and a cellar hole, and around a slow curve. Now she saw that the road wasn't unmarked, after all. At one time somebody had painted a piece of scrap wood and nailed it to a tree: Coffins Neck. But scrub had grown up around the tree, little popples and pin cherries, so the sign was nearly obscured and the paint faded and leached into the grain of the wood.

No tire tracks on the road: no one had come from or gone to Coffins Neck since the snow. Sunday, everybody hunkered down, sleeping off Saturday night. The road seemed much longer than she remembered, hard going since the snow cover concealed patches of ice, potholes, rocks. Spruce and fir grew close to the road on both sides. They badly needed thinning. Many were spindly, many were dead or dying, their trunks splotched with lichen, their brittle branches trailing old-man's-beard. Ravens in the woods screeched, sounding like crazed humans. After a while Kori began to worry that she'd missed the turn, would eventually wind up at the tip of the peninsula and have to retrace all her steps.

But then she came to a narrow drive off to her left, and through the trees could just make out the black pickup. As she approached the trailer the dog inside began to bark. She guessed sooner or later the barking would roust him, so she didn't go any closer, just stood there in the clearing and waited.

The trailer was an old one, streaked with rust. It had two metal doors, blank as closed eyes. A cinderblock stoop led to one door, nothing led to the other. You'd need to jump a foot and a half or more off the ground to get through it. Empty bottles and cans, tires, a rotting overstuffed chair, other assorted junk partly under snow littered the clearing.

Now that she wasn't walking, she felt chilled. Her socks were wet inside her boots, and her nose began to drip. She found a tissue in her pocket and wiped it.

Relentlessly the barking went on. He must be some heavy sleeper, she thought. Either that, or out cold. She didn't consider leaving. She thought she might put down roots right there, like a willow twig idly stuck into marshy ground.

Then Pete opened the door above the stoop, holding the black dog by the choke collar. "It's you," he said. He was wearing a rumpled shirt, mostly unbuttoned, and the bottoms of long johns. His feet were bare.

"Can I come in?" she asked.

"Sure you want to do that?"

"I didn't walk all this way to stand out here."

"Things might be different this time."

"I know that."

He yanked the dog back from the doorway by its chain and she passed by. It was the way you feel going into the fun house at the Millettsville Fair, she thought. Right away the ground under your feet isn't level, so you think you're going to careen into a wall. The mirrors give you back a picture of yourself you don't recognize. Squat like a pig with a smeared-out nose, or skinny and rubbery like a noodle. Then you notice that's your jacket! Your hat! You don't really want to go on in. But you don't want not to, either. And anyway you've already paid for your ticket.

SUICIDE

My jacket gapes open because the zipper's jammed, and my hair whips around my face, flying into my eyes and mouth. It's February, a raw wind blasting up from the harbor, gravel-encrusted snow heaped along the sidewalk. Most of the shops on Market Street are still boarded up for the winter. I'm on my way to my usual afternoon haunt, Leonie's.

Leonie's is a café with straggly plants in the window, meant to lure tourists, I guess, and week-old newspapers abandoned on the tables. I don't know why the place stays open all year round, except that otherwise the fat old hippie, Leonie, would have nowhere to go. Local people don't come here much. But it's warm inside, and I can stay as long as I want without anybody giving me a hard time. At home my mother would think up chores for me to do or hassle me about my homework.

I pour myself a cup of coffee from the carafe. It's honor system at Leonie's. I've been sitting at one of the gimpy-legged tables for a minute or two when the door opens, jingling the strap of sleigh bells hanging from it, and a man comes in. He's in his fifties, maybe, with a face cratered as a battlefield, thinning grayish hair, bony ridges over his eyes. He walks directly to my table, carrying a folded piece of paper. "I saw you drop this the other day," he says. "I've been watching for you, to give it back."

He must have seen me on the street and followed me here. "It's not mine," I say automatically—never admit to anything you don't have to—though the paper could have escaped from my backpack. I haven't missed it.

"I'm sure it was you."

"Nice of you to take the trouble, but it really doesn't belong to me."

"All right," he says, shoving the paper into the pocket of his overcoat. It's wool, dark and heavy, and smells like it's been hanging somewhere damp. "Do you mind if I sit down?" he asks.

Why not? This is a free country. He scrapes back one of the mismatched chairs, which were white when the café opened but are now chipped, revealing a variety of other colors underneath, and pulls himself up to the table.

"I'm in town for the winter," he tells me. "Working. I'm staying in the studio on the Haskell property."

"Studio" is a ridiculous name for the place. It's an ancient rusty trailer a couple of miles north of town, clumsily situated on the edge of the marsh, as if a tornado picked it up from somewhere else and dropped it there. Denny Haskell, who's a scalloper and famous for his meanness, had his father-in-law living in the trailer until the old geezer departed for the hereafter, his only way out. Nobody in their right mind would choose to live there. "Are you an artist?" I ask.

"Writer."

Broke writer, I figure. That, or crazy. Over by the glass case Leonie is hunched over like a troll, moving slices of spinach pie from one plate to another. Her limp cotton skirt dry-mops the floor.

The man takes the piece of paper out of his coat pocket and unfolds it. The paper is lined, obviously torn out of a three-ringed notebook. It reads: *You'll cry for me but it will be too late, I'm heading out to cross the final gate.* The handwriting could be anybody's. "Did you write this?" he asks.

"Not me," I answer, passing the paper back to him.

"Look," he says. "I was walking behind you. I saw it blow into the hedge by the library. I thought it might be a homework paper you hadn't turned in yet, and you'd have to do it over. I called after you, but you didn't hear me. By the time I got the paper out of the hedge, you'd gone. Then I read it."

Intently he gazes at me. What he's seeing is a gap-toothed fourteen-year-old, messy hair, cheap Kmart clothes. A girl without hope? Friendless? Suicidal?

Mulling the situation over, I stir my coffee with a fork handle. If this writer has gotten it into his head that I'm planning on checking out, where might the idea carry him? The scenario could take an interesting turn, and God knows, things are pretty dull around here. "Maybe I wrote it," I say, "and maybe I didn't."

Before he knows what's happening I grab my jacket and backpack and am out of there. No crowds to disappear into, no other shops open on this part of Market Street. Behind me I hear bells jangle as he leaves the café, and then the door slamming shut.

I run across the street and down the sidewalk a few blocks and duck into the park. Leaves are off the bushes, trees bare, nowhere good to hide. So I make for the public toilet down by the pond, backpack bumping against my spine. Crows in the trees screech as I pass under. I'm sure he's after me, determined to save me. I tear around the corner of the Ladies side of the cinderblock john and find the door in there chained shut.

Now I hear his footsteps . . . not running . . . hesitant on the pavement. He must not've seen which way I went. In this dark place is a cold, sour stench of piss, and under my feet dirty ice. The footsteps stop. I've got a stitch in my side.

Maybe thirty seconds pass. Then he moves on, in the direction of the rose garden, which will now be nothing but thorny canes stuck in mud hard as concrete. I smile.

~

"I asked you to be home by four," my mother says, "so you could watch Jason while I went to the dentist."

I drop my backpack on the kitchen floor and take a banana from the imitation-wood bowl on the counter.

She watches me strip off the peel. "I had to take him with me," she complains.

So? Jason's your kid, not mine. "Something came up," I tell her.

"What came up?"

My mother has a blocky body and a pinched, sorrowful face. Two men have married and then left her. She and Jason have a different last name than mine. From snapshots my mother keeps in a drawer, I can tell that I take after my dad: same skinny frame, same frantic dark hair. His name is Nolan Bragg and he's living down South with his current wife and a bunch of kids. Every once in a while a child-support check comes in the mail with an Edneyville, North Carolina, postmark on the envelope. No letter, just the check. I wouldn't mind seeing my dad sometime, but not the wife or kids. One half-brother is plenty.

"You're not in some kind of trouble, are you?" my mother asks. Last summer I got caught lifting a silk teddy from a boutique. The cops just gave me a warning, first offense, but she never lets me forget it.

"No, I'm not in any trouble," I say, biting off a hunk of banana.

"Then where were you, Lynette?"

I'm certainly not going to tell her about the writer living in Haskell's trailer, who has taken such a great interest in me. That will be information I'll use in my own way, in my own good time. Before answering I chew slowly and swallow. "Pep Club rally." My mother knows me so little she doesn't get it: I wouldn't be caught dead at a Pep Club rally.

In the front room, I can hear the TV playing a *Home Improvement* rerun and Jason jumping on the furniture, doing Turbo Megazord Power Rangers sound effects. My mother rubs lotion into her hands. She's got any number of allergies. Nerves, she claims. "I wish you'd called to let me know."

"I didn't have any money for the pay phone."

Sighing, she says, "You better get started on your homework."

I pick up my backpack and climb the stairs to my frigid room under the eaves.

~

A couple of times that week I spot the writer in his long wool overcoat: once in the Kwik-Stop convenience store buying cigarettes, another time near the high school just walking along the road. Apparently he doesn't have a car. I wouldn't be surprised if he's in Leonie's in the afternoons, looking for me, but I'll let him wait and wonder awhile before I go back there.

Friday, sure enough, he's sitting at a table by the window, next to a hairy cactus and some dusty, spiky plants in clay pots. Behind him there's also a few geraniums straining against the glass in search of sunlight. Good luck. I shed my jacket and drop my backpack on a nearby table, pretending I don't notice him, then pour myself a cup of coffee from the carafe. When I'm settled I open a book I picked up in the school library this afternoon, the thinnest one on the paperback rack. I have to do a book report for English on a novel "of my choice." No sci-fi or fantasy allowed. What kind of choice is that? These rules tick me off.

I slog through about four pages, in which nothing much is happening except for a man named Mr. Pontellier lighting a cigar, while the writer is over by the hairy cactus with his eyes boring into me. Finally he clears his throat and says, "One thing you should know. That's not the title the author gave it."

Innocently I glance up to see who might be speaking.

"Chopin's publisher forced this title on her," he says.

I shut the book and look at the cover. *The Awakening.*

"One of the countless stupidities in the long history of publishing," he goes on. "It completely distorts the author's intention."

A book called *The Awakening* could be about finding out that while you were asleep aliens turned you into a different person, with a brand-new reflection in the mirror. Or about opening your eyes one morning and noticing you're on a weird and mysterious planet somewhere else in the universe. The picture on the cover tells you to forget that idea. It's a painting of a stiff-backed, beaky-nosed woman wearing an old-fashioned long white dress. Her hair is braided into a bun. From her expression, my guess is that the story doesn't have a happy ending, not that I necessarily buy happy endings.

"It was originally titled *A Solitary Soul,*" the writer says.

I'm beginning to have the feeling this book is not for me, no matter how short.

"The novel has some wonderfully evocative passages." Leaving a newspaper open on his table, he sits down at mine. "May I?" He reaches for the tattered paperback, and I hand it over. Eagerly he riffles through some pages, one or two of which threaten to fall out. "Listen to this: 'The voice of the sea is seductive,' " he reads, " 'never ceasing, whispering, clamoring, murmuring, inviting the soul to wander for a spell in abysses of solitude; to lose itself in mazes of inward contemplation . . . ' "

A regular comes into the café, a retired naval officer who left his wits behind him on the ship. Leonie brings him his usual, a piece of pineapple upside-down cake, and the old man starts to devour it, muttering, bits of cake snagging in his yellow beard.

"Do you like to read?" the writer asks.

"Nothing much else to do around here in the winter."

"There are worse things than reading."

His skin is so pitted he must have had terrible acne once. I bet that's why he became a writer, shunned on account of his oozing zits. I know something about how that feels: I'm not the most popular girl in the ninth grade. Actually, I don't give a rat's ass what they think at school.

"I was disappointed when you ran off the other day," he says.

"I had, you know, things to do."

He pats a pocket of his heavy wool coat. Obviously he craves a smoke, but the troll has a big sign on the wall warning you not to light up. You'll turn into a frog or a stone. "I've been thinking about the message on the notebook paper," he says.

"I don't know if that was a *message*."

"What was it, then?"

The loony naval officer lurches out of his chair and stumbles toward the door. Sleigh bells crash behind him.

So the writer will think I'm too shy or nervous to answer, I lower my head and shove the novel into my backpack. He gets up when I do, forgetting all about his newspaper.

On Market Street he walks along with me, in the direction of my house, which is the opposite direction from Haskell's trailer. From Market Street you can catch glimpses of the harbor at the cross streets. In the summer the bay is speckled with white sails and fishing boats. Now the water is granite-gray, so cold that if you fell in you'd die of hypothermia in minutes.

A girl from my class, Terri Michaud, comes out of the Kwik-Stop and stares at us. Who can that guy be? she's thinking. Not Lynette's old man: them Braggs all look the same, wild black hair and a space between their front teeth you could drive a truck through.

Terri Michaud is a geek. I don't hang out with geeks. I'm not that desperate, even though my best friend moved to Lincoln last fall. Stinkin' Lincoln, people call it. It's a mill town, way up north of Bangor somewhere. Jen and her mom had to go live with relatives when her mom's hours at Walmart kept getting cut. She couldn't find another job.

For now, at least, the writer has dropped the topic of the notebook paper and is asking me about myself, about my life. But I have no interest in describing my obnoxious little brother and mistake-prone mother and our junker of a car that's held together with duct tape and the threatening letter that came yesterday from Bangor Hydro. I'm certain he doesn't really want to hear about those things, either. So I just shrug and act mysterious. I'm a princess incognito, for all he knows.

He's quiet for a while, walking along beside me, his wool coat flapping around his legs. Then he's telling me about Grand Isle, the summer colony in the Gulf of Mexico where *The Awakening* is set. Years ago, he says, he spent a semester as writer-in-residence at a college in New Orleans and made a point to visit the island. He remembers weather-beaten old houses hinting of secrets from the exotic Creole past. A picnic on the beach, wine and white cheese and oranges. Someone playing an accordion in the distance. The softness of the humid air, the lure of the sea. " 'The compellingly seductive sea,' " he recites dramatically, " 'pulling away from the sand with the moon-driven tide.' "

Here it's still frozen February. Beyond the defunct cannery, Market Street turns into Route 1A, a two-lane road with practically no shoulder to it, crusted with rock salt and gravel. If two trucks happened to pass you at the same time you'd have to dive into the ditch, and it's awkward to keep pace with this guy. He's taller than me and walks with a kind of lurch. Now he's talking about his travels in various countries, the important writers he's met. One man's name I recognize and I'm sort of impressed. "Wasn't he married to Marilyn Monroe?" I ask. "Did you get to meet her?" No such luck, by then she was dead and he was married to somebody else.

Half a mile out of town, I stop at a mailbox. The driveway winds away from the road to a big Victorian amid oak trees. The house needs paint and numerous repairs and for somebody to take a chainsaw to the scrub that's encroaching on the lawn. Politely I thank him for keeping me company.

He tells me his name, John Scarano, and I tell him mine. Only my first name, though.

"Are you famous?" I ask.

"I did have a book that was nearly a best-seller once."

He looks up at the house, no doubt picturing me at a window in one of the turrets, gazing suicidally out to sea. His hand touches my shoulder. "Lynette, things are never as bleak as they seem," he says.

Without answering, I give him a mournful little smile and turn away. I have to admit I'm getting a charge out of being the heroine of the story he's making up.

He's watching from the road as I walk up the drive and around to the rear of the house. No one lives here now, since Doc Whitley went into the nursing home. Behind the barn I cross a stubbled cornfield, fight my way through a patch of alders, and finally end up in the backyard of my family's dinky bungalow.

~

Sunday afternoon my mother wants me to do a load of laundry and after that clean the bathroom, including scrubbing the floor and the shower stall. She thinks work improves character, especially mine. While the wash is agitating in the basement, the machine generating enough noise to wake the dead, I ease out the kitchen door and lift the old bike down off the porch. In a second I'm aboard and weaving around the corner of the house. The bike pops in and out of gear with a mind of its own, the chain makes balky ratchety sounds, and the brakes are mushy. But the tires have, by some miracle, enough air to get me where I'm going.

This bike, a Raleigh with a man's crossbar, used to belong to my dad. He left it behind. I have a memory of him teaching me to ride a kid-size bike, running in back of me with his hand gripped on the seat and shouting "Go for it!" while I careened terrified and ecstatic down the pebbly driveway. My mother's story, however, is that I was only eighteen months old when he took off with "that woman."

There aren't any snapshots to disprove what she says, though the man I remember picking me out of the hedge when I smashed into it had curly black hair same as my dad's. Since we aren't on speaking terms with any of the Braggs—my mother says they're all on *his* side —I don't have anyone else to ask. Can it have been Jason's father, not my own, that taught me to ride a bike? Hard to imagine, because he hated me, and he wasn't around for very long.

When I was nine I quit riding the kid bike. Jason won't touch it because it's pink and has no crossbar. I learned to ride my dad's Raleigh all by myself.

I pedal a mile on Route 1A, passing through town, which is silent as a tomb except for Delaney's Pizza, the Kwik-Stop, and Burger King. Even Leonie's isn't open on Sundays. Another two miles and then I leave 1A and wobble along the rutted driveway, not much more than a path, that leads to Haskell's trailer. It's a foggy, drizzly day, and I'm soaked by the time I get there. In reasonable weather you'd be able to see the sea beyond the marsh. Not today, but you can smell the salt and decaying shellfish and hear the black ducks on the water, laughing like madmen.

I lean the bike next to the trailer and knock on the door. When he answers he blinks in the light as if I'd turned over a rock he was under. "I don't want to bother you, if you're busy," I say, my eyes cast downward at the flimsy aluminum step I'm standing on.

"No, no, come in."

The trailer is in confusion, papers and books everywhere. On the dining table, a typewriter that doesn't plug in—John Scarano is out of the Dark Ages—and disorderly heaps of typed pages. He must eat standing up. Unwashed dishes by the sink and, on the counter, boxes of cereal with their tops flapping open and stacks of soup cans and a giant economy-size bottle of Jim Beam. Stink of cigarette smoke.

"You're wet," he says. "Let me find you a towel." When he does, it's slightly damp, and as musty as the rest of the place. Since he went to the trouble, I give my hair a few passes with it.

In the kitchenette he drapes my jacket over a chair, then runs water into a kettle and puts it on the stove. He's wearing a shirt that was white at one time but must have gotten washed in a load of coloreds at the laundromat. Sinewy freckled forearms and bony elbows poke out of the rolled-up sleeves. The nakedness of his arms is almost embarrassing.

We sit in the living-room part of the trailer waiting for the water to boil. There's an oriental rug on the floor, a feeble attempt to cover the stained wall-to-wall carpet squares. Above the couch is an oil painting that for sure never belonged to Denny Haskell: slashes of red, purple, and gray, with blotches of pink. It makes me think of a slaughterhouse or a car crash. "What's that a picture of?" I ask him.

"It's called *Resurrection*. The artist is quite well known."

Seems like a strange thing to name this painting. But I've never been to church except for the day my mother married Jason's father, so what do I know?

On the coffee table is the lined notebook paper. It's wrinkled from being in his coat pocket. I assume he's been studying it, fabricating my story out of the smeary ballpoint words. He looks at the paper and says, "I think you ought to tell me what this is all about, this little poem."

The kettle whistles, and I sit quietly while he makes tea out in the kitchenette. I notice that on the side table beside my chair is an odd carving, made of ivory looks like. It's flattish, about the size of a pocket watch. There's a carved spider on one corner. I remember seeing something like the carving in the window of an antique shop in town.

"I'm afraid I don't have any milk," he says when he returns with two mugs. "It spoiled, and I never seem to remember to buy more."

The tea is hot and bitter. I take a small sip and put the mug on the side table next to the carving. He's nervous, which is amusing, because he's old—older than my dad, even. Why should he care whether my tea has milk in it or not?

"You don't have to worry that I'll reveal your secret," he says. "I barely know anyone here."

I take another sip of tea and carefully replace the mug. "What do *you* think the poem means?" I ask. This is the method I use for dealing with my mother when I want to string her along. She always falls for it.

"I think we have here someone sad. Someone who feels that no one cares about her." From beside him on the couch he picks up a pack of Camels and digs one out and lights it. "Possibly she believes there's no way to cure her unhappiness."

I hear myself saying, "What if there isn't?" For a second I'm confused about whether I supposedly wrote the poem or not and whose story I'm in, exactly. "There's always a way, Lynette, believe me."

I look at my boots, which have dried mud on the heels. He's expecting me to spill my guts, but I don't do that. I don't show my belly, like a dog that's too scared to fight. That's when people take advantage. "Did you know Denny Haskell from somewhere?" I ask, just to be changing the subject.

John Scarano smiles, rubbing his pot-holed face. "Why would you think that?"

"Why else would you come here?"

"I picked the town on a map, because I wanted to be near the water. This was the place I could afford." He begins to tell me about the book he's working on, how slow it's going, how he'd hoped the spare winter landscape would get him on track. He'd counted on having a first draft done by now, but he's plodding in circles, making little headway. I watch him drag on the Camel, rub it out in a saucer, start another.

His last book didn't sell, he says, problems with distribution, and the *Times* reviewer must have had a grudge against him for some reason. His editor doesn't return his phone calls. He's low on cash, has about run through his puny advance. And then there's the money he has to pay his wife . . .

"You have a wife?"

"It seems to make her happy to make me unhappy."

I gaze at his naked freckled arms, feeling a little sorry for him, against my better judgment.

"Sometimes," he says, "I've had thoughts like the girl who wrote the note: how much easier it would be simply to give up. Yes, let them regret all their sins of omission and commission after you've gone, after it's too late. There's a certain grim pleasure in that notion, which I understand very well. But you can't give up, Lynette. It's your duty, your *duty,* not to let the goddamn bastards win."

Pinching the cigarette between thumb and forefinger, he looks at me so hard that a laser beam shoots out of his colorless eyes, curves around the universe a million times faster than the speed of light, and in almost the same instant nails him in the back. His body twitches when it hits.

"Well," I tell him, "my mother's expecting me home."

"Come any time you like. I mean it." He puts out the butt and goes to the kitchenette for my jacket. Surprising myself, I slip the ivory carving into my jeans pocket.

~

Up in my room, I lock the door and turn on the radio, which is tuned to Lucky 99: One Hundred Percent Country, a station my mother detests. I pull the carving out of my pocket and examine it. It's just the right size to fit neatly into my palm, caramel-smooth on the underside. The design is of a pony half caught in a web, and on the web a spider waits for its victim, ready to pounce.

"Lynette!" my mother yells up the stairs. "The laundry! You didn't forget about the bathroom, did you? Where'd you go off to, anyway?" but I don't pay any attention. I run my finger over the old ivory with its hairline cracks, trace the intricate web, feel the pony's plump breast and muzzle and the curls of his mane, the double bump of the spider's body.

The pony doesn't look at all worried about the fix he's in. Maybe he hasn't figured out yet what the spider has in store for him.

"Lynette, are you listening to me? Turn that thing down!"

The next day I carry the carving to school tucked inside my bra. In the afternoon, curious to find out whether John Scarano is going to try to get it back from me, and, if so, how, I stop by Leonie's. Sure enough, the writer is at the window table next to the pathetic collection of plants. Enjoying living dangerously, I bring my coffee to his table and drop my backpack onto the floor, drape my jacket over a chair back.

But I'm not going to get to play cat and mouse, after all. Right away he tells me that after I left his place yesterday, he decided to walk into town for milk and cigarettes. While he was gone, trespassers entered the trailer.

"You didn't lock the door?"

"It never occurred to me that would be necessary."

I feel the carving pressing hard against my breast. "What did they do?"

"Took something."

"Something valuable?"

"It might have kept me going for a few months, if I'd been willing to sell it."

"But you wouldn't have?"

"It was very old, museum quality, irreplaceable. A relic of happier days. Selling it . . . I'm not that close to the edge yet."

My underarms tickle. Something flutters in my crotch. If only John Scarano knew where his precious carving is right now.

"Did you call the cops?"

"Not yet. I'm not sure what to tell them. After I discovered the theft I remembered that I'd heard voices in the marsh when I was walking along the path, but I'd thought at the time it was gulls. Or ducks." He smiles wanly. "That's not much evidence to go on." Behind him, the sun is sending a few weak rays into the storefront window.

"There's kids in this town with nothing better to do," I say, "than break into camps and cottages and steal whatever they can find. Sometimes they wreck the place, too. They don't care who they hurt, and the cops hardly ever catch them. What can you do?"

He takes a deep, ragged breath. "What you can do, Lynette, is refuse to let them defeat you."

But he looks defeated already, and I feel a twinge of guilt. He begins to talk about *The Awakening*, which is buried unread in the depths of my backpack. The book report is due Thursday. "Edna Pontillier may have been a victim of society, and of her own desires," he's saying, "but that's a work of fiction. In real life, there's no such thing as tragic destiny. You don't have to be a victim."

Who is he trying to convince, me or himself? He leans forward and lays his hand on my arm. "Are you all right?" he asks.

On the far side of the room Leonie heaves her bulk into a chair and falls upon a wedge of strawberry chiffon pie as if it's her last meal. Without answering his question, I hotfoot it out of there.

~

It's way after midnight and I'm lying under a pile of quilts and army blankets with the pony carving closed in my fist. I'm thinking about whether John Scarano has called the cops and whether they'd be numb enough to believe the tale about juvenile delinquents lurking in the marsh. The hole in the story is that the supposed thieves did not steal every blessed thing in the trailer and then trash it, the standard m.o. of the local punks. They'd have had plenty of time to do the job right, since from his place it's two miles to town and two miles back—at least an hour on foot—plus whatever time it takes to pay for a quart of milk and a carton of cigarettes in the Kwik-Stop and chat with ditzy Krystal the checkout girl while she struggles to make the scanner scan. If the cops don't buy the j.d.s, and they start asking questions about who else might have been around the trailer Sunday afternoon, then what? I don't need the law bugging me again. But something tells me he hasn't called the cops and isn't going to. He's more the type to decide the robbery must be his own fault in some way. I don't know if that makes me feel better or not. Up here in my room, which is basically the attic, with slanting ceilings and wallboard nailed to the rafters, the wind sounds like it's going to rip the roof off and pitch me onto the frozen mud in the yard.

In the morning I have such a hard time waking up I feel like I've been drugged. It takes me forever to find a shirt that's not too wrinkled and a pair of pants that will pass the dress code. Meanwhile my mother is shouting up the stairs that I'm going to be late and she can't drive me to school because something's wrong with the clutch, and bratty little twerp Jason is whining and carrying on, like always.

It's not until I'm halfway to school that I remember the ivory carving, which is still somewhere in my bedclothes. It's sleeting, the wind is fierce, I've lost my gloves, and I haven't done my math homework. Not my day. After school I consider going to Leonie's. I know he's there, bent on saving me from myself, but the hell with it, I'm not in the mood. I head on home.

My mother's in the kitchen cleaning the stove. She jerks her head out of the oven as soon as I open the back door, and right away I can tell something is up. "On the table," she says. "I found it this morning when I was changing your sheets."

What was she doing changing my sheets? Every other damn week of the year she shoves them into my arms when I'm on my way up to the attic or just leaves them on a step. The carving looks ridiculously out of place on her ugly, cheap, stupid plastic tablecloth from Reny's. "It's mine," I say.

My mother rises, a Brillo in her hand, filthy soapy water dripping onto the newspaper she's spread over the linoleum. There's smudges of grease on her broad, bland face. All over again, I'm glad I take after my father. "You stole it, didn't you?" she says.

"No, I didn't steal it. Somebody gave it to me."

"Please don't lie to me, Lynette." She's about to begin crying now. "I can't bear it."

"I'm telling you the truth."

"Who is this person, then?"

"He lives over to the Haskell place, in the trailer."

"What?" she asks, pulling awkwardly at the tips of her rubber gloves. They are suctioned onto her sweaty hands. "Nobody lives there."

"Somebody does now. A writer."

"Why would he give you such a thing?"

"Because he likes me," I say. "I know that's hard for you to believe."

"Oh, Lynette . . . "

I climb the steps to my room, the carving in hand. Whether she believes my story or not, she isn't going to do a thing about it. The last thing she needs is another complication in her life.

~

I keep expecting him to be at Leonie's when I get there in the afternoons, that wool coat giving off its mildew smell, empty cups littering the table, his sparse hair eggbeatered by the wind. But he never is.

Sitting there sipping my coffee, I think about what I'm going to do with the carving. I imagine myself hitching to Bangor, getting on a Trailways bus. There must be antique shops galore down in Boston. I'd have to convince them it was mine to sell, I know that much. I glance over at the retired naval officer, who's dragging a great dirty handkerchief out of his pocket. I could tell them I inherited the carving from my grandfather, a retired naval officer, who picked it up in his travels in the Orient, and now I'm forced to part with it because (the old goat is hawking something up into the handkerchief) my mother has a bad lung disease, and my father took off with his pregnant girlfriend, and we're living on AFDC and food stamps, and we have to have the money, we just have to.

I can feel the piece of ivory in my bra, that poor pony never noticing the spider lying in wait.

I picture John Scarano out in the trailer, the sour milk in the fridge, a mess of books stacked everywhere. He can't stop worrying about the trespassers who snuck into the trailer while he was gone to buy cigarettes. He doesn't know who they are, or why they have it in for him, or when they'll strike again. If he leaves the trailer, they might do anything. Tear his books at their spines, smash his typewriter into a heap of rubble, let the wind scatter his papers among the cattails. He stares at the stains on the carpet squares and doesn't remember they were already there when he rented the place from Denny Haskell. It was the trespassers who made those stains, he thinks now. Through the smeary windows of the trailer he looks past the marsh, out to the narrow gray strip of sea.

~

Jason is hunched on the porch steps in a small patch of sunlight reading a comic book he's read a million times before. Looks like Mom put him outside to get some "fresh air and exercise." I run past him and heave my backpack onto the glider. "Mom says to tell you—" he begins, but I've spirited the bike down the steps and am on it and away before he gets a chance to finish.

The marsh weeds are brittle with frost. I pound at the cold metal door until my hand is sore, but nobody answers. The door is locked.

Shades are pulled down over all the windows.

My plan was to get myself invited in and, while he's fussing over the teakettle, slip the carving back among his things. Obviously, that's not going to work out. In a pile of junk behind the trailer I find a cinderblock and lug it over to one of the windows so I can stand on it and peer beneath the shade. It's too dark in there to see a thing. For some reason I feel kind of sick to my stomach.

I'm weaving back down the rutted driveway, and a big black pickup turns off the road and barrels toward me, braking with so little room to spare that pebbles fly up and ping against my spokes. It's Denny Haskell. He leaves the engine idling and gets out of the truck. He's carrying a homemade For Rent sign and a hammer. Ignoring me, he goes over to a nearby popple tree. I watch him pick a nail out of his pocket and with three whacks attach the sign to the tree.

"You happen to know where he went?" I ask Denny's broad back. The imitation fur on his jacket collar and his scrawny neck and shaved head make me think of a turkey vulture, like you see pecking at squashed porcupines on the road.

He studies his sign for a while, admiring its artistic merit, I guess, then turns and squints at me. Recognition slithers across his wattled face. He's concluding that I must be related to them Braggs and wondering what I, a numb Bragg, would have to do with a writer, even a writer down-at-heels as this one. He grins. Obviously he's not going to tell me anything, even if he knows. Denny Haskell is as mean with his words as he is with his money. "He didn't mention any plans," Denny says, climbing back into the pickup.

"Are you sure?" I yell, but of course he can't hear me. He revs the engine so that I get out of his way in a hurry.

~

On my way home I turn off Market Street at Burger King and pedal over cobblestones down to the wharf. It's deserted, no boats on the bay, not a soul in sight. I drop the bike, leaving its tires spinning, and walk out to the end of the dock. The tide is foaming, swirling around the barnacled pilings, smelling of seaweed and rotting fish. I reach inside my jacket and dig the ivory carving out of my bra. I look at it curled in my hand one last time. Then I hurl it as hard and far as I can into the water.

IN THE MARROW

In the john Amy filled her palms with the gritty soap powder and rubbed her hands together until the skin was about to come off. The ballpoint pens always leaked on her fingers, and the print on handbills and flyers stuck to her hands like blurred tattoos no matter how careful she was. Two minutes to twelve. Back in the front office she yanked open the humidity-swollen desk drawer and took out her lunch bag, praying Georgene wouldn't find one more thing for her to do before she could escape.

"Be back at twelve-thirty sharp," Georgene said. She worried about the girl, felt she was her responsibility, one she hadn't asked for. Amy's grandmother thought she ate her lunch right here in the office, and Georgene had to cover for her when the old lady telephoned: "She just went in the bathroom, I'll have her call you back." Or "I had to send her over to State Street, rush job." Georgene didn't like to tell falsehoods, wasn't good at it, feared getting caught.

Amy pulled the jangling door shut behind her. She knew Georgene would turn on the radio and eat her sandwich at her desk. Georgene had been working here since before the Flood. Never got married, had no life except the print shop, and the Baptist Church, and the Thursday night card game with the "girls." Amy would rather die than have a life like Georgene's.

Or Gapp's. Her grandfather worked in the back where the presses were, fed paper into them, made sure they were oiled and aligned, fixed them when they jammed or broke down. When she was a kid, before she had to spend every summer in the print shop as a regular job, Amy thought operating the presses was exciting. She'd beg to go to work with Gapp, to hang around and watch. Magic the way the blank sheets leaped into one end of the machinery and flipped out all printed at the other, faster than your eye could follow. The sweating men tossed jokes above her head. "Remember that cute little blond girl worked here once?" they'd say. "Hair got caught in one of the presses and she came out scalped."

Now, though, Amy thought of Gapp as being chained to the machinery, a prisoner. He'd gone deaf from the din and did his work as if in a coma.

Amy sprinted across Water Street, making a guy in a florist's van jam on his brakes and swear at her, and cut between two factory buildings. The brick one had long ago been abandoned, birds flying in and out of the broken windows. The other, an auto muffler factory, was a metal prefab, corrugated iron streaked with rust.

On the river side of the buildings the air felt different. Cool on her skin, and if she licked her arm she'd taste salt. She followed a rough dirt path down to the bank and sat on a crate that bore a peeling, weather-soaked label from Guatemala.

Fumes from the factories and mills hung over the river. The water, scummy with oil and algae, sawdust and bits of straw, lapped against the bank. Gulls shrieked. Eating her sandwich, Amy watched a convoy of scows filled with gravel proceeding in a stately way down the river. She'd like to be riding on the tug, feeling the powerful engine rumble underneath her. Even better, she'd like to be on a really fast boat, heading far out to sea, the wind whipping her hair.

After a few minutes she heard someone coming down the path, a man she'd never seen here before. He was smoking a cigar not much bigger than a cigarette, and he wore a faded blue work shirt, the sleeves rolled back to the upper arms. His arms swelled there, making her think of a snake that has swallowed something large. His hair was nut-brown, thinning. He must be thirty, at least.

"I saw you from the window," he said. He meant from the muffler factory up on the rise. "I noticed you because of your skirt."

Amy glanced down at her cotton skirt, which had a pattern of multicolored *Xs* and *Os*, like a tic-tac-toe game gone out of control. The material fell loosely around her bare calves.

"I like that in a girl," he said. "Wearing a skirt." That was a lie. What he'd noticed was her hair—pale, lit by the sun, curling wispily on her thin shoulders. It made you want to stroke it the way you'd pet a young animal.

The man's green eyes, the intent way they studied her, unsettled Amy. Cigar ash fell near her sandal. She rolled her sandwich crusts into the paper bag and got up from the crate. So as not to have to pass by him, she walked away among weeds along the riverbank.

"Hey," he called, "I don't bite."

~

Amy promised herself she would not go back to the river. The guy from the muffler factory made her nervous because he was so old, even though he was cute, or at least the girls at school would think so. But at lunchtime the next day she couldn't face eating in the messy front office with Georgene, who would be leaning greedily over her tuna fish sandwich, the wax paper spread out on top of order blanks, crumbs stuck to her cheek. Anyway, Amy had as much right to be by the river as the muffler guy did.

In the night it had rained, bringing out the melon smell in her crate. She imagined a ship landing on a tropical island. A beach with the shells of giant snails on it, pink and pearly and smooth as silk inside. Footsteps in the sand, not her own.

She started to eat her sandwich and soon she was aware of the smoke of his cigar. He said, "We meet again."

She looked up at him. In the breeze off the river her skirt flapped around her calves. Her breasts swelled gently under a hideous blouse, out-of-date rayon or some fabric like that, heart-shaped imitation mother-of-pearl buttons, machine-made embroidery on the pressed collar. How old could she be? Sixteen? Seventeen?

"You work over there?" she asked, lifting her head at the stained corrugated rear of the muffler factory.

He explained that he was in shipping, not the greatest job, but it was okay for the time being. So long as he succeeded in keeping the supervisor off his back. "What about you?" he asked. She worked in a print shop, she said, filling out order slips and filing. Sometimes she made deliveries, which she liked, because it got her out of the shop. In moments, it seemed, a buzzer went off inside the muffler factory, and she watched him stroll up the hill. His head had a bald spot on the crown, she noticed.

It became his habit to take his break outside when she sat on the riverbank, her skirt spread out around her, and they'd exchange a few words. One day he casually let slip that he'd done a tour in Vietnam. He wondered whether that would scare her off, almost hoped it would. But she wanted to hear about the war—*Did you ever kill anybody? Were you ever afraid you were going to die?*—more than he wanted to reveal. The next day he told her he'd spent some time in a VA hospital downstate. The sky was overcast, beginning to drizzle.

She turned her head away, toward the river, and he saw droplets of rain caught in the fine-spun web of her hair. He imagined she was guessing where his scars might be.

Another day he mentioned that he lived in a furnished room over a used clothing store. When she finally asked his name he considered lying—safer to make up a new one—but for some reason told the truth. Jack. "As in rabbit," he said, mock-leering, and she didn't quite get the joke. In a way he was glad she didn't, but at the same time her innocence made him uneasy. He could tell she was attracted to him, and it had been a long time since a pretty girl opened herself to him. Amy, her name was.

Back in the print shop she thought about how he'd looked standing near the crate, smiles crinkling the corners of his eyes. How would you describe the color of those eyes? She bought a notebook on her way home. She'd write down all the details she collected about him, to preserve them. Two and a half weeks she'd known him now. In her room after supper she opened the spiral-bound notebook and wrote in careful backhand: *Things About Jack.* Underneath, she wrote, *Jack's eyes.* She thought for a while and then wrote, *Green. Not transparent, like emeralds. Green like bright stones that you find at the beach, worn smooth by the waves, still wet from the sea.*

His hair is straight and medium brown, parted on the left side. You'd find it soft if you touched it.

He always wears a blue work shirt.

In fact, she guessed it was the same shirt, washed out at night with bar soap and hung over a bathtub to dry, because, along with the smell of the cigar, he gave off, very faintly, the aroma of sour washcloth. She could summon him at night by burying her face in her own washcloth.

He was wounded in the war, but you can't see any scars, and he doesn't limp or anything.

He hates working in the muffler factory.

He has a brother in Los Angeles.

Someday he's going to raise Labrador retrievers. He likes the black ones.

The brand of cigars he smokes is ________________. (On Monday she'd be sure to notice when he tore off the cellophane wrapper. Maybe save it and tape it into her notebook.)

But Monday he didn't appear. She couldn't even find any of his old cigar wrappers amid the rubbish near the crate. Bite by tiny bite she ate her sandwich, telling herself that something had held up his break. Probably the mean supervisor chewing him out. By the time she finished her lunch she'd hear his work boots hurrying down the path so as not to miss her. She threw the crusts to a gull and turned toward the factory. Maybe he'd be at a window and call to her or wave. Nobody there, though, no sign of life at all. She waited, watching the gull gobble the crusts, then poke hopefully at a fast-food wrapper. At last the buzzer sounded, the end of break.

She thought he might be sick, stricken by a summer cold or the flu. He'd be all alone in his hot little furnished room over the used clothing store, too sick to go out and buy food. He could be too weak to dial the emergency number. Maybe he didn't even have a telephone.

He didn't appear on Tuesday, either. On Wednesday, she worked up enough courage to go right into the front door of the factory. In the big open area stacked with boxes, a man in a jumpsuit was riding around on a forklift. Over the noise of the machine she asked him if he knew somebody named Jack who worked there. "Jack? What's his other name?" Well, she wasn't exactly sure. He gave her a quick amused look and directed her to a partitioned cubicle at the rear.

Inside she found a woman wearing a blouse so tight the sleeves cut into her plump arms. When she finally got off the phone, Amy asked her about a person named Jack. "Jack?" Lazily she flipped through a card file and then said, "I find a Jack Gilley. That the one you mean?"

Amy said she supposed so, and the woman told her he'd been terminated, as of the end of last week.

"Terminated?" The word sounded awful to Amy. "Why?"

The woman shrugged.

"Do you have an address for him?"

"We don't give out that information," she said, picking up the phone again.

"But it's important."

Over her eyeglasses the fat woman peered thoughtfully at Amy. "You in trouble, dear?"

"Trouble?"

The woman ripped a sheet off an order pad and scribbled down an address on the back. "You make sure he helps you out. Then, if you want my advice, you'll tell him to get lost."

Four days after that, a Sunday, Amy dressed as if going to church so as to deceive her grandmother. She walked up State Street and across the old bridge, over to Exchange and Park and Center Street, up Center as far as Cobb. The whole way she was worried that he wouldn't remember who she was. That he'd laugh at her the way the man in the jumpsuit had. That he'd be with somebody else. That he'd have moved to another apartment or away from Bangor altogether and left no forwarding address. Out of her purse she took the page from the order pad, though she'd read it so many times she knew it by heart. 11B Cobb.

When she found, at 11 Cobb, a used clothing store, she felt a thump in her chest like a mallet blow. The store occupied the ground floor of a two-story frame structure, an ordinary building you could walk by every day and never notice. Hanging in the shop window were wrinkled suits and dresses with ragged hemlines, bravely trying to tempt passersby inside. Somebody'd left a donation of old clothes in the doorway—the bag had fallen over and was spilling slips and bras and rumpled dresses onto the sidewalk.

Around at the back she found 11B. The name on the mailbox said Phipps, not Gilley, but she pressed the doorbell anyway. For ages there was no answer. A kid who was delivering Sunday papers, pushing them along the driveway in a rusty supermarket cart, stopped to stare at her as she waited. "Looking for somebody?" he called out to her. She turned away and pressed the bell again, but even after she heard the shopping cart's wonky wheels scraping over the sidewalk on Cobb Street, the kid's insolent voice echoed in her head: *Looking for somebody?*

The sky, which had been a brilliant blue when she started out, was now clotted with low clouds, and she began to be chilly in her Sunday dress. The summer's over, she thought in despair. She'd be back in school and . . . And then suddenly there he was at the door, a day's growth of beard on his face, his soft hair unbrushed. He held not a cigar but a half-smoked cigarette in his hand.

Christ, it's the kid, he thought. The blue taffeta affair she wore made her look like she was playing dress-up in her mother's clothes. "Hi, Amy," he said, not very pleased to see her. The riverbank was one thing. A full-scale invasion of his place was another.

"You stopped coming," she said. She felt her face go red.

"I don't work there anymore."

"I know, I . . . "

He put his cigarette to his lips and inhaled. Now what? He considered telling her he was busy and shutting the door. He pictured her limping away in those ridiculous high-heeled shoes, puffy raw blisters forming on her feet. So instead he asked, "Do you want to come upstairs?"

At his question she realized all at once what he must think, the reason she'd come here. "No," she said, "that's not what I want." She wasn't going to fling herself on him. She'd die of misery first.

She backed off the stoop and ran up the driveway and along the uneven sidewalk, half stumbling, and then she heard footsteps behind her, and she knew he was coming after her. At the corner she had to stop, halted by traffic, and when he caught up to her he grabbed her arm. "What's the matter with you?" he asked, panting. His fingers tightened on her upper arm, and it occurred to her that she didn't know him at all.

"I made a mistake," she said. "I'm sorry." She hated herself for whimpering. She needed to get a tissue out of her purse, but his fingers held her. "Please let me go," she said, and when he released her she fumbled inside the purse and several coins and pens and a lipstick fell out and went bouncing onto the pavement. He made no move to pick them up. He just waited while she wiped her eyes and blew her nose.

"You're acting like an idiot," he told her, and she answered, "I know it," and hiccupped. "Why don't you come on back," he said.

She followed him along Cobb Street, stumbling a little in her heels as she tried to keep up with him, forgetting all about the objects she'd left on the sidewalk.

The steps were dark, narrow, unswept, sagging a little under their feet. She smelled mildew and stale smoke. Inside his apartment he ordered her to sit and she obeyed, pulling a chair up to bare

Formica. She didn't want to look at the bed, on which was a tangle of yellowish sheets. While he did something at the stove she fixed her eyes on an electric guitar propped against a wall.

"You can let go of your purse," he said, placing a mug of coffee in front of her. "I'm not going to steal it."

She realized she'd been clutching the purse so hard the black grosgrain had moist smeary spots from her palm. She set it on the table, the damp side down, and carefully lifted the mug with both hands. Her fingers were trembling.

But he wasn't watching her, he was digging into his cornflakes. She must have interrupted his breakfast. The cereal looked totally soggy by now, and he was going to punish her by ignoring her. She didn't know how much of the acrid coffee she was going to be able to put on an empty stomach, but she had to keep her hands clamped on the cup so they wouldn't shake. After some minutes, desperate for something to say, she asked, "Do you play?"

"Play?" He turned the word around in his head, amused at the possibilities.

"That," she said, nodding at the dusty, ruby-red instrument.

"No, not me." He reached across the table for a matchbook, and she saw again how firmly muscled was his upper arm. "My brother left it behind when he moved to LA, and I've been lugging it from pillar to post ever since." He tore off a match and rubbed it against the matchbook three or four times before it would light. "I don't know why I bother. I doubt the thing's worth more than a few bucks."

"What does he do in LA, your brother?" She thought about her spiral-bound notebook, how she'd be able to enter this information when she got home.

Putting the match to his cigarette, he told her Lee's idea had been to get into the film business, on the technical end. He knew something about lighting, used to do lighting for a band. Jack laughed and dragged on the cigarette. "Last I heard, though, he was working in a carwash. I don't know how serious he was about the movie industry, as a matter of fact. I think it was just something Lee told people, an excuse to go to the West Coast."

Jack's brother works in a carwash, she wrote in her head. No, cross that out. *Jack's brother plans to work in the film industry. His name is Lee.*

Jack leaned back in his chair and drew smoke into his lungs. The girl's stiff dress stood away from her chest, so without even trying he was able to see the strap of her white bra, part of the cup. Her breast made him think of a scoop of vanilla ice cream.

"What are you going to do?" she asked.

"Do?"

"Now that you're not working in the factory anymore."

Suddenly she was sure he was going to the West Coast, too. People did that all the time, just got into cars or vans or pickups and took off. The older brothers of people she knew in school. Her own mother, so long ago Amy had almost no memory of her. Mostly those people never came back.

Jack didn't say anything for a while, just went on drawing on the cigarette and blowing out the smoke. She looked at the mug he'd given her and saw that a duck carrying a red umbrella was painted on the side. Why would a duck need to carry an umbrella? she wondered.

He got up from the table and tapped his cigarette ash on top of rinds and coffee grounds in the garbage pail. Why not tell her? She might be just a kid, but it wasn't like anybody else gave a shit what he did. "The thing is," he said, "the deal's not signed, sealed, and delivered yet."

"I can keep a secret."

He looked at her innocent face, lightly freckled, without guile, and felt impelled to trust her. He told her about the piece of land out on Gooseneck Road, in Holland. Kind of swampy, but it had a little house on it. It would do all right. He found himself telling her about Panther, the perfect bitch, won best-of-breed at a show in western Massachusetts a couple of years ago. Only four years old and already'd whelped a couple of gorgeous litters, brought top prices.

Amy imagined him stroking Panther's silky black coat, the dog's tongue licking his fingers.

"I'm going to pick her up next week, Wednesday or Thursday," he said. "She's at a kennel downstate." He dropped the cigarette into the pail, and it sizzled against an orange rind. Before he knew what he was saying, he asked, "Why don't you come along for the ride?"

She'd have to cut school, which she'd never done in her life. She'd have to lie to her grandmother. "Okay," she said.

~

On a Sunday afternoon a couple of weeks later they were putting up bread and butter pickles, Amy and her grandmother. Amy hated being stuck in that dim and congested kitchen, the old linoleum so coated with damp from the boiling vinegar that her shoes kept sticking to it or skidding on it as she tried to maneuver around Gam's bulk . . . while Jack, her lover, was out in the cool countryside cutting down trees to make space for his kennels, the muscles in his arms flexing as he manipulated saw or axe or winched out stumps. He could be pausing now for a cigarette. If she was with him, he could be lifting her skirt, touching her, his hands smelling of earth and spruce gum . . .

One of the quart jars failed to seal. Impatiently Amy wiped

mustard seeds off the rim and replaced the lid, returning the jar with a splash to the canner.

"I'm not going to let you wreck your life," Gam said, "over some pimply boy."

Right out of the blue, she said that. Well, Jack wasn't pimply and he wasn't a boy. Amy had already made love with him twice and felt the jagged row of stitches winding in the small of his back. She was certain she knew far more about such things than her grandmother ever had. "There isn't any boy," Amy said.

"I'm not deaf and dumb, Amy." Her grandmother wiped her hands on her apron.

"I won't wreck my life."

"When I was your age I had nothing."

"I know, Gam." Of course she did, knew the story by heart. Hard times. Leaving the potato farm as a girl, traveling down to Bangor on her own and living in a room in a rich family's house, scrubbing floors and washing dishes to pay part of her rent. Humiliating jobs that hardly paid enough to keep body and soul together, but at least she wasn't trapped on those few acres of dirt, which produced more rocks than potatoes. Amy'd heard her grandmother's story so many times she was sick of it.

"You have it easy, compared to me. Don't thumb your nose at your luck the way your mother did."

"I *won't,* Gam."

Ethel looked at her granddaughter's thin arms, her tangle of wheat-colored hair, the secretive downcast eyes that were altogether too much like Ruth's. Under her grandmother's gaze, Amy pulled a damp dish towel from her shoulder and threw it on the table.

"You haven't finished here, Miss. Where do you think you're going?"

"Nowhere. Where is there to go?"

Down the hall the girl's bedroom door opened and slammed shut. Ethel made herself a cup of tea and sat at the table, thinking. She felt a pain inside her, imagined the mouth of a worm attached to her stomach lining.

Ruth, the beloved child of her middle age, somehow grown up wild and defiant. Wanting it all and wanting it *now,* and see where it got her. Ethel groaned and heaved herself out of the chair. In a kitchen drawer, amid a jumble of rubber bands and thumbtacks and milk-bottle wires, she found an old key. She carried it into the hall and turned it in the lock on her granddaughter's door.

Amy heard the rough scrape and whine. For a second, absorbed in her notebook, she didn't understand what the sound meant. Then she ran to the door and pounded on it. "You can't do that! Let me out!"

Silence. Just crickets in the crabgrass outside her window, the television set in the neighbor's house, the faraway drone of a lawnmower. She lifted the window as far as it would go and pulled at the rim of the screen, but it was rusted in the frame. Frantically she searched the room for something that would cut it. Everything blunt in here, soft and bendable, as if she'd been deliberately stripped of weapons. Finally she took her nail scissors from the top of the dresser and jabbed them into the screen. While she was cutting she thought about her mother. Now Amy understood how her mother had been driven to pay such a price—her baby daughter—for her freedom. So what if in the end she'd died alone in a rented room? At least she'd lived first.

Amy took with her a few clothes in a plastic shopping bag, the dangly gold earrings that had been her mother's, and her birth certificate. Climbing down through the pricklebushes that grew against the foundation, she scratched her arms and legs. For once in her life she was grateful for the overgrown cedars under which the house cowered in darkness, since their thick branches hid her from prying eyes. She got her bicycle out of the shed, stuffed the bag of clothes into the saddle basket, and rode away.

⁓

They stopped for gas just over the state line, and she used the pay phone to tell her grandmother not to worry about her. She would be needing her money, Amy said, the money she'd been working for every summer, which had been saved in the bank for her future.

"You won't see a dime of that money," Gam said. "Not unless you come to your senses."

Amy was sick into the toilet in the Ladies. She rinsed out her mouth under the tap and combed her hair and ran out to the truck where Jack was waiting for her, his fingers tapping on the steering wheel. He didn't ask what her grandmother's reaction had been, and she didn't say. It was September, and already the leaves were turning, and as they drove along the mountain roads the smell of wood smoke drifted in Jack's open window along with the chilly, foggy air.

For three days they stayed in a motel on a back-country route. Their cabin had two metal lawn chairs out front, which they never sat in on account of the bugs, and plastic flowers in a vase on the bureau. They ate carry-out meals sitting on the chenille spread of the saggy double bed—he'd drink beer and she'd drink sodas—and a dozen times a day they made love. She'd wake him in the night she was so hungry for him. She never felt like she got enough.

On the fourth day they went to a justice of the peace in a nearby village, and Jack took a plain ring out of his jacket pocket and put it on her finger. They'd bought the ring in a secondhand shop, must have been gold-plated, at least, because it didn't turn her finger green. It was a little too big, and she worried she was going to lose it.

After they got back to Holland, to the cape hastily furnished with things bought at flea markets and the thrift store in the basement of the Union Church, he asked about the nine hundred dollars in her bank account. Bills coming due for the chain-link fencing, the concrete, the wood planks that lay stacked in the yard.

"I won't be able to give it to you, after all."

He thought she was kidding.

"When I called her from the pay phone, she said if I married you I wouldn't see a dime of it."

"She didn't mean it. She flew off the handle, that's all."

"She meant it, Jack."

"But the money's yours," he said. "You earned it."

"What can I do? The account's in her name."

"Get your grandfather to help you."

"Gapp always does what she tells him."

Jack walked out of the house and she heard the rented machine start up. He was drilling post holes for the first lot of fencing. All afternoon he worked without stopping, and she thought the sound of the drilling was going to drive her crazy. She felt her bones vibrate, thought her teeth would be shaken out of her head.

Later, in bed, he said, "The old witch will come around."

~

The next Sunday she got Jack to shave with a new razor blade and to put on a dress shirt she'd laundered by hand and hung out to dry on a rope strung between two trees in the yard, then pressed with a clumsy, heavy old steam iron from the church thrift store. He combed his hair with water. It was chilly as they drove along Gooseneck Road, the swamp maples flaring red, a touch of frost on the dry weeds in the meadow. The love she had for him was like the way you feel when you haven't eaten breakfast. A vague uneasiness, something's missing or forgotten but you're not sure what.

Jack parked the pickup in front of the house on Knollwood Lane and turned off the ignition. It'll be okay, she said to herself. I'm not like Ruth, my mother, coming home with a bastard baby in my belly, itching to take off again the minute the kid is born. Jack is nice-looking, well spoken. He'll listen to Gapp talk about the new press, imported at great expense from some foreign country. He'll clear his plate and say yes to seconds, praise Gam's cooking. They'll see how serious he is about their future.

She ran up the front steps and took her house key out of her purse. But she couldn't make it go in the lock. "What's the problem?" Jack asked.

She laughed. "I've been gone so long I've forgotten how to work the key."

"Let me do it." He tossed his half-smoked cigarette into the bush under the window and fiddled around with the key, turned it over and tried it upside down. "You sure this is the right one?"

"Of course," she said.

He swore under his breath. "They must have had the lock changed."

She couldn't believe Gam would do that. She rang the bell, rapped on the door. They never went anywhere on a Sunday morning, that's why she picked Sunday for the first visit. Gam would be in her housedress, scraping the vegetables for midday dinner. Gapp would have reached one of the back sections of the paper by now. There'd be a pot of cold coffee on the stove, the smell of meat roasting in the oven, fat sputtering into the pan. Always enough food for leftovers on Monday, for the sandwiches Gapp took to the shop.

After about five minutes the window next to the front door was raised a little. Furtively Gapp leaned down into the crack and said she'd better come back another time.

She saw that the unshaven stubble on his cheek caught the light like grains of white sand. His eyes were watery, the sockets the color of a bloody cloth soaked and wrung out. How much he seemed to have aged in only a couple of weeks. "Gapp, open the door. It'll be all right."

"She says when you come back, come by yourself."

"Tell her I'm not going to do that," Amy said.

Turned out she did, though. She needed cold-weather clothes from her closet, her winter boots. And the truth was she felt homesick for Gapp, and for her grandmother too, couldn't bring herself to make a complete break. At the beginning of November she drove the pickup to the house, ate a meal with them. Before she left Gam rummaged through the kitchen cupboards and gave her an old mixing bowl Amy had always liked, the color of caramel with a blue stripe under the rim, a well-seasoned iron skillet, a handful of mismatched utensils. But her grandmother wouldn't talk about Amy's husband, refused to hear his name mentioned.

"What about the money?" Jack asked when she got back.

"I didn't bring it up."

Anyway, even if she'd been able to talk Gam out of the nine hundred dollars, it wouldn't go very far, she realized. She knew she'd have to look for a job, and before long she found one, pecking out contracts and letters to clients on the old Underwood in Ewell Dyer's law office. Only paid minimum wage, but she didn't even have a high-school diploma, and she guessed it was better than cooking up burgers in a truck stop.

~

She thought it was the flu, because it was March, and everybody was talking about how bad it was that year. She couldn't put anything on her stomach, and she felt faint as she stood at the stove frying Jack's bacon. She had to sit on the toilet with the cover down and put her head between her legs, the wretched fatty smell of the bacon seeping around the bathroom door.

"What's eating you?" Jack asked. "You look like death warmed over."

"I must be coming down with something. The flu."

Ewell Dyer's wife had it, and the woman Amy talked to sometimes in the laundromat. Amy overheard somebody in the post office say it had killed her mother in the nursing home. Some kind of special Asian strain of virus nobody had any resistance to.

"Well, for Crissake don't give it to me," Jack said, thinking about Rosie in heat and the appointment he had to keep with her down in Massachusetts. How was he going to drive down there with the flu?

So that night, and the night after, Amy lay on the couch in the living room, trying to sleep, listening to the black bitch Rose of Tralee whining in the kennel outside the window.

Amy didn't come down with the other symptoms—sore throat and fever and cough—and gradually she realized she wasn't going to get the flu. Her nipples chafed inside her bra. She felt pressure in her bladder. In the late afternoons, sitting at the old Underwood in the office, she felt so exhausted she thought she'd be able to sleep with her cheek resting on the keys.

Then it was April, and one day, with that tiny clump of life in her belly, she got in Jack's pickup and drove way out in the country, somewhere north and west of town. Now if she looked at a map she'd never be able to trace the route, and she couldn't have at the time, either. It was almost as if she invented the countryside as she drove along and it disappeared after she passed through it.

She left the pickup by the side of an unpaved road and walked through a field. It wasn't soggy, like the open land on Gooseneck Road, and everywhere in the field some kind of tiny wildflower was blooming, acres of billowing white. She thought it was a sign that it would be okay, he wouldn't mind. He'd be pleased, even.

When she got home she blurted out the news. The dirty dog food pan he was carrying dropped into the kitchen sink and clattered against the enamel. "Well, you'll just have to do something about it," he told her, "because we can't afford it right now." He bent to unlace his boots. "You know that as well as I do."

Silently she went to the sink and picked up the dishrag and started washing out the pan. Her neck muscles would be clenched, her jaw tight with the effort of not speaking. A strong streak of the martyr in her, he thought, annoyed. "It's the wrong time, Amy. Maybe next year."

She couldn't press him, she mustn't. After all, it was her own decision to be here, she could blame no one but herself for that. And she knew he was right, they couldn't afford a child. Later he made love to her. She felt his heart beating hard an inch away from hers and the rough snake of stitches winding across his spine.

The next day she asked her friend in the laundromat if she knew a doctor who'd understand a woman's problems, and the friend understood what she meant and wrote a name on the back of a candy wrapper she found on the laundromat floor. At the office Amy looked up the name in the phone book and called and made an appointment.

She tried not to think about it, but couldn't get rid of the image of the little black-handled paring knife she'd bought for a quarter in the church basement. She pictured the knife coring the offending cluster of cells, like a rotten spot in a piece of fruit. Afterward she felt sick for days, dizzy and sore and passing clots trailing scarves of membrane, but went to work anyway.

Not long after the abortion she tripped on the stoop and chipped a front tooth. Punishment, she knew.

~

Rose of Tralee had her pups, five coal-black wriggling blind babies, at the end of May. The summer was the hottest in living memory. In July a nearby barn burned, and the fire spread into neighboring fields. Jack told Amy to get in the pickup. "I'm not going to leave you," she said. "The hell you aren't," he replied. He loaded Rosie and the pups into the truck bed, ordered Amy to drive fast as the vehicle would go to the opposite end of Gooseneck Road. He stayed and held the hose, ready to douse the kennels if the fire should leap from tree to tree through the marsh and reach their place. When the firemen finally got the blaze under control and it was safe to come home, she found Jack drinking a beer in the kitchen. Specks of cinder had fallen from the sky and burned tiny holes in his shirt.

She wanted to talk about it then. Say something like: Shouldn't we stick together in times of trouble? Impossible to come up with just the right words, though. She knew how irritated he'd get by what he labeled "hearts and flowers." And she was afraid if she asked who he'd been rescuing from the fire, her or the dogs, he might tell her something she didn't want to hear.

In August Gapp retired from the print shop. The owner planned on throwing a party for him at the big Italian restaurant out on Broadway Extension, all the workers and their families invited. Amy told her grandmother she wouldn't go without Jack, and Gam said she wouldn't go if Jack went. In the end it didn't make any difference because Gapp died in his sleep a few days before the party. Just like him, Amy thought. Never liked being the center of attention. Couldn't stand fuss.

After Gapp was in his grave the arthritis that had troubled Gam for years grew worse. With cold weather came attacks in her knuckle joints and knees, in her spine. Other pains came out of nowhere, stabbing her for no reason in heart or groin. She took to using a big black cane she found in the attic, could hardly make it as far as the corner store.

Jack complained about Amy's spending so much time at Knollwood Lane.

Now they had three bitches, a yelping gaggle of half-grown pups. He could use more help hosing down dog runs, mixing up the vitamin-laced puppy mash the vet recommended, brushing the dogs' coats. "The more you wait on the old bag, the more she'll demand," he said, and Amy answered, "I have to. She doesn't have anybody else."

Amy couldn't explain it to Jack, but she discovered a kind of pleasure, or maybe it was only relief, in trying to make up for past sins.

March. At the house on Knollwood Lane there was still a crust of snow, tough and dense as asphalt, under an overgrown cedar in the yard. In one trip Amy hauled the two bags of groceries from the pickup—enough, she hoped, to keep her grandmother going in the week until her return. All week Gam pored over the ads and coupons in the supermarket flyers that came in the mail, making lists of instructions for Amy to carry out at the IGA and the Super Value. Lists written in her crabbed, nearly illegible hand, the pen pressed down so hard it punctured the scrap paper.

Most of the stuff Gam didn't even need. Squirreled away on closet shelves, in the attic and down cellar, she had toilet rolls and bars of soap and cans of food enough to last her a hundred years. She must figure she's immortal, Amy thought. Yet in a way Amy could understand the kind of hunger that fueled Gam's hoarding. *Things* don't go away and leave you. *Things* don't die.

"That you, Amy?" Gam called from the den, where she'd probably been dozing in her chair.

"Yes, it's me." Amy shed her coat and carried the kettle to the sink to fill it. She was dying for a cup of coffee. Tedious day in the office, and then the hassle of two supermarkets, crowded as they always were at that hour of the day.

While the kettle was coming to a boil she began to unpack the groceries onto the counter and kitchen table. She didn't put them away, since Gam would examine each item and check it against the list. Each week something was wrong, Amy had made some mistake. She'd be doomed the following Wednesday to stand in line at the customer service counter in Super Value or IGA with the flyer and the offending item in hand. The kettle whistled thinly, and Amy fixed two cups of coffee.

Her grandmother, wearing a crocheted hair net like a fish seine and flesh-colored cotton stockings, limped into the kitchen. Leaning on the big black cane, of a size made for a man, she lifted her cup from the table and slurped the milky coffee. "You didn't get boric acid, I suppose."

"Boric acid? It wasn't on the list, was it?

"I didn't realize I was almost out until this morning."

No point in asking why she didn't call the house. Jack might pick up the phone. Or the office—the woman they had answering the phone needed a hearing aid, Gam claimed, she couldn't understand a word Gam said. Instead, Amy was supposed to be a mind reader. "I'll bring some by tomorrow."

"Pain's bad today, right in the small of my back."

"I'm sorry, Gam. Did you remember to take your pills?"

Of course she didn't take them. The pills made her dizzy, Ethel didn't know why Amy kept forgetting that. Amy's long-suffering expression was like a dose of gall to her, smile as false as a three-dollar bill. When the girl opened her mouth she couldn't help showing the chipped front tooth. Ethel did not doubt that man gave it to her, the only thing he would ever give her.

The old woman set the cup down, rattling it dangerously in its saucer, and started to sort through cans and boxes with her arthritic claw of a hand. "I saw your husband has an ad in the paper," Gam said.

Amy sat at the table with her cup, untied her shoes, and pulled them from her feet.

"It's not about dogs for once. Bicycle. Garden tools. Fishing gear. I don't remember what-all else. Must be hard up for cash."

Always, Amy thought. Always.

"That wouldn't be the bicycle you stole from the shed, would it?"

"It was my bike. Gapp gave it to me."

"Not to run away on, he didn't give it to you for that."

"It's old and rusty."

Ethel remembered unlocking Amy's door and finding torn pieces of screen littering the floor, the ruined manicure scissors open beside them, the room swarming with mosquitoes. "Wouldn't be old and rusty if you'd taken care of it."

"That's like saying you wouldn't have rheumatism if you'd taken care of your joints."

Gam lifted the big black cane and brought it down hard on Amy's forearm. The cup flew out of Amy's hand and crashed against the stove, breaking into four or five pieces. Amy was so surprised that for a moment all she could do was stare at the brownish liquid dripping off the oven door onto the floor. The old woman calmly resumed checking off the items on the table against her list. If it hadn't been for the pain in her arm and the broken cup on the floor, Amy almost would not have believed it happened. Then Gam muttered, "Time you learned to keep a civil tongue in your head."

Amy stood. Her hands were shaking. She said, "Gam, I'm not a little girl. I'm twenty years old, a married woman."

"Twenty years old and stuck like a fly in a web."

Amy cleaned up the coffee and broken china, then set about preparing her grandmother's supper.

~

More litters of pups were born and then, after eight or ten weeks, sold through classified ads in the paper. *Black Labs, excellent bloodlines, all shots, wormed.* Amy never got used to the expense involved in the raising of pedigreed dogs: stud fees, show fees, vet bills, propane gas to heat the kennels, kibble by the hundred-pound bag. Each new statement that appeared in the mail made sweat collect in her armpits as she tried to figure out which creditor could be stalled a month or two, which corner cut. She'd get a sick headache and swallow so many aspirin she imagined them corroding her stomach lining, but Jack seemed indifferent to the invoices collecting in a pile on the kitchen counter. Apparently he assumed that God would provide. Or failing that, Amy.

One year a virus wiped out two entire litters, except for an ugly runt that Jack never found a buyer for. Clumsy and fawning, the animal hung around in the back kennel, a daily reminder of their bad luck. Another year a young bitch Jack paid a thousand dollars for developed a brain tumor and had to be put down. All that money gone, might just as well have flung it into the dustbin, Amy thought, put it out with the trash.

Neither of them ever mentioned it, but the plain truth was that without Amy's job to pay the mortgage and the electricity and fuel bills, buy the groceries, they would have no home. They'd starve.

Often Jack had terrible dreams, which he refused to talk about. As far as he was concerned, she'd imagined the screams that woke her in the night. He'd push the bedcovers back and get up. She'd hear the toilet flush, the kitchen door open and close, footsteps outside crunching dead grass. She didn't know whether he was checking on the dogs, smoking a cigarette, or just looking at the stars hanging over the marsh. Still inside his war dream maybe, too scary and dark a place for her to go.

Of course, he was a solitary, private person. She'd loved that about him, because it made her special that he'd allowed her into his life. Now, though, she wondered why he had no friends, scarcely left the place except to exhibit the dogs in what she'd come to realize were third-rate backwater shows. Even a blue ribbon didn't mean much, wouldn't result in more sales or higher prices.

~

Spring, just past mud season. Amy raised the kitchen window back of the sink and smelled the mingled odors of dog and the paper mill upriver. Days like this one—damp, low cloud cover—held the poisonous, acrid stench close to the soil. Near the edge of the yard was a granite boulder the size of a car. It just sat there for no reason, abandoned during the last ice age, too huge and heavy for anyone to think of moving. "Imagine how long that rock's been here," she'd said the day Jack brought her here to show off his new property. Seventeen years old she was.

"And how long it will be here after we're gone," he'd replied, his hand lightly caressing the back of her neck. Her hands in dishwater, she shut her eyes, remembering. In no time they'd been inside the empty house, lying on the bare, hard living room floor, and she'd felt for the first time the jagged war scar on his back. He'd hurt her, but she hadn't cared. She'd wanted him so much.

Now she heard him outside in the dooryard, stamping his feet on the rubber mat, opening the storm door, pulling off his work boots, slinging his keys onto the table. She dipped a plate into the dishpan and rubbed it with the sponge. Amy always took care of the breakfast dishes before going to work, not only washing them but drying them and putting them away. It was one of the many things about her that baffled Jack.

"Vicky's gimpy this morning," he said, unwinding the red strip of cellophane from a fresh pack of cigarettes. Victory, the pick of

Rose of Tralee's last litter, six months old now.

"It's not her hip, is it?"

"She's walking like she has a thorn or something in her left hind paw, but I couldn't see anything. Maybe you'd take a look."

She'd be late for work, but she told him she would. It was going to be a bad day, anyway. She had on brown slacks and a yellow pullover that was pilling under the arms, ugly as sin, but too good yet to get rid of. All she had to make her lunch out of was the heel of a block of processed cheese she'd bought on sale. Jack hadn't cared for it, so she'd ended up eating most of it herself. The rotten-egg smell from the mill would linger in the office all day, putting everyone in a foul mood. All right, admit it, she was feeling sorry for herself. But give her credit for not whining out loud, at least.

Amy put the last dish on the drain board and as she turned to get a towel from the rack, she saw him sitting at the table. Just sitting, doing nothing.

She left the towel on the rack, pulled a chair away from the table, its legs scraping harshly over the asphalt-tile floor, and sat across from him. He looked at her, mildly surprised, his green eyes squinting in the light from the window behind her back. He lit a cigarette while he waited for her to say whatever she was going to say.

"Jack, I want a baby," she told him. "It's time, past time."

Behind him she could see the wall of bundled insulation, naked and now fraying because he'd never put the plasterboard back up after the brief foray into home improvement soon after they'd moved in. She hadn't once nagged about the plasterboard, because she'd hear her grandmother's voice in her own.

"You're the one pays the bills," Jack said. "You know how much is left in the bank at the end of the month." They'd been through all this before, a million times it seemed like. What if there weren't so many dogs? she'd say. If we had only half as many to feed, we'd have enough for a baby, more than enough. Well maybe so, but how did she think he was going to develop a good breeding stock if he sold half of it off? It would be like killing the goose that laid the golden egg, before it even laid one goddamn egg. Besides, babies didn't stay little. Before you knew it they were needing braces on their teeth, ten-speed bicycles. Demanding to be taken to Disney World.

Sometimes Jack thought about how much easier it would be to forget about breeding the best damn Labrador retriever the world has ever seen, just get in the pickup and head out. Stay for a while with his brother Lee in LA, maybe. He still had that old guitar around somewhere, he thought, unless they'd sold it in one of their yard sales. "What happened to Lee's guitar?" he asked.

"Lee's guitar! What has Lee's guitar got to do with this?" Amy knotted her hands together under the table. "Listen, Jack. Every damn bitch on the place has litter after litter. Except me."

"You aren't making sense," he said. "Pups bring in money. Babies don't."

"But pups don't bring in *enough* money, do they? So I have to type contracts and wills and divorce petitions until my fingers fall off. Until I croak."

"Maybe next year."

"No, Jack. This year. Now. Or I'm going to leave."

He exhaled, a long thin stream of smoke that trembled slightly in the draft of air from the window and then wrapped itself around the overhead light fixture. Inside the frosted glass were the carcasses of flies that had somehow found their way in there in summers past, though he knew how tight the globe was screwed into the metal base, how tight the base was jammed against the ceiling.

In truth it wasn't just a baby Amy craved. Or maybe not a baby at all, not really, not any more. She felt crazy with restlessness, with a yearning she didn't know how to deal with. "You don't believe I'd leave, do you?"

"Where would you go?"

The voice he used was one in which he might ask if it was going to rain today or whether she'd remembered to gas up the truck. She shook her head, not trusting herself to speak.

"What about Vicky's paw?"

"You'd just have to manage it yourself."

He knocked ash into a saucer. If he stayed cool, he thought, she'd calm down and admit to herself the foolishness of leaving. Maybe he could even laugh her out of it. "Better not go to your grandmother's house," he said. "The old witch would drive you nuts."

Amy got up and went to the sink, stared out the window. She imagined the boulder suddenly starting to move, flattening the wild azaleas that grew there, picking up speed as it rolled down the slope toward the house. The picture in her head was so vivid that for a moment she stood with her hands gripping the edge of the sink, bracing herself for the crash.

~

Amy took the first apartment she looked at, the cheapest advertised in the paper—a furnished attic efficiency in Bangor, near the old gas works. It had a low, pitched ceiling and on three walls beige wallpaper stained by roof leaks. Crammed against the back wall were a stove, a tinny icebox, and a sink. The landlord had stowed the toilet behind a particleboard partition so you couldn't see it, but she'd always hear it, the water in the tank endlessly dribbling.

The narrow, dark steps reminded her of the steps to Jack's room on Cobb Street, over the thrift store. If only she hadn't gone up those steps. If only she'd picked up the change and ballpoint pens from the sidewalk and walked back home and left him be.

She didn't give Jack her new address, or anybody else in Holland, and she didn't tell her grandmother that she'd left her husband. Why listen to the old woman crow. "About time you came to your senses," or "I'm not one to say I told you so, but . . . " She quit typing for Ewell Dyer and took the GED exam and passed it. Then she found another position, in an insurance office on Exchange Street. For that job she had to learn to use a computer, but after the first few weeks she'd have been able to run the programs in her sleep. She bought a car, a serviceable hatchback with some body rust but low mileage for the price and reasonable monthly payments.

Sometimes she went out to lunch with another girl who worked in the office, who'd recently broken up with her boyfriend and was eager to have someone to unload her troubles on. A few times Amy was asked out on dates. One of the men, an adjuster, took her to a bar and ordered whisky sours. She drank half of hers and felt her face grow numb. Another man, who worked in a discount shoe store, talked to her about leather uppers over a meal of sweet and sour pork and shrimp fried rice. A third took her to a free movie at the business college and afterward tried to unbutton her blouse in his van. She wore her mother's gold earrings on these dates, but none of the men asked her out again. She wasn't sorry.

Spring turned to summer and summer to fall. She thought about Jack, wondering how he was managing without her, without her paycheck. Perhaps the rapidly dwindling bank account had forced him to look for work. Or perhaps he'd found someone else to pay his bills.

Often in her mind she'd get into the hatchback and cross the city, picking up Route 239 east of the old bridge. After eleven miles she'd bear right at the country store with the Getchell's ice chest out front and the sign in the window advertising Taylor's worms and crawlers for sale, then head out Gooseneck Road. Another six winding miles past some down-at-heels trailers and collapsing barns, fields with goldenrod blooming in them, acres of woods, an old granite quarry called Devil's Hole because so many kids have drowned in it, some more fields, and a marsh where alders and winterberries grow. Then the road stops being paved.

You wouldn't notice the house unless you were looking for it, a poky cape set back from the road, near a spindly growth of spruce and white pine. Attached to a chain-link cage next to the house is a weathered sign: *J. Gilley. Labrador Retrievers. Pedigreed. AKC Registered.* And under that, hand-lettered on raw plywood: *Dogs boarded. Pet supplies.* Amy hears dogs barking behind the house. The one Lab she can see, in the first run, is a pup, born since the spring.

There's something a little creepy about the place. Maybe it's the half-dead trees, some of which have knots of fuzzy moss adhering to naked branches. Or the mournfully aimless barking, or the shades pulled in the windows.

The concrete path is crumbling, with weeds forcing their way up through the cracks. What little grass there is between the side of the house and the woods needs cutting. The smell of dog smothers everything. The pup has risen to its haunches and gazes at her as she knocks on the door frame.

After a while a man opens the inner door. Through the screen she sees that he's got a day's growth of stubble on his jaw, which seems to have gone somewhat slack. As she anticipated, he doesn't recognize the person at the door. "Yes?" he says.

She wonders what to say. Finally, as he's about to close the door on her, she tells him, "I came about the ad in the paper."

"Wait a minute."

He shuts the door in her face, leaving her to stand on the stoop. Then he reappears, a short leash in his hand. He leads her around the house to the rear, where there are five or six more chain-link dog runs, some sheds and outhouses, a little weed-choked garden plot, and a granite boulder that has lichen growing in its crevices. All the dogs—more than twenty of them—are now barking and hurling themselves against the fencing, obviously hot to get at her and rip her throat open. They don't recognize her, either. She glances back at the house, almost expecting to see a young woman with a round face and flushed cheeks and light wispy hair and a chipped front tooth staring at the stranger who is talking to her husband, but all the windows have their shades pulled down to the sills.

Jack is oblivious to the racket. He raises the latch on one of the cage doors and opens it just enough for a bitch to squeeze through. She's smaller than the others, but not a puppy. As he's clipping the leash to the chain around her neck, he begins to talk about her. "She's not a show dog," he says, "I'll be straight with you. You wouldn't want to breed her because she's got a genetic fault." He pauses, his luminous green eyes on the dog. "I'm not sure where it came from—must be some quirk in the dam's bloodline."

"A throwback?" Amy asks.

He shrugs. "Not bad enough to cripple her, you understand, but she can go a tad lame in wet weather. You have to take care to look for fractures."

He's scratching the dog's head and fondling her ears, and her eyes become slits in pleasure. "A good house dog, though, if you know how to handle her."

Tentatively, Amy pats the dog between her ears. The bitch lifts her head, nudging it into Amy's hand. The nap of the fur is so short and smooth Amy's aware of the bony ridge of the dog's skull just beneath it.

"If you're interested, I can make you a deal. Frankly, I'm a little pressed for cash right now. I said one-fifty in the ad, and she's actually worth at least two, but I'll let her go for a hundred. A check's okay if you don't have the cash."

The bitch begins to lick Amy's hand and she backs off from the dog, puts her hand in her pocket. "I'm not sure," she says.

"Better make your mind up pretty fast. She won't hang around long at that price."

Now the bitch has caught wind of something in a nearby tree, a squirrel maybe. She strains at the leash in Jack's hand, her neck pinched by the choke collar, her toenails scrabbling in the dirt.

"You seem kind of familiar," he says to Amy. "You been here before?"

~

The plastic film bag on her grandmother's newly dry-cleaned drapes read: *WARNING: To avoid danger of suffocation keep away from babies and small children. This bag is not a toy.* Amy ripped the bag from the hangers over which the curtains were folded and knotted it several times and threw it into the wastebasket. She began to jab the hooks into the strip of buckram behind the pleats. From the sun porch, which received no sun because of the cedars that hovered over the house, came her grandmother's snores. With any luck Amy would have the curtains hung by the time Gam arose from her nap.

But in only a few moments the old woman was stirring, the rubber tip of her cane punching the linoleum as she braced herself, hobbling. "Thought I heard somebody in here," she said in the doorway. She eyed the knotted plastic in the wastebasket. "I could have used that bag to protect my winter coat."

"But you never wear your winter coat." Amy poked a hook into the tough, tightly woven material. "You never go outside in winter anymore. Or in summer, either."

"What if I had to?" Gam said. She made her way to the shabby upholstered chair that was once Gapp's favorite. A puff of dust rose from the cushion as she took possession. "The trouble with you is, you do things without thinking."

Impulsive girl, Amy. And stubborn. Never satisfied. Her mother's girl, through and through. What's in the marrow can't be knocked out of the bone.

"Sorry," Amy said, not sorry at all. The last hook in, impaling the last pleat, Amy pulled a footstool over to the window and climbed up, the heavy curtain dragging from her arm. She took a deep breath and, reaching up, maneuvered the sharp end of the hook into the metal eye dangling from the rod. One, two, three hooks into their eyes. The curtain felt a little lighter on her arm. But a muscle near her elbow trembled, unused to this kind of job. Four, five, six, seven, eight. The coarse fabric, stinking of dry-cleaning chemicals, chafed the skin of her inner arm. Nine, ten, eleven, twelve. That's one panel up. Three to go.

Amy stepped off the footstool and picked up the second panel. Her grandmother's eyes were three-quarters shut, the old woman peaceable as a toad sunning itself on a rock. Then she leaped. "Your husband's looking for you," Gam said.

"What?"

"Called me on the phone, Sunday I think it was." Amy's cheeks flushed, and for a moment Ethel thought she was going to fall right off the footstool. "Said you'd left him a year ago or more. That true, Amy?"

Amy pulled out a hook that wasn't straight, forced it back into the stiff buckram. "Yes, it's true."

"Where've you been living, if you haven't been with him?"

"I took an apartment. Over by the old gas works."

"You've got a room here."

Whenever she had to open the door of that room Amy was sickened by the odors of unaired bedding, cold rusty water in the radiator, nail polish remover, pink acne cream, underarm odor, dime store cologne, foot powder spilled in the rug. The drawers of the imitation-maple dresser were stuffed with bras and slips and blouses that fit a young-for-her-age seventeen-year-old. A *True Confessions* magazine must still be hidden inside a sanitary napkin box in the closet, along with the spiral-bound notebook she'd bought with grocery money on her way home from the print shop. The lined pages filled with her backhand would be yellowed by now, her gushing dopiness humiliating to reread, even to recall. She detested the faded pink wallpaper splashed everywhere with daisies, so busy it made the room seem to close in on you.

"You could've come here," Gam repeated.

"I thought it would be good for me to learn to live alone."

That possibility hadn't occurred to Ethel, though God knows she'd spent enough time mulling over the situation after the shock of the man's news wore off. Maybe there was some merit in what the girl said. Ethel could not live forever. She limbered her fingers by rubbing them, the way her own mother had done, and watched her granddaughter stretch to work a hook into a metal eye that dangled from the rod. To Amy's back she said, "Make sure you don't give that man any money. Remember how he tried to get mine away from me."

Gam was confused. That was *Amy's* money Jack hoped to wangle out of the old woman. But what difference did it make now?

~

The doorbell surprised her. It was a buzzer, actually, in a metal box mounted in the stairwell. The noise was shrill and threatening, and Amy resolved not to answer it. Who'd come calling on a Sunday morning? Probably Jehovah's Witnesses or somebody trying to find a tenant who'd moved out a long time ago. Then the buzzer went off again, and she knew. Gam must have spilled the beans. No, she thought, she wouldn't see him. He could send her a letter if he had something to say.

A third time the buzzer rang, a long high-pitched bleat that was probably going to short out the wiring and continue to scream forever like a deranged car alarm. She set her empty coffee mug in the sink and went down the two long flights. Through the glass pane in the door she saw Jack's face.

His hair was thinner. He smiled in that way he had, mostly with his eyes, his tongue lodged against the lining of his cheek. "Hello, Amy," he said when she opened the door.

There was a pause, and because the porch was down a step from the doorway where she stood, their heads were at the same level. Finally he said, "Can I come in?"

She smelled the raw turpentine odor of spruce gum on him. He must have been felling trees around the place, the way he'd done when he first bought the property. Hard to wash off, spruce gum. So many times she'd felt the stickiness on her skin when he took hold of her body and probed it. She backed up into the dark hallway, her heel catching on a curled loose end of flooring, and said, "I'm just going out."

He guessed she was lying. "I don't have to stay long."

"A few minutes."

Jack followed her up the two flights of narrow steps and into the apartment. Early spring light seemed to give the room a greenish cast.

"Not enough room in here to swing a cat," he said. The sink was the kind on legs he remembered from the crummy apartments his mother rented when he and Lee were kids. Surprisingly, there was a small stack of dirty dishes in the sink. He sat on the couch, from behind which the wall sloped toward a sharply pitched roof. It gave him the feeling he'd crack his skull if he sat up straight.

He failed to understand how she could prefer this pokey attic room to the house in Holland, which might not be a palace but at least you had air to breathe. She always did enjoy the role of martyr, though, being the victim of other people's failings.

He took a pack of cigarettes out of his jacket pocket but didn't light up. For a while they listened to the toilet tank dribbling behind the flimsy partition, a baby crying somewhere, her cheap battery-operated traveling clock ticking away on the window sill. Finally she said, "What is it you want, Jack?"

He would have asked her to sit beside him on the couch but was afraid if he laid a hand on her she'd stiffen. Arch her back. His mouth felt dry. "I'm having a hard time . . . " He realized that he'd bunched the rug up under his feet. With the heels of his work boots he made an effort to straighten it.

"I don't think I can help you," she said.

Pollen or something in his eyes, like somebody'd tossed grit into them. He dug at the inner corners with his thumbs. The room looked blurry. "Jesus, Amy, you're my wife. Why don't you just come on home with me?"

Home. The alders in the marsh would be strung with catkins, the shadblow soon to unfold its delicate blossoms.

"Things could be different. If you came back, my luck would turn."

"We don't make other people's luck," she said. "We make our own."

He got up from the couch, his work boots heavy on the floorboards. "Think about it, okay?"

"I'll think about it." She figured she must owe him that much. She heard his footsteps receding down the two flights.

~

Amy found her grandmother in the yard, on her knees, the cane beside her on the ground. Over her house dress the old woman was wearing an ancient cardigan that used to be Gapp's, and in her hand she held a serving spoon. "Gam, what in the world are you doing?"

"I buried it here, but now it's gone."

Amy shifted the grocery bag to her other arm and saw a shallow depression that her grandmother had managed to scrape out of the cement-hard soil. "What? What did you bury?"

"Money," Gam said. "Silver dollars in a tin box. Twenty of them. I know I buried them right in this spot. He stole them."

"Who?"

"You know who," she said. The hole looked like a dog made it, scratching for a bone.

"Gam, please stop. You're going to catch pneumonia."

"You know who. He came in the night while I was asleep."

Amy set the bag on a front step and came back and crouched next to her grandmother. "I don't understand," she said.

"That man you were married to, he took my money."

"But that's crazy. How could Jack know you had money buried here or where to look for it?"

Her grandmother's neck was bent, and sparse hair was escaping from under the crocheted hair net. The backs of her legs were shiny, hairless, yellow. Feebly she tried to clean dirt from the spoon with her gnarled fingers. "He must have found out," she muttered. "Evil men have their evil ways."

"Jack's not evil, Gam. He's just ordinary."

Her grandmother tried to answer, but Amy couldn't make out the words. The only sound that came from her throat was a weak gurgle, like congested plumbing. The old woman struggled to heave herself to her feet, fell back, tried again. Then she allowed her granddaughter to help her up and brush the dirt from her knees. How light she felt, leaning on Amy's arm, as if suddenly she weighed nothing at all. The cane was left lying by the hole.

~

Knollwood Lane was a one-block dead-end street south of the river, not easy to find without a map, but Jack had been here once before. The houses were frame, mostly two-family, with straggly scraps of lawn. Nothing special about any of them, except the one down at the end. A bungalow with dark brown siding, hunkered down under enormous shaggy evergreens of some kind. He stopped the truck and turned off the ignition.

The last time he was here was right after they came back from getting married. They'd walked up the front steps and Amy tried the door. Wouldn't open, her key didn't fit the lock. Amy rang the doorbell, knocked on the frame. He'd said, "Come on, forget it, let's go," but then a grizzled old guy lifted a window. Looking scared, he'd said to Amy, "You better come back alone. Some other time." Jack hadn't known if the old witch was lurking inside or not.

Now Jack pocketed the keys to the pickup and started down the sidewalk. Snow had fallen during the night. The neighborhood seemed deserted. No traffic on the street, no other cars parked on it, even. No sounds coming from any of the houses. All the windows dark.

The brown bungalow was the quietest of all the houses, almost swallowed up under those huge trees, the branches scraping against the windows. He mounted the steps and pressed the bell, but no one came to the door. Why didn't she answer? Maybe the bell was busted. She had to be here. "Paid her last month's rent back in July," the landlord told him yesterday, when he went to look for her. "Went home to nurse her grandmother. Stroke, she said."

The door was warped or locked. Either way, he couldn't pull it open. The windows on either side of the door had venetian blinds, and the slats were pulled tight. Jack trudged around to the back of the house, shoving through interwoven branches, clumps of wet snow pelting him like clubs. One window back there had its blind raised, but it was too high for him to see in. Amid the junk in a falling-down shed he found a lawn chair, the old-fashioned metal kind that didn't fold, made no compromise with your spine. The chair reminded him of the motel they'd stayed in when Amy ran away. He hadn't known what to do with her, but after three days of serious fucking, what else could he do but marry her? Just a kid, counting on him. He dragged the chair through the snow to the window and clambered up through the pricklebushes that guarded the foundation.

Inside, an ugly old woman wearing a black string hair net sat propped up in bed. Her head lolled to one side, her mouth open. Amy was lifting a spoon to it, cupping the old woman under the chin, gently tipping the contents of the spoon onto her tongue.

Jack rapped on the window and Amy turned toward him, the spoon in her hand. Her hair had grown long enough to pin up off her neck, darker than it used to be, the color of buckwheat honey. She was no kid anymore. He wanted her like he'd never wanted her in his life.

He imagined breaking the glass with his fist, climbing inside through the shards of glass, smothering the old witch in her bedclothes, carrying his wife to the pickup and back to the house in Holland. "Look," he'd say, showing her around. "The plasterboard is up in the kitchen. The front walk is mended. There's brand-new asphalt tile on the bathroom floor."

Amy didn't turn away from him, and for a moment he believed it would be all right. She'd understand how determined he was to make a good life for her. But as he gazed at her, something in her expression, as sealed and self-contained as an egg, let Jack know that she was simply not taking him in. He was no longer real to her. Her thoughts were fixed on a point far in the distance, a place much farther away than he could ever reach.

BENT REEDS

APPROACHING THE CREST of Spindle Hill, Grace saw seven or eight cars parked higgledy-piggledy on the left-hand shoulder of the road, as if the drivers had dropped everything to respond to some emergency. Wonder what's going on at Millard's? she thought. She didn't stop to find out, though; she didn't want the milk to turn or the eggs to poach right in her knapsack. Instead she headed for the house across the road from Millard's, wheeling her bicycle over the crushed stone that had recently been dumped in Owen's driveway. She leaned the bike against a popple tree and wiped her forehead in the crook of her arm. Maybe I'm getting a little long in the tooth for this form of transportation, she thought. From the rear of Owen's house came the sound of steady tapping. Finally getting those last shingles up. Two hammers at work, she judged. She went on into the house.

When she'd unpacked the groceries she climbed the stairs to the back bedroom and poked her head through an open window. "What's transpiring over at Millard's?" she asked.

The land was lower on this side of the house than in front, and below her, balanced on some rickety scaffolding, nails sprouting from his mouth, stood Owen. Also Perley Pinkham, one of the deacons. Owen didn't look so good. His face seemed kind of pinched. Oughtn't to be outside in this heat, on that bad leg all day, but just try to keep him from working on his house. Perley shifted his weight to hammer a nail and the scaffolding swayed. "Garage sale," he said.

"What did he do, clean out his attic?" Grace asked.

"Guess so," Perley said.

"Whoever heard of doing spring cleaning in August?"

The two of them looked so uncomfortable she thought it must be more than the cockeyed plank they were perched on or the heat. Perley spoke. "You know Millard don't do things by other people's calendars."

Owen took the nails from his mouth and said, "Did you remember to pick up that extension cord, Grace?"

"Course I remembered. Got you some eggs, too; I saw yesterday you were almost out. Owen, why did Millard clean his attic?"

"Reamed the whole house out," Perley said. "Stem to stern."

"Why don't you go on over there and take a look?" Owen said, rummaging in the pocket of his carpenter's apron. "I bet he's got some great bargains."

"If you fancy old junk," Perley said.

"Owen, I want to know what's going on."

Owen positioned a nail and focused busily on the shingle in front of him. Tap tap *tap*. "He's moving," he said, not looking up.

"What do you mean, moving? Where to?"

Perley took out his handkerchief. He lifted his feed cap and mopped the crown of his head. "Going to live," Perley said, "with his married son. Over to Aurora."

"I don't believe it. Millard always says the only way they'll get him out of that house will be in a pine box."

Perley glanced sideways at Owen. "I reckon his boys want him where they can keep an eye on him," Perley said finally, "on account of his ticker."

Then she got it. *Owen* was the one supposed to keep an eye on old Millard; that had been the unspoken agreement when Millard sold Owen the parcel of land across the road at a price well below its market value. But since Owen's operation . . . "Maybe Millard's jumping the gun a little," she said. "Plenty of life left in the old geezer, seems to me."

Perley shook his head. "Nobody tells Millard what to do."

Including his boys, Grace thought, though his "boys" must be pushing sixty. Funny that Millard would knuckle under without a fight.

"Any red tomatoes out yet at your place?" Owen asked.

"Tom says next week."

"If it don't turn cold and rainy on us." Perley stuffed his handkerchief into a rear pocket of his overalls and resumed hammering.

She could stand a break in the weather, she thought, as she drew her head back into the bedroom. The room still smelled of paint, a dazzling yellow, picked out by Owen himself. Whichever parishioner painted it had left a handful of brushes soaking in a coffee can full of turps, figuring women's work: let one of the women come along and do the tidying up after. With a sigh Grace stooped and lifted the can. She wasn't in much of a mood to do somebody else's scut work, but she'd better get it out of the way so Owen wouldn't go stumbling over it in the middle of the night. She had an idea he didn't sleep much, that he spent a lot of time wandering in his house after everybody'd gone home. Thinking over ideas for sermons, maybe. Or just thinking.

Down cellar, she found some rags and drenched them in turps and began to clean the brushes. Fumes made her remember the hours she'd spent down here late in the winter, February it must have been, when Owen was still in the hospital. She'd volunteered to dip the shingles that Owen wanted on his house in that preservative stuff. Quite a job it turned out to be, clipping the wire on the bundles, discarding the split ones, dousing the shingles one by one in Cuprinol and standing them in rows in a piece of plastic gutter she rigged so the excess would run back into an empty can. Splinters. And small cuts the Cuprinol would find and work its way into, in spite of her rubber gloves. And the fumes, enough to knock you out, nearly.

Tom had said she was nuts to do the job in February, no way would that bunch of arthritic old-timers and assorted do-gooders the Reverend had building his house get around to shingling until well into the summer, if then. She'd freeze down in that cellar. No, she told him, she'd collect that old kerosene heater from Grammy's house. Right, he said, blow yourself up, then. Be my guest. People who perish doing God's work go straight to heaven, that the deal?

Naturally Tom missed the point. She couldn't explain it to him, didn't even try. She thought—no, it was more she *felt,* deep in her bone marrow—that if she took pain and danger on herself, even in a small way, she could force God to take away some of Owen's. Owen would have scolded her, if he'd known, for entertaining such a sacrilegious notion. But Owen made his home in the New Testament. Her experience and intuition drove her to dwell in the Old.

Dipping those shingles had been something like dipping sheep, she thought now, that spring ritual they performed on the farm when she was a girl. *He shall feed his flocks like a shepherd,* she began to hum, *and carry the young lambs in his bosom . . .*

It was shepherds that got saved in that avalanche, she remembered.

~

Last March, a couple of weeks after Owen had come back from his stay in the hospital, she heard on the radio that there'd been an avalanche in Turkey or somewhere. Tons of snow loosened by a thaw slid down a mountain onto a village, burying hundreds of people, and the ones who survived were those who were at prayer and the shepherds out in the fields. A perfect idea for a sermon, she'd thought, and she'd given Owen a call, but there wasn't any answer, and he hadn't turned on that fool answering machine of his, which wasn't like him. Must have forgot, she supposed.

Well, when Tom got home from work she took the car to do one or two errands and returned the long way through town, figuring she'd stop at Owen's and tell him about the sermon idea in person. He still rented that shabby apartment over the Bargain Box back then, waiting for his house to be finished. But he didn't answer her knock, and she didn't see his van in the place he always parked it. She had to start supper in a hurry because Monday was Tom's lodge night and he had to be there early to polish the swords or something, and then after supper that woman from the recycling committee dropped by with the envelopes she'd mousetrapped Grace into addressing and stayed on to unburden herself on hazardous wastes and seepage. So with one thing and another Grace didn't get around to calling Owen again until after eight. Still no answer. She began to have kind of a shivery feeling, and Tom wasn't around to reason her out of it, so she decided to give Millard a call even though she risked dragging the old grouch out of bed. But if anyone would know where Owen was, he would.

Those two had grown so close after Millard's wife died and Owen's wife, seized by some women's liberation fancy, took it into her head to toss him out of the house and sue for divorce. An odd friendship, everybody said so: the dig-in-your-heels chair of the deacons, whose family had lived in town for six generations, and who wouldn't water his garden because God knew best—and the easy-going doctor of divinity, who'd happened into town one July on vacation from the community college where he taught philosophy, and never left because the parish needed a preacher. The two of them, thick as thieves, making the rounds of public suppers and fish-fry nights from one end of the county to the other, more night life than they'd had in their two lives combined up until then, Grace guessed.

So she'd dialed Millard's number. "Haven't seen him," Millard said.

"What about the Monday meatloaf luncheon special at Uncle Nippy's? You two never miss that."

"Told me he couldn't make it this week."

"Why not? Did he give you a reason?"

"Nope."

Damn the man. "Millard, Owen doesn't answer his phone. Or his door. His van's not in the lot by the Bargain Box. It's not like him just to disappear."

"Van's here."

"What?"

"Across the road. Parked in the driveway."

"But he can't be staying there."

"Course not. Wood stove ain't been installed yet."

"Well where is he then?"

Grace could hear the old man's sinuses reverberating as he mulled all this over. Maybe he'd turned off his hearing aid.

"Millard," she shouted, "did he tell you anything about what . . . the doctors said?"

"Doctors?"

"After the operation. Do you know anything about Owen the rest of us don't?"

"Can't say."

She recognized the intonation. It was the same way he said "Blest be the reading of God's word" every Sunday morning at the end of the scripture lesson. Trying to drag any more out of him would be futile.

She was about to hang up when he muttered, "Grace?"

"Yes?"

She listened to him breathe some more. Then he said, "He don't have a gun. Not that I know of."

Grace flew into her coat and boots and out to the drive before she remembered that Tom had taken the car. She ran up the Strouts' porch steps, nearly falling on the ice, and grabbed their car keys off the hook inside the kitchen door. "Explain later," she shouted.

She maneuvered the old boat of a car across the bridge, braked at Spindle Road, cut the corner, and floored the accelerator, which raised the Oldsmobile's speed from seventeen to seventeen mph. "Damn. Damn. Damn." With each explosion of breath the windshield clouded over more. *Just like a Maine man . . .* Furiously she rubbed at the fog with the heel of her hand—her gloves were still on the floor of the mud room—creating a smear that furred house lights along the road . . . *to think the only way you can kill yourself is with a gun.*

At the top of the hill she found, sure enough, the van squatting in the drive, an inch of snow on it. Snow that had fallen the night before. He must have preached his sermon, shaken the hand of each of his parishioners, and then driven here and . . .

With a start Grace recalled the text of the sermon. *Lo, thou trustest in the staff of this broken reed.* One of the prophets. Isaiah. But what had Owen preached on the text? Rummage through her brain though she might, Grace knew she'd never be able to reconstruct it. She must have woolgathered, as she often did during Owen's meandering conversations with the text and with God, allowed her thoughts to turn toward some such question as whether she should make new slipcovers for the chairs in the sitting room, and if so, what color? Floral? Stripes? Grace cursed herself for failing to pay attention.

Owen's house would be locked, but Grace knew the whereabouts of a cellar door key. She'd used it all those days she dipped shingles. Hard going under foot: beneath the layer of new snow that slipped like quilt batting was mud frozen into ruts. She hugged the side of the house as she made her way, tarpaper snagging her coat. The penlight on the Strouts' keychain flashed a feeble dime of illumination on the snow.

At last she got to the bulkhead. The toe of her boot nudged the section of clay drainpipe where the key lay hidden. With fingers so numb she could scarcely move them she groped inside and found it. Now to open the bulkhead door. Tough enough to manage in daylight, the key stiff in the new lock, the heavy metal doors sloping at an awkward angle. Knees braced against the bulkhead, she brushed snow off the door with her coat sleeve, directed the penlight at the keyhole, and tried to poke the key into it. No luck. She backed off, pocketed the key, and rubbed her hands together to get some circulation into them. Try again. She leaned forward, key in hand, and as she bent to kneel on the door one foot slipped out from under her and she landed flat on her belly. The key skittered against metal and fell somewhere in the snow.

"All right, if that's the way you're going to be!" she yelled at the sky, or the chink of it she could see, a leg or something of Orion's. "Let somebody else find him! I quit!"

She didn't, though. She found the key, got the door open, and searched the house, every cranny, with the penlight. He wasn't there, of course.

How could she have imagined he'd give up on life so easily? It must have been her own chicken heart made her react that way. She returned the car keys to the Strouts with some lame excuse, never mentioned to Tom she'd gone out, never confessed to Owen that she'd tried to break into his house, expecting to find a corpse. Even after she found out where Owen *was*—had a few things to talk over with his ex-wife, he said; left the van in the driveway on Spindle Road and went on foot the mile and a half to her house because he didn't want people to see the van parked there and jump to the wrong conclusions—Grace didn't say a word.

Only Millard—sleepless, maybe, gazing across the road, wondering about guns—might have seen the car entering the driveway, seen her bundled stubby figure groping its way toward the house, and guess what she'd done.

Now Grace laid the paintbrushes out on newspaper to dry, disposed of the turps-soaked rags, and left the house. Wonder what the old goat's got for sale? she said to herself as she unhitched her bicycle handlebars from the popple trunk.

Behind her, on the crushed stone, she heard Owen's footsteps. Unmistakable, his gait, ever since they cut the muscle in his thigh to get at the tumor lodged against his pelvic bone. She turned and let him catch up.

"Do you really think he'll do it—move to Aurora?"

Owen's face opened into its grin, which only made her realize how slack his jaw had become. "You know Millard when he makes up his mind about something."

"But he built that house with his own hands." The bike wobbled as she steered it over the gully at the foot of the drive. "His kids grew up there. His wife died there."

Owen waved at the driver of a pickup that passed in the road and then said, "We all do what we have to do, Grace."

She leaned her bike against Millard's mailbox post and they walked across the grass, dry blades crunching under their feet, past the jungle of raspberry bushes that year by year ate up a little more of Millard's lawn. The crop hadn't been good this year; she'd heard that for the first time in living memory Millard had neglected to fertilize them. Must be getting past it, somebody'd said. Beyond the raspberries lay a vegetable garden—pumpkins the size of boulders sprawled on the tough clay—and beyond that his acreage gradually sloped down to the rock-strewn river. Cattails and reeds by the riverbank looked dry enough that the next tide might snap them off. No rain to speak of had fallen since June.

"Garden sure is parched," she said. "I have half a mind to sneak out here some night with a hose and water those poor desiccated beans myself."

"He'd probably take after you with a baseball bat if he caught you. The way he does with porcupines."

"He wouldn't catch me." She rolled up the cuffs of her dungarees. "Thick skulls, porkies. Funny how they keep coming back for more."

"He claims all he does is stun them a little."

They turned and began to walk toward the garage, where five or six customers stood pawing through Millard's goods and chattels. "You in the market for anything?" Grace asked him.

"He mentioned he was putting his boys' old bunk beds in the sale."

"What would you do with those?"

"Set them up in the back bedroom for when Celia and the kids come to visit."

Celia, Owen's daughter, lived in Cincinnati and was married to some kind of engineer. She'd made herself pretty scarce all those months Owen was in Bangor under the knife and being pumped full of poisonous chemicals. Of course, she had a job and those kids, and airline tickets cost money. Still, Grace wondered if Celia would ever stay in his house, bunk beds or no.

Millard had moved his pickup and tractor-mower out of the garage and set up boards and sawhorses inside. On the planks, in heaps and stacks, was all manner of old rubbish. Dozens of those canning jars, the kind with glass lids that clamp on. His wife, Aldina, had been noted for the quality of her preserves, and she'd apparently assembled quite a stock of jars. Pairs of rubberized boots in various sizes and stages of decay. Primitive-looking power tools. At one time Millard used them to make toys to sell at the church fairs, trains and pull-toys and such. The toys hadn't gone over very well lately, except to the summer people; kids nowadays went for bright plastic, not wood. Cords on the tools looked dangerously frayed. A pair of bedroom dresser lamps, milk glass painted with roses, their ruffly shades on crooked so it appeared their necks were twisted out of whack. Everything musty-smelling and strung with cobwebs. At the back of the garage, in a lawn chair, presiding over the dispersal of the earthly remains of his whole past life, sat Millard, glowering.

"Well, Millard," Grace said, "this is a surprise."

"Guess you don't read the paper."

"Not the yard sale ads." She picked up a dented aluminum six-cup percolator and peered underneath. "You didn't put prices on, Millard?"

He grunted. "Make me an offer."

Oh no, she wasn't going to play that game. Offer too much and he'd think you a fool. Offer too little and he'd take it as an insult. She set down the coffee pot and began to examine some Christmas tree ornaments in a flimsy box stamped *Made in Occupied Japan.* "I'm surprised you decided to move," she said. Meanwhile, Owen had put on a pair of hunting boots and was stomping around in them. He spotted someone he knew on the lawn and went traipsing out of the garage, rawhide laces trailing behind. "Aurora, is it? The *real* sticks."

"Those're antique," Millard told her.

1946? Well if that's antique so am I. She had to admit the ornaments did have a certain something about them, though. Maybe the forty-odd years of grime. "How much do you want for them?"

"How much are they worth to you?"

Oh well, why not let him think her a fool? "How does seven dollars sound?" she said, figuring that was the absolute tops he could expect for them in his garage.

"Eight," Millard said.

"Seven-fifty."

"Done," he said. He hefted himself out of the lawn chair and moved over to the plank that displayed the Christmas decorations. "What about Rudolph?" he asked, pointing to a plastic reindeer with one missing hoof. Millard's plump hand squeezed the tail and a bulb at the end of Rudolph's nose flickered. "Fella from the realty told me confidentially this here's a collector's item. Probably worth upwards of a hundred, fella said, but I could let you have him for seventy-five, keep him here in town."

"I appreciate that, Millard, but I think just the ornaments will do me." As she was counting singles out of her wallet to pay for them,

Owen came limping back into the garage, the rawhide laces dragging on the concrete. They'd collected some twigs and a shriveled leaf.

"Those boots suit you?" Millard asked. He was back in his lawn chair.

"A little snug," Owen said.

"That's because they're stiff. Nobody's been wearing them lately."

Forty years or so, Grace thought.

"You walk around in them, they loosen right up."

Or he could always lop his toes off.

The bunk bed parts, boards of varying widths and lengths, leaned against a wall of the garage. If it hadn't been for the scuffed blue paint on them, you'd probably have thought they were just a bunch of old planks stacked together for no particular reason. Millard noticed Owen eyeing them and said, "You interested in those beds?"

Right away Grace saw that Owen wasn't going to play games with Millard; in fact, the idea would never enter his mind. They were friends, buddies. Eating companions. Companions in misery. Those are the kind of people you're above-board with. "Sure am," Owen said.

From the depths of the lawn chair Millard said, "Make me an offer." It was so dim in that garage you couldn't see the expression on his face.

Grace stopped breathing. She sensed that something awful was about to happen.

"Fifty dollars," Owen said heartily. Generously, or so he must have believed.

Millard scrunched down farther into the lawn chair. "Made those bunk beds," he said in a voice you could hardly hear. Nevertheless, a summer person inspecting one of the frilly-shaded lamps swiveled her head to catch what he was saying. "For my boys."

"I know," Owen said, his face bright and cheery. "It's good they'll be put to use again."

"I don't accept your offer," Millard said, dropping each word like a wad of biscuit dough.

"Fifty dollars, and not a penny less."

Oh my God, Grace thought. Owen must think Millard's angry because he offered too much! How could Owen be so numb, even if he is from away? Grace wanted to sprint over and drag Owen out of the garage, but three long planks balanced on sawhorses and loaded with possessions intervened.

Slowly Millard rose out of the lawn chair, like a backhoe out of a bog. The inner corners of his eyes almost met and his wattles quivered. "I do not. Accept. Your offer," he said.

Grace gripped the box stamped *Made in Occupied Japan.* One or two ornaments crunched sickeningly in the box.

~

The following day, for the first time since the weekend his wife died, Millard did not appear in church. As the choir was filing in singing the processional, someone grabbed Perley Pinkham, shoved him into the aisle, and pointed him toward the pulpit. Poor Perley stumbled over so many words in the scripture lesson it was agonizing. The text: Ecclesiastes 3:1-8. *To every thing there is a season . . .*

At Grace's prodding, on Monday and then again on Tuesday Owen limped over to Millard's to make a higher offer on the bunk beds. But both days Millard had risen at dawn to drive his pickup loaded with furniture the 120-mile round trip to Aurora and back. Damned if he'd pay a moving company to do what he could perfectly well do himself, he explained to Vi Leighton in the post office, when she ventured to inquire why his pickup was idling out front, crammed to the gunnels with bed frames and kitchen chairs and supermarket boxes. Just asking for another heart attack, Vi said on the phone to Grace, stubborn old skinflint.

Quarter to six Wednesday night Owen drove across the road to pick up Millard, just as he'd done every Wednesday night since the fall of 1989, except when he was in the hospital. But Millard said, from behind the screen door, no he didn't think he'd be going to the all-you-can-eat fish-fry tonight, Uncle Nippy's haddock just hadn't been settin' well on his stomach lately. He was sorry, but Owen should go on without him.

Very well, Owen replied, why don't you let me know when your stomach *is* up for haddock? Briskly he got in his van and drove back across the road and microwaved one of the frozen pot pies Marvella Look had baked for him.

That was Owen's version, as he reported it, a mite sheepishly, to Grace—men of the cloth were expected to turn the other cheek, after all. Nobody knew Millard's side of the story. Millard wasn't talking.

It went on that way for weeks: Owen mad at Millard for abandoning him by fixing to move to Aurora, and Millard mad at Owen for abandoning him by fixing to die. After the first week nobody could summon the courage to mention the name of one to the other. Spindle Road became like a moat between the two houses, which were in fact almost within spitting distance of one another.

Millard's Ellsworth Realtor erected a big sign next to the mailbox and took out ads in the county newspaper and, buckling under pressure from Millard, in *The Boston Globe.* Of course nobody bought the property because Millard had put way too high a price on it. The trailer on his son's land in Aurora was all spiffed up, ready for him to move in, but Millard lingered on in his house, camping out with just a few sticks of furniture and a pot or two. If you'd run into him in town he'd confide that a couple from Boston, professional couple, had made an offer on the house and were waiting to hear on their mortgage—but nobody believed him. Every once in a while, Owen told Grace, he'd look out his kitchen window and spot Millard propping up the Realtor's sign, which had blown to the lawn in the wind.

Meanwhile, Owen's sermons were becoming even more disorganized than usual. Truth was, you couldn't make head or tail of them. And he looked strained, his hands gripping the lectern, almost as if he'd keel over if it weren't there. He'd forget to show up for Church Council meetings or Bible study. One Sunday morning Grace went into the bathroom in the church basement right after Owen had used it and found blood on the floor. She decided just to mop it up and not say anything, since Owen had made it clear that a possible recurrence of the tumor was not a topic open for discussion. He was cured, and that was that.

October arrived. The maple in Grace's front yard shrank into itself and discarded its leaves like so many sandwich wrappers. Grace stood on the porch steps, broom in hand, and noticed Owen's van bumping over the bridge. Off to that meeting of the people trying to organize a soup kitchen, Grace thought. When the van turned below her house and chugged up the drive she figured he had in mind roping her into yet one more save-the-world rescue operation. Definitely not, she thought. This time I'm going to say no and make it stick. She waited for him to burst out of the van and yell hello, how are ya, Grace, but he just sat there in the driver's seat. She leaned the broom against the railing and walked over to the window.

He'd rolled it part way down.

God, he looked awful. Cheesy yellow patches under his eyes. She sucked her breath in.

"Grace, do you think you could drive me to Ellsworth in this thing?"

"I don't know, Owen. It doesn't look very reliable," she said, but when he didn't smile, she said, "Sure. I'll just get my jacket."

"I set out, but I realized I wasn't going to make it without help."

"I'll only be a minute."

As she was grabbing her jacket off the hook in the mud room she realized that before the silly squabble over the bunk beds, Millard would have been the one he'd have asked. He wouldn't even have *had* to ask. Somehow Millard would have known and had the pickup all gassed up for the journey.

At the hospital in Ellsworth they didn't bother to admit him; instead they sent him on to Eastern Maine Medical Center in Bangor in an ambulance. CAT scans and other complicated tests were performed and the deacons scrambled to find a substitute minister. While Owen was in EMMC Millard finally locked his doors, loaded the last items of furniture into his pickup, and moved to Aurora.

The following day, when Grace and Lizzie Pinkham went over to Owen's to clean out the refrigerator, they found, neatly stacked against the bulkhead, a number of planks of various shapes and sizes, freshly painted blue.

ELWOOD'S LAST JOB

THEY DIDN'T HEAR him over the roar of the washers and the flopping of clothes in the dryers, so he said it again, louder this time. "Nobody move. This is a stickup."

The Widow Balch looked up from the afghan square she was knitting and saw Elwood Tibbetts standing in the doorway with a plaid cloth suitcase in his hand. In the other he held what appeared to be a gun. Mrs. Balch peered over her half moons. "Stop that foolishness, Elwood," she said.

"It ain't foolishness." He stepped into the laundrymat and set the suitcase down. Then he turned the lock in the glass door behind him.

By now Elwood had the attention of Rena Guptill and Mandy Clukey, who were seated in molded orange chairs near Mrs. Balch's. In her third-grade-teacher voice, which she hadn't lost in twenty years of retirement, Mrs. Balch said, "Put that away, now, Elwood. It's not polite to go waving guns around, even if it is a toy."

"This ain't a toy," Elwood said.

True, the gun had the heavy, black, sober look of an honest-to-goodness weapon. "Where'd you get it?" Mandy asked.

"Never you mind."

Must have sent away for it, Mandy thought, from one of those mail-order places that advertise in gun magazines. She pictured Elwood laboriously penciling the address on a rumpled envelope, enclosing a money order he would have bought at the post office.

Elwood worked there, sweeping the place out and emptying the trash bins. You could also see him shoveling snow at the Congregational Church or in summer mowing its lawn and trimming the hedges. He was a hulking, paunchy man with little in the way of a chin and shoulders sloped from decades of menial jobs.

"Why would you want to rob a laundrymat?" Mandy said. "Nothing worth taking in this crummy place."

"She's got that right. Left my diamond tiara at home, ha ha." Rena found a cigarette and lit up, in spite of the flyspecked sign that forbade bare feet, shirtlessness, smoking, overloading the washers, dyeing, and loitering.

Suddenly Elwood took aim at the change machine, pulled the trigger, and fired. BLAM. Mrs. Balch dropped a stitch and Mandy the damp copy of *House and Garden* she'd been thumbing through. In the center of the machine was a hole like a belly button where once a lock had been.

When their eardrums had recovered from the blast, Mrs. Balch said, "My stars," and Rena said, "Well, there. I guess you showed that ole change machine. Just let it try to cough back our raggedy bills now."

From his pocket Elwood drew a black plastic garbage bag. "You," he said to Mandy, "over here." Mandy was eight months pregnant, her first kid, and these days you practically needed a winch to budge her. In addition, she was not used to taking direction from Elwood Tibbetts. She had trouble wrapping her mind around this departure from the normal order of things. However, she heaved herself out of her chair and waddled toward the change machine.

Elwood handed the bag to Mandy and pried up the machine's hinged door. He ordered her to scoop quarters out of the three metal troughs inside the machine, which were the size of smallish shoeboxes, upended. "Holy shit," she exclaimed. There were way more quarters inside this machine than Mandy would ever have imagined, enough to do the whole town's wash, maybe the whole county's wash—and dry it, too. Encouraged by the sight of the gun, she got to work, and fistfuls of coins began to go tumbling into the bag, ringing merrily. The bag got heavier and heavier.

In fact, Elwood had underestimated the combined weight of a serious quantity of coinage. As Mandy was finishing emptying the last trough, the bag's bottom seam burst open, and a torrent of quarters poured onto dirty linoleum. Some rolled under the chairs Mrs. Balch and Rena were sitting on.

"Drat," Elwood said. "S'posed to be a heavy-duty bag." Pointing the gun in turn at all three ladies, Elwood looked around the laundrymat. He seized a pillowcase from one of the baskets and tossed it to Mandy. "Okay," he said, "pick up them quarters."

"Why don't you get Rena to do it? I'm in no condition to go crawling around on the floor."

"I've got a bad back," Rena said. "Elwood knows about my back, don't you, Elwood? Remember how I always mention it when I see you in the PO?"

"You won't get away with this," Mandy said to Elwood. With a groan she knelt and began to gather heaps of quarters into the pillowcase. She wondered how come nobody in Clip 'n' Curl next door had heard the shot. She wondered how come nobody arrived with their laundry and pulled on the door handle and peered through the glass and sized up the situation and ran to call the sheriff. It seemed like everyone in town had magically vanished, leaving the three ladies to the mad whims of Elwood Tibbetts.

"What are you going to use the money for?" Mrs. Balch asked conversationally, fishing for the dropped stitch.

"I ain't sayin'."

Mrs. Balch noticed Elwood was sweating in the moist heat of the laundrymat. His sparse straight hair was all mussed. She remembered when he was in her third-grade class and he always hid slumped in the back row so as not to be called on. The other boys picked on him because he was slow and because he couldn't throw or catch a ball to save his soul, and she'd felt sorry for him, but when teachers butted into children's affairs it only made life worse for the victim. You just had to pray the tormentors outgrew the nonsense before too much damage was done. Mrs. Balch recalled that one of Elwood's classmates was killed in Vietnam. Another drowned, dragged from his lobster boat by his own gear. But most of them moved away, because they couldn't find work here that paid enough. Elwood was one of the few left in town.

"I bet you're running off with somebody," Rena said. With her pinkie nail she picked a shred of tobacco out from between two front teeth. You could see the gold inlay in her dog tooth. "The new check-out girl in Conklin's Variety, maybe."

"No girls," Elwood said with conviction, as if he'd already considered such a plan and decided a female companion would be more trouble than she'd be worth. Based on his experience with his mother, Rena thought, he'd be right. Nasty old biddy, Gladys Tibbetts. One of the washers screeched to a halt, and Rena said, "That's my load. Mind if I put it in the dryer?" She squashed her butt under her shoe. "I'm in a hurry. I have to bake a lemon meringue pie for the Vets Club supper."

"I guess that would be okay," Elwood said reluctantly. "Just don't try anything."

The gun trained on her, Rena wheeled one of the laundrymat's carts over to the washer and removed a tangle of sheets and underwear from its innards. Behind her, Mandy crawled under a chair to retrieve a quarter. The knees of her maternity pants were now filthy from the floor, which hadn't been mopped in years, possibly decades. Her bleached hair was coming undone from its rollers.

This is like a movie, Mandy thought, dragging the heavy pillowcase behind her. She tried to picture what would happen next. The sheriff would burst in, guns blazing. Or the most unlikely one of the hostages—yes, she decided, they were actually hostages—would disarm the gunman and save the day. That would have to be Mrs. Balch, but Mrs. Balch was proceeding with her afghan as calmly as if this was just an ordinary occurrence on an ordinary day. Mandy's baby kicked her bladder, and she realized she had to pee.

Rena stuffed her wash into one of the dryers, then remembered she was out of change. She waved a dollar bill, which looked as if it had been through some previous wash itself, in Elwood's direction. "Could I turn this in for some of the quarters in the pillowcase?" she asked. "As you know, the change machine has a little problem at the moment." Without waiting for a reply, Rena handed the bill to Mandy and received four quarters, which she deposited in the coin slots. Her sheets and underwear began to rotate behind the dryer's foggy window.

Back in her chair, Rena said, "So, are you planning on taking the loot over to the Union Trust? You know what Monica's going to say when you show up with that pillowcase there? Monica's going to say, 'Where'd you get all them quarters, Elwood? Whaja do, rob the laundrymat? Ha, ha.' "

"Ain't taking 'em to the bank."

"What *are* you going to do?"

Not that it was any of their business, but he'd be on the 11:45 bus to Bangor, he told them. And from there on the next bus out of town. Never coming back, neither.

All three ladies absorbed this for a while. None of them could imagine the town without Elwood Tibbetts cutting the church lawn in crooked swaths. Or standing in front of the nursing home in a red and black wool jacket and matching hat with earflaps, selling homemade crafts like reindeer lawn ornaments he'd constructed out of birch logs. Or raising a cloud of dust in your face in the post office, smiling bashfully if you bothered to pass the time of day with him.

Mandy hauled herself to her feet and thrust the pillowcase at Elwood. Must be hundreds of bucks worth of coins in there, she thought, but he was so numb he didn't know he wouldn't get very far on that. She plunked herself back in a chair, hoping she'd get to pee soon, now that he had what he came for.

Not quite yet, though. The next thing Elwood did was to extract a wad of paper money maybe three inches thick from the machine. The ladies' eyes bugged. Here they'd thought all he was getting was quarters, a lot of quarters to be sure, but still, pocket change. Actual bills—including fives and tens—were a whole different kettle of fish. Calmly Elwood dropped the wad into the pillowcase. While they were still digesting the size of the take, Elwood held the sack open in front of the three ladies, who sat in a row in their molded orange chairs. He was like a kid trick-or-treating, a large middle-aged kid toting a gun. "Put your stuff in," he said. "Money, any jewelry you got on you, any other val'ables."

"Why Elwood," Mrs. Balch said. "Robbing the laundrymat is one thing, but robbing us is quite another. We're your friends."

"Naw," he said. "You ain't."

Mrs. Balch remembered the D minus she'd given the boy in penmanship, although he'd struggled so hard even to hold the pen properly, never mind form the letters. She wrestled her wedding ring off her finger and dropped it in the pillowcase. In her pocketbook, she knew, was a ten-dollar bill and some singles. She added the pocketbook, then the garnet earrings she'd inherited from her mother. Mrs. Balch wondered sadly if she'd ever see them again.

Rena remembered all the times she'd walked past Elwood's pitiful little stall in front of the nursing home and never bought a thing—well, why should she have? Bunch of junk. Into the pillowcase went her purse with the forty dollars she'd been about to spend for the week's groceries, then her diamond engagement ring, which she'd been wearing on her right hand for three years, ever since she and Phil went their separate ways. Dammit, she might not be married anymore, but she'd *earned* that ring. She didn't like the way this was going at all.

Mandy remembered how she and her friends used to shout *Hey, Smellwood, where'd you lose your chin?* at him as they rode past on their bikes. She didn't have a wedding ring, not yet, but she had two hundred dollars she'd just taken out of the ATM to give to Donnie Dorr, who was adding a porch onto her trailer and would work for less if you paid him under the table. She put the wallet containing those crisp new twenties into the pillowcase, plus her beloved gold chain anklet engraved with her initials. Geez, she needed to pee so bad. And now she felt sort of sick to her stomach, nervous sick. She always thought Elwood was harmless, poor old doofus, but maybe she'd been wrong.

"Elwood, dear," Mrs. Balch said, "if you go your mother will miss you terribly. Why don't you reconsider? Maybe the laundrymat people will overlook the damage you did to their change machine if you give the money back directly."

Rena glared at Mrs. Balch. Reminding him of his witch of a mother was the last thing to convince him not to bolt.

"You'll be leaving behind witnesses, you know," Mrs. Balch went on in a kindly voice. "The police will put up a roadblock and arrest you long before the bus gets to Bangor."

Christ on a crutch, Rena thought. Why did she have to bring up the subject of witnesses? Who knew what Elwood was capable of, bashful grin or no? He could shoot them as easy as any change machine. "Shut the hell up, you old windbag," she hissed at Mrs. Balch.

"There's no need to be rude," Mandy said, beginning to sniffle.

"You can shut *your* mouth too," Rena said, "like you should've shut your legs when that worm digger came around, and would've if you had any sense."

Mandy wailed.

"That was not at all a kind thing to say," Mrs. Balch said to Rena. "No wonder Phil Guptill took off the way he did."

"Get up," Elwood said.

"What?" Mrs. Balch asked.

"Get up. Now." Keeping the gun on them, Elwood went to the glass door and unlocked it. Then, the pillowcase slung over his shoulder as if he was some kind of deranged Santa Claus, the plaid suitcase in his left hand, he marched the ladies past the rows of washers to the back of the laundrymat and out the rear door. Behind the laundrymat was an alley surrounded by a plank fence, where none of the ladies had ever been. It was empty except for two dented trash cans and some dead leaves from last fall. Chilly out here, for May, on account of a breeze off the bay. Blackflies had already hatched, and a few of them began to menace the ladies' ears.

"My driver's license," Rena said suddenly. "You've got my driver's license in that pillowcase. And my MasterCard."

"Don't worry. You won't be needing 'em anytime soon. You and you," he said to Rena and Mandy, "sit." Elwood took a roll of duct tape and a pair of scissors out of the suitcase and gave them to Mrs. Balch. Pointing the gun at her, he explained how she was to tape up the other ladies' mouths and wrists and ankles as they huddled on the cold concrete.

"My back," Rena whimpered, "you remember about my back, don't you?" but Elwood paid no attention. Mrs. Balch had prided herself on the values she taught her third graders (*a job well done is worth two half done; a job worth doing is worth doing well)* and she executed a thorough and efficient job of disabling the other witnesses. Then Elwood taped up his old teacher, every bit as competently as she could have done it herself. Humming a cheerful but unrecognizable tune, he unzipped the suitcase. He took out a floppy denim hat and clapped it on his head. Then he returned the duct tape and the scissors to the suitcase, along with the gun. With effort he crammed in the pillowcase. Once he'd zipped up the suitcase the bulge wasn't that conspicuous. It could have been his winter jacket and some of his mother's fruitcakes, wrapped well, packed to give him sustenance on his journey. "You have a good day now," he said to the three mummified ladies. Suitcase in hand, he unlatched the rear gate and closed it securely behind him.

The ladies heard cars and trucks go up and down Main Street. They heard the Bangor bus roar to a stop in front of Clip 'n' Curl and shortly thereafter take off again. Gulls screamed overhead. Black flies swarmed and bit the flesh below their ears. Rena was dying for a cigarette. Mrs. Balch thought about her laundry mildewing in the washer and the chicken parts defrosting in her kitchen sink, probably going to end up spoiled. Mandy made a sorry little puddle on the cement beneath her.

Finally they heard a squad car's siren approaching from Route 1A, turning the corner onto Main Street, and abruptly terminating in front of the laundrymat. The sheriff must have been at the other end of the county when he heard about the heist over his shortwave radio, up to Lubec or Calais, and that's what took him so long to get here. They'd be rescued now. But nobody came to the rear door of the laundrymat. After a while they heard the squad car drive away.

They thought Elwood might get pretty far, after all.

DEMONS

January 2000

Denia heard the church basement door open and slam shut, rattling glass in its window. Boots slapped across linoleum as though they were unlaced or the wearer had overlarge feet. The girl appeared in the doorway of the makeshift cubicle that constituted Denia's office and stood there for a moment. A ratty imitation-leather handbag dangled from her shoulder. Under the fluorescent light, snow sparkled on her pale hair.

"I'm so sorry, but my office hours are over. I'm expected at the nursing home," Denia said, visualizing the dear old souls being wheeled into a circle around the piano so they could gum the words to "Sweet By-and-By."

Paying no attention to this, the girl seated herself in the metal folding chair next to Denia's desk. She was long-limbed, sturdily built, pretty in an unwitting way. The girl looked around. Her eyes fixed on piles of theology books that had found no room on the few shelves, folders of clippings and sermon notes that still needed stowing in the file cabinet, the framed diploma from Bangor Theological Seminary propped against the wall, Denia's black robe hanging from a coat rack, inside its plastic bag from the dry cleaner.

"So you're a preacher now," the girl said. "Diploma and everything."

Where could Denia have encountered this person before? She'd remember the hair, so blonde it was almost white, if not the girl's face. Denia wasn't especially good with names or faces. "I'm afraid I'm not sure who you are. Please remind me."

"Good question. Who am I?"

Denia clicked the point of her ballpoint pen. She'd been called to this congregation just after the new year, at the dawn of a new millennium; the ceremony of laying-on-of-hands marking her ordination went backward in time, in an unbroken line, for two thousand years—an omen, Denia liked to think. Her first ministry, at the age of forty-five, and a long hard road to this place. Now, having at last arrived, she could not simply turn the girl away. She did her best to smile. "Is this a riddle?"

The girl leaned forward. "I bet they made you read the Gospel According to Saint Mark, over there at the seminary."

Ah, the Gospel of the Obtuse Apostles. Denia wondered more than once how the disciples could have been so clueless, Jesus's parables sailing right over their heads. "Yes, I'm familiar with Mark."

"So you know all about King Herod." The girl's eyes were a very light, watery blue, and her skin was flushed by the warmth radiating from Denia's electric heater. She hadn't unbuttoned her pea coat or taken off her gloves. "How he married his brother's wife. Probably an impulsive act, even though they both happened to be married to other people."

Were they? The girl knew the story better than Denia, but she certainly wasn't going to admit her ignorance to this scruffy teenager.

"Well, that's how it is with kings," the girl went on. "They tend to do things on a whim, just because they can."

What's the girl's angle? The pastorly patience Denia had taken great care to cultivate began to slither out of her grasp. She breathed deeply and smiled again. "I'm due at the nursing home in moments.

If you could come back another time . . . "

"But then a certain prophet advised Herod that he shouldn't, actually, have married his brother's wife. It was unlawful, for starters, not to mention how the cast-off spouses might feel about the situation. The prophet, by the way, was John the Baptist."

Denia noticed that the fluorescent light overhead had begun to flicker. She put down her pen, feeling somewhat muddled. Who *is* this girl? she wondered.

"The more the king's new wife thought about the way that busybody John the Baptist had butted in, the angrier she got. It's like she was possessed. First she made King Herod throw John in prison. Then, on the king's birthday, she sent a daughter by her first husband to dance at Herod's party."

"The daughter," Denia said, in the graciously authoritative tone she'd absorbed at seminary, "was named Salome."

"True, but Mark doesn't bother to mention that. Anyhow, the girl did a bang-up job. The king was so enraptured by her dancing that he promised, 'Whatever you desire, anything at all, it's yours.' So she went to her mother and said, 'What shall I ask for? Half of the kingdom maybe?' and her mother answered, 'No, not half the kingdom. You must demand the head of John the Baptist.' "

The steeple clock began to strike the hour. "This is all very interesting," Denia said. "However—"

"The head of John the Baptist! Half the kingdom sounded like a better deal to the daughter. But if the prophet's head was what her mother wanted . . . So the girl ran back to King Herod, and that's what she requested. Now, the king wasn't particularly eager to comply, because he rather liked John the Baptist, shaggy hair and all, but he'd given his oath, what could he do? So he sent for the executioner and ordered the head of John the Baptist to be brought, and it was carried into the birthday feast on a big platter. Exit one inconvenient prophet."

"Why are you telling me all this? Why have you come here?"

The girl groped in her handbag, pulling out a rumpled tissue. "Here's the thing. Seems like the king's wife won. Seems like, in spite of all her sins, she lived happily ever after. But did she? I'd really like your opinion. As a preacher. With a diploma from the seminary and all."

Melted snow had made a puddle all around the girl's rubber-soled boots. Denia would have to get some paper towels out of the john and wipe the muddy mess from the linoleum herself. The half-blind old sexton wouldn't even notice it, should he deign to lug his mop and pail down to the basement.

"I've no idea," Denia said briskly. "I don't believe the gospel reveals that information."

"See, I'm thinking that such an evil person couldn't possibly live happily ever after. I'm thinking the demons she unleashed tormented her soul every minute until she died."

"There's such a thing as redemption."

"Only if she atoned for her sins. Sincerely."

"That isn't for you or me to judge." Denia smiled. "It's up to God."

"And God acts in mysterious ways, doesn't He?"

"I really must leave now," Denia said. She rose and reached for her coat. "I'm already very late." Devoutly she hoped this was the end of it. Then she saw the knife.

November 1999

He was a skinny little man with a sparse mustache. Setting a carrier on the counter, he said, "How much does it cost to have a cat put down?"

"Put down?" Molly said. "What's the problem?"

"My wife told me to bring her here." He glanced over his shoulder, as if the woman might be hovering behind him. "She scratches carpets and we just got new wall-to-wall."

"Did you think of taking her to the Humane Society?"

"All the way to Bangor? Look, I don't have time for that right now. My wife . . . "

"You need to fill out a form," Molly said, attaching it to a clipboard and handing it to him. "The fee is fifteen dollars, plus thirty for the cremation."

"Cremation? Can't you just put the body in the garbage?"

"The Health Department isn't real keen on that. You could come back later and dispose of it yourself." She thought of telling him he better not get caught trying to sneak it into the bin over at McDonald's—there's a good stiff fine for unlawful disposal—but decided to let the jerk find out the hard way.

She took the carrier into the back room and coaxed the cat out. Six-toed tortoiseshell short-hair, rigid with fear. Molly put her in a cage. The cat made no sound, just scrunched herself into as small an object as she could. Doc would dispatch her after he finished with his surgery schedule.

When Molly returned to the reception area, the man gave her the form and a check for forty-five dollars. "Her name is Mittens," he said.

"Why are you telling me her name if you want her put down?"

"I thought you might need to know for some reason."

"No."

"It won't hurt her?"

"She won't feel a thing after the needle prick."

"You can keep that," he said, motioning to the carrier, maybe hoping his generosity would let him off the hook, maybe wanting to be rid of the reminder of what he'd done.

"No, thanks."

Molly watched him walk out with the empty carrier banging clumsily against his leg. Poor little wuss, totally under his wife's thumb. Bitch. She was the one who deserved the needle.

After work, Molly pulled on her gumboots and the pea coat she'd found in a thrift store for only ten dollars, still almost good as new. Now that she was working full-time she felt less worried about money, but she saved every cent she could. Someday Molly would need it for Ma.

Cold out, nearly dark already. Earlier it had been raining, and the streets were wet, leaf-choked puddles along the curb. She drove to the big hardware store at the other end of town and sat in the parking lot, gazing at stacks of brick under overhead lights that turned them a bluish color.

Shortly before five-thirty a Taurus wagon entered the lot and pulled in right in front of her. Molly noticed shiny stickers on the rear bumper: *Jesus on Board!* and *Prevent Truth Decay, Read the Bible!* Leaving the engine running, the driver yanked the rearview mirror toward her so she could see her own chinless face and fidgeted with her perm like a bird poking twigs into its nest. Exhaust fumes spewed into the air. Soon a tall balding man in an overcoat shuffled around the corner, his shoulders hunched. Uncomfortably he folded himself into the passenger side of the Taurus and they drove off, going north on 1A.

Molly put the pickup in gear and turned out of the lot, following a few cars behind the Taurus. They headed out of Ellsworth, past the wooden toy maker's shop and the apple store. At one time Ma was a picker in that orchard, fitting the work in around her other jobs.

After a few miles the Taurus bore right off the highway, onto an unpaved road that wandered past a couple of trailers and a dilapidated farmstead. The truck's window was stuck halfway open, and Molly smelled damp woods, felt the cold wind flaying her cheek. She tried to keep well behind the Taurus, though she was pretty sure they wouldn't notice the pickup anyway, just one more rust bucket rattling along on this country road in the dark.

The Taurus turned into a driveway. Molly eased to a stop a ways farther down the road and watched the garage door jerk upward and the car disappear inside. The short chinless woman and the balding man left the garage through a side door and walked toward the house. Molly didn't know what she'd expected, but this modest bungalow wasn't it. He was carrying a supermarket bag full of groceries.

Molly waited ten minutes by her watch and then climbed down from the truck, shutting the door as quietly as she could. She decided to approach the rear of the house by walking through some weedy brush rather than heading across the lawn or down the gravel driveway. The legs of her jeans got drenched. Brambles snagged her clothes, and she was glad she was wearing gumboots instead of sneakers. No moon to help her out. She could see a light on at the back of the house—the kitchen, she guessed.

She thought about Ma, maybe starting to get hungry, maybe wondering in a vague sort of way why Molly wasn't home yet. Cautiously, hoping a dog wouldn't begin to bark or security lights flash on, Molly crossed the patch of grass in the backyard. She paused and then stepped onto a concrete patio, where there was a metal trashcan, some folding lawn chairs leaning against the siding, a charcoal grill whose rack nobody'd taken a wire brush to in a while. A plastic line with clothespins clipped to it dangled from the overhang, nearly catching in her hair as she approached the window.

Yes, this was the kitchen, all right. Molly peered past ruffled café curtains and saw him unpacking groceries onto the table: a box of cereal, a bunch of bananas, a few cans of soup and tuna fish, it looked like. She could make out a spice rack, a wall calendar, a philodendron trailing from a shelf. The woman was bent over in front of the open refrigerator, brown polyester pants stretched over her big butt. She turned to say something to her husband, but Molly didn't try to hear what. His face looked cowed, woebegone.

It was all so ordinary. No children baking in that oven, no cauldron of poisonous brew simmering on the stovetop. Still, there *was* evil here, Molly could smell it: spoiled chicken hearts and gizzards in the trashcan, crumbling concrete soaked with rain, rotting leaves, burnt flesh. She shivered, feeling queasy.

He wouldn't have told his secret to this woman, his wife. He wouldn't have withheld even a dime of his measly salary. He would not have dared.

Molly crept across the lawn to the pickup, turned on the engine, backed into the driveway and drove up the road.

At home Molly unlocked the door with two keys and locked it again behind her, turning a key in the bottom lock and throwing the deadbolt. She hid the keys in the kitchen, in the flour canister. Molly kept having to change hiding places. Ma didn't cook anymore—she wouldn't be getting out the flour to mix up a batch of biscuits—but she had an uncanny way of homing in on the keys when she was ranging around the house in the middle of the night, almost as if she had a special radar.

"Ma?" she called. No answer. Molly poured water into a saucepan. She'd soft-boil an egg for her mother's supper.

Ma wandered into the kitchen, her hair askew, wearing a black cardigan that was missing most of its buttons. She hadn't put her arms through the sleeves. Her hair was no longer the exact same shade of blonde as Molly's, but the color of the ash that's left when you burn white paper. She wouldn't let Molly trim it anymore, and it ended up in horrible tangles.

Something about her mother's expression made Molly remember the tortoiseshell cat in the cage, but then Ma's face went blank again. "I'm making you something to eat," Molly said. "Are you hungry?" She set the saucepan on the stove and turned on the electric burner.

Her mother began to sing a little rhyme that Molly knew from her childhood. "Bat, bat, get under my hat . . . " Ma stared out the window, her black cardigan wrapped around her, the empty sleeves hanging down from her shoulders like broken wings. "And I'll give you a slice of . . . "

"Bacon," Molly prompted.

"Bacon. And when I bake I'll give you a . . . " Her mother turned from the window and looked at her helplessly.

"Cake," Molly said, tears stinging her eyes. "I'll give you a cake. If I am not mistaken." But by now her mother had lost the thread and was dancing on unsteady feet to a tune only she could hear.

Let the devils go out from my mother, Molly prayed. Let them go back wherever they came from.

September 1999

Marty saw a girl down at the end of an aisle, next to the shelves of adhesives and sealers. Her hair, the pinkish silvery color of raw wood, caught his attention. She was tall, big-boned, wearing a faded T-shirt. He felt that he'd seen her before, and more than once, but couldn't recall where.

As he passed she stared at him, her hand on the hip of her jeans. His scalp prickled. Had she purchased an unsatisfactory product here? Or been shortchanged and blamed it on him for some reason? The impression that he knew her reminded Marty of the way especially vivid dreams keep sliding into your waking hours the whole of the next day.

August 1999

At two in the morning Molly woke and realized her mother's bed was empty, the sheet dragged onto the splintery floor. Finally she found her down by the road in her nightgown, trying to hitch.

Where are you going, Ma?

To work. I'm late for work.

You don't work anymore, Ma.

I do. I'm going to be late.

Where do you work, then?

Fear belly sin. Fly bite sting.

What are you talking about, Ma?

I'll let him down if I'm late.

Who, Ma? Who?

I can't let him down.

That's when Molly began to figure things out.

November 1990

Lengths of white plastic pipe, wooden dowels, poster board, sandpaper, duct tape, all manner of odds and ends covered the card table set up in the middle of the front room. Teresa picked up a little round mirror and looked into it, but the person she saw wasn't herself. "Is this a trick mirror?" she asked.

"Trick?" Molly leaned over the table, cutting into a length of pipe with an old saw she must have found in the shed. Strong hands she had. Big bones. Teresa didn't know how she managed not to bang her hand against the wall whenever she put her arm in her jacket. Only twelve years old, but she was like Jack's beanstalk, growing so fast you couldn't guess where she was going to end up. "It's convex," Molly explained.

"Oh. What's all this for?"

"My science fair project. I'm making a model of the space telescope." The pipe came apart into two, and Molly started sanding the rim of one of the pieces. "It sends pictures to Earth, pictures of things no one's seen before."

"Like what?"

"Planets, galaxies, nebulae. Whatever's up there."

Picturing those mysterious things swirling overhead made Teresa feel weirdly dizzy, like too many trips on a merry-go-round. Scared she was going to faint, she went into the kitchen, pulled a chair away from the table to sit, and dropped her head between her knees.

November 1990

Denia's head hurt and a stitch worried her side. "You go on," she said. "I'll wait for you here."

"Are you sure?"

"Of course."

For a moment she watched Marty hurrying to catch up with the others, his long legs pumping, his rear end urgently clumsy as he negotiated the rough trail. Silly fool, pushing fifty, just asking for a broken ankle or a heart attack. She turned her back and sat on the bench, huddled in her old goose-down parka. This vista overlooked a cove, where icy saltwater licked shale. Stunted jack pines leaned precariously from the cliff. Decaying vegetation in the woods behind her gave off an unpleasant smell, something like dog shit.

Insane, this spur-of-the-moment expedition into the wilds of Quoddy State Park, a misguided impulse to show off the splendors of Maine to Marty's cousin and his wife up from Billerica. Denia had drunk too much the night before and then awakened at five, hours before dawn, jittery and sick to her stomach.

She felt the chill of the wood bench through her pants and began to regret her decision to stay here, where the path looped back on itself. The others would be hiking through the wilderness for an hour or more. She wasn't happy in their company, hated their stupid chitchat, but the truth was, she was even less happy in her own company.

How spare and unrelentingly dull was the landscape, how unforgiving. Not even a hint of sun behind low clouds. She stared down at the stony, seaweed-strewn beach fifty feet below, trying to empty her ears of voices—theirs, and also her own.

For warmth, Denia dug her hands into her pockets. She became aware of something in one of them, a scrap of paper. A grocery list from some previous time she'd worn this coat, could have been last winter or the year before, even. "Milk," it said in her own absentminded scrawl. "Bread. Eggs."

A simple diet, easily digested, rich in nutrients. A diet for a pregnant woman.

After the last miscarriage—or spontaneous abortion, as the doctor called it—Denia refinished all the floors in the house, the electric sander screaming in her ears, the dust clogging her lungs. Then down on her hands and knees, her back aching like crazy, breathing the fumes of stain and varnish. The house was upside down for months on end, and she barely paused even to eat. Marty made himself scarce. When the floors were finally done she couldn't enjoy them. She knew where the flaws were, the places the sander scoured too deep, the smudges in the finish.

She couldn't enjoy anything, in truth, hadn't for a very long time. Nothing worked out the way she intended—there were always complications she hadn't prepared for, hadn't counted on. Like the bedspread she began to crochet, but the yarn kept tangling into knots, and the pattern turned out to be fiendishly complicated. To this day, in the back of her closet lurked a bag full of that expensive, unused yarn.

There was the boutique she opened on Water Street. She'd gone to so much trouble to find hand-woven scarves and hats, wooden toys, crackle-glazed pottery. But people around here didn't care about owning such things, even if they had the money. Sales to tourists hadn't even paid the rent on the shop, and she ended up reducing the merchandise to half price and having to swallow three months' rent on the lease.

Another year she took a still-life class on Wednesday nights at the high school, imagining that she could be an artist. The fruit she'd carefully chosen and arranged rotted before she could make it look right on the canvas.

Sitting there on the bench Denia thought about all that wasted fruit, pears and melons and plums and nectarines. Their cloying odor seeped around her. She couldn't get the fruit out of her mind; it was like having a fever and being tormented by images and smells that won't go away. She gagged. Her stomach in turmoil, she lurched from the bench and threw up such a quantity of thin yellow fluid that it seemed nothing could be left inside her. "Please," she whispered.

When at last she was finished Denia crouched at the edge of the cliff, her head pounding, her stomach muscles sore, her throat raw with the sour bile. Below her, the tide was receding, leaving glistening flat rocks in its wake.

Then she felt better. She used her foot to cover the mess with dead leaves and returned to the bench. The old grocery list, she realized, was still crumpled in her hand. Eggs, bread, milk. Biblical in their simplicity. Denia was aware of a powerful yearning for her life to be that uncomplicated, that pure. The air seemed warmer now, and dryer, and the sky had begun to glow with a faint pearly luminescence.

After a while Marty came stumbling down the path. "I was worried about you," he said, laying his big hand on her shoulder, "left here all alone."

"I'm fine," she said, and she prayed it was true.

August 1978

Teresa set her suitcases on the floor and looked around. The place wasn't so bad. Hot, though. She reached over the kitchen sink and forced up the window, which screeched in its corroded aluminum frame. No screen. She guessed she must have ended up somewhere near the sea, but all she could see out there was high grass and weeds.

The sink enamel was stained, worn right down to the rough brown surface underneath. She turned on the tap and air spurted. A trickle of rusty water ran out of the faucet.

The fridge was unplugged and when she opened it she smelled mold. Black spots in there. Didn't matter, the food she'd brought wouldn't need refrigeration anyhow: crackers and peanut butter, packets of dried soup. Sure could use a cold drink, though. She found a jar on a shelf, wiped out bits of dead insect with the hem of her blouse, and let some tap water run into it. Ugh. Metallic-tasting, but better than nothing.

Teresa felt the pain creeping up on her and she sat down in a kitchen chair. 3:19 in the afternoon by her watch. She knew she was supposed to time them, but then what? Her understanding of how this was supposed to go was fuzzy, because she hadn't really believed it would happen. Something would put an end to the situation before it got this far, a tumble down a flight of stairs or a car crash. Yet when she woke up this morning she found the bloody smear on her nightgown, and here she was.

Packing her suitcases, she'd heard about the pope's death on the radio. She remembered being a kid and eating tuna fish on Fridays and pondering Limbo, and bread turning into Christ's body, and venial sins, and mortal sins, and the fires of hell, and eternal damnation. During Mass, silly words would pop into her head: *Pious Pope Pius's sow has psoriasis.* A miracle lightning didn't strike her dead right there in St. Joe's, but for His own reasons God took that pope instead, and then the fat jolly one, and now today the tall skinny sour one with the bushy eyebrows.

Her brother Ed, up in Houlton, mailed her the key to the trailer. His directions were like a treasure hunt. Left at the landfill. Right at the sign for bloodworms and crawlers. Another right at the house that's nothing but a cellar with a roof on it. Straight for a mile, past a giant half-dead oak. Left at the fork where the road becomes dirt. The beater of a car she came in she owed to Ed, too. Last spring Ed picked it out at a used car lot and tinkered with the engine until it ran.

Ed said in his letter she should go to the hospital, he'd find a way to help her with the bill. Of course she couldn't do that, because if you went to the hospital they'd ask you all kinds of questions and print your name and your baby's in the newspaper, rubbing your nose in your shame like a bad dog's in its mistake.

She didn't want anybody else to know about it. Especially him. He'd count back, begin to worry. He was a nice guy, and none of this was his fault.

The trailer was all right. Ed's friends used it for hunting in the fall, but she wouldn't be here that long, just until she could figure out a place for her and the kid to go.

The pain came again. The pains weren't the way she'd thought they would be, not like when you cut your finger and accidentally vinegar got into it. That kind would have been better. This was more like being wrenched apart with a crowbar, or having something pumped into you that sooner or later was going to make you explode. Sweat ran into her eyes. This pain lasted a long time, and she could feel the muscles in her thighs jerking out of control.

When finally the pain eased Teresa walked to the rear of the trailer and into the tiny bedroom, where she found a mattress on the floor. She went back to the suitcases and opened one and took out two sheets. She'd brought clean towels, too, and the knife from the kitchen, and a bar of soap still in its wrapper, and a hank of twine. At least she knew to do that much. She made up the mattress as well as she could and took off her blouse and drawstring pants and underwear, piling them neatly on a straight-backed chair in the corner of the room.

Between the pains she slept a little, dreaming in snatches. She felt so hot. She couldn't budge the window in the bedroom, and she thought of dragging the mattress into the kitchen area, but another pain came, and she knew she wouldn't be able to manage it. She went and lay, naked, on the linoleum floor. Grit stuck to her. Flies had come in the open window, and she listened to them buzzing. Sometimes they landed on her and crawled on her damp skin.

Desperate for some kind of relief from the pains, she returned to the mattress. *Hail Mary, full of Grace, the Lord is with Thee,* she murmured automatically, but she wasn't really counting on any help from the Virgin.

Sometime later she felt a hot sea of liquid spill from her, bathing her legs, drenching all the bedding. After she dried herself with one of the towels, Teresa went to the kitchen for a drink of water. The sun was low in the sky. Through the open window she smelled salt air. A light breeze cooled her.

Soon afterward, her baby came in a burst of slime and blood, clotted with something like cottage cheese. It cried right away, and Teresa found that she was glad, after all.

November 1977

Marty stared at the inventory sheet. Two hundred thirty-nine bags of bone meal in the warehouse. Bone meal didn't move the way it used to, people wanted the cheaper chemical fertilizers. He pictured those bags in some dark corner, draped with cobwebs. The figures blurred out of focus, and he took off his reading glasses and rubbed his thumbs into the corners of his eyes. The phone rang. Marty reached for the receiver and said "FBS," but although the line was live no one spoke—a mistaken dialing by some person too stunned by their error or too polite to hang up on him, he assumed. Anyway, it was closing time and he didn't want to deal with questions about kerosene heaters or radial arm saws at this hour, even if there really was an actual customer at the other end, so he replaced the receiver. He thought about Denia at home, relentlessly grieving. Everything he did to try to comfort her only made things worse.

He headed for the back room to retrieve his coat and was startled to see Teresa in one of the aisles, on her knees, dusting under bottles of Black Flag and rearranging them on the shelf. "What are you doing here?" he asked. "You should have been gone half an hour ago."

She glanced up, her eyes pale. Her hair was pale, too, a very light blonde that when she first came to work here he'd thought must be fake, but then realized must have been God-given, because she wasn't the sort of person who would go to a beauty salon or even choose a color in a drugstore. The hair hung limply on her shoulders. She was small and angular and she dressed badly, maybe out of poverty or maybe because she didn't know any better. The stock-girl—or stock-woman, when you looked closely you realized she must be in her thirties—had been slipping into his dreams lately, or her ghost had, strange and silent. He could never quite remember these dreams when he woke, but her presence lingered in his mind, troubling him.

"I'm about to lock up," he said.

"Okay," she replied in a voice so soft he could hardly hear her. She folded the dust cloth and stood.

In the back room he helped her into her coat, a ragged parka from Kmart or somewhere, and wisps of her hair brushed across his hand.

"See you Monday," he said and let her out the rear door, turning the deadbolt. He shrugged into his own overcoat and walked through the store, making sure all was in order, then set the alarm before exiting through the front door. Cold out, and windy. Gritty flakes stung his cheeks. A film of new snow covered the sidewalk, making the footing slippery. Either the weather guys hadn't predicted snow, or he hadn't been paying attention.

The big FBS sign on its wooden stilts planted in cement shuddered in the wind. FBS was short for Fickett Building Supply, but Fickett's heirs had long since sold out and departed Maine for gentler climes. The business had been dealing in general hardware and other related lines for so many years that few people remembered what the initials once signified.

Marty rounded the corner of the store and entered the parking lot. Surrounding it, stacks of building supplies lay hulking under tarps. To his surprise, he saw that Teresa was still there, looking uncertain. The only car in the lot was his own. "Do you need a ride?" he asked, hoping she'd say no, that she was waiting for somebody to pick her up. He had the impression that Teresa lived way back of beyond, with some relative or other. Reluctant though Marty was to go home, he felt even less like driving around the countryside in the snow, accompanied by this woman who had been invading his dreams for some reason he could not fathom.

"That's okay. I can call a cab."

But either he'd have to re-open the store for her, disabling the alarm and all that rigmarole, and wait while she phoned, or else let her cross 1A and make her way down the road to the strip mall, where there was an outside phone next to the pizzeria. He doubted she could afford a cab, especially to the hinterland, and maybe she had no intention of calling one. Marty imagined her hitching partway, walking the rest. Under the harsh security light Teresa's hair glittered with snowflakes. Sighing, he unlocked the passenger door of the Escort and said, "Get in." At first she hesitated, then did as she was told, and he shut the door after her.

He started the engine, waiting for it to warm up, and adjusted the defroster. "You Light Up My Life" was playing on the radio. Nowhere on the airwaves could you escape it. He switched the radio off and listened to the directions Teresa gave in her whispery voice: back through town, left at McDonald's, straight on Route 1 for a few miles and left at the gravel pit, then . . . "It's too far," she said suddenly. "I don't want to make you do this."

Knowing he was in for it, he put the car in gear and turned on the wipers. Once on the road they were quiet for a while. Then Teresa said, "I heard Fred talking this afternoon, by the coffee pot."

"Fred Dunphy? The accountant?"

"He said the owners are planning on selling. If they can't find buyers, they might shut the place down. Think it's true?"

"Who knows? They don't share their plans with me." The possibility was something Marty had tried to avoid contemplating. But Thanksgiving was almost upon them and no cartons of Christmas tree lights had yet arrived from the supplier. Inventories of the more popular items had been dwindling, and some merchandise seemed to stay on back order for months on end, until he'd begun to suspect orders had been mysteriously cancelled. Everyone hired in the past year or two was part-time and minimum-wage, Teresa included. They came and went in a hurry, as if the store had acquired a curse they were fleeing from. "What will you do if it closes?" he asked.

She laughed, a sound deep in her throat that made him wonder if she was a smoker, though she didn't give off that cigarette stink. "Move on someplace else. I don't expect much."

"Why not?"

It was snowing harder now, and Marty turned the defroster up to max. Ahead in the slush he saw tracks where some vehicle had started to skid and nearly hit the curb. He slowed to a crawl. They passed the IGA, Merrill Furniture, Gold Star Cleaners, the Shop 'n Save, before she finally answered. "It's easier that way."

Marty thought maybe if he'd taken that view things would have been easier for him, too. He hunched forward to see, his nose practically touching the windshield, because the wipers weren't doing their job. He should have had them replaced when he took the car in for an oil change last month. Tires were pretty bald, too. If FBS went belly up, what would he do himself? He couldn't imagine giving news like that to Denia, especially now.

"Know what FBS stands for?" Teresa asked. Before he could explain about the Ficketts and how the name had faded from local memories not long after they decamped to Myrtle Beach, she said, "Forget benefits, suckers."

Marty smiled, surprised that she'd think it up, even more surprised that she'd say it to him, her superior.

At McDonald's he made the turn, realizing that now he was driving directly into the wind. He could barely see the road and thought it was fifty-fifty whether or not he would crash into something. Teresa sat silently beside him, her hands clasped loosely in her lap as if she were prepared to go with him into a ditch, over a cliff. Halfway up the hill he felt the car begin to slip. "I can't do it," he said. "I'm sorry."

She was staring out her side window and didn't say anything.

He reversed direction in a used car lot, then prayed he wasn't going to go slamming into a truck on the way back down the hill. Luckily, at the yield sign no traffic was coming from the left. Driving back along High Street, he tried to figure out what to do. The motel next to Rosie's Restaurant was $19.95 for a single, according to its sign, but he didn't have that much cash on him, and he didn't want to ask Teresa to pay for it. She probably had no more than a few bucks in change in her shabby purse. He wasn't about to put it on MasterCard and have to explain to Denia when the bill came.

They passed the strip mall, and a quarter of a mile beyond it was FBS. Marty pulled into the parking lot. "There's stuff in here we could use," he said. "Camping stuff."

She looked at him for a long time, her skin sallow under the security light, her hair bleached of all color. Marty waited for her to say that she didn't want to stay here alone with him, wouldn't feel right about it. He didn't see what choice they had, but if necessary he'd try to come up with some other plan. "Would we get in trouble?" she asked.

At first he was confused about what she meant.

"Using their things."

"We'll put them all back the way we found them. Nobody'll ever know."

She nodded, trusting his word, and he turned off the engine. In their absence, no more than half an hour, enough snow had fallen that it was packed inside their shoes before they got to the front door. He unlocked it and they rushed inside so the alarm wouldn't go off. Teresa stood close to him, unzipping her parka, shaking the snow from her hair. He felt his heart pulsing in scary little leaps. And then, he wasn't sure how it happened, he was pulling her scrawny body against his own, as if she were a small injured animal that needed his protection, but at the same time he knew that he was the one most desperately in need.

August 1977

Denia watched membranes swirl like streamers around the clot in the toilet bowl. Four months she'd carried this one. No way was she was going to put herself through this nonsense ever again.

She went into the kitchen and opened a beer to kill the cramps and calm her nerves. Two pork chops lay draining on a paper towel on the counter. It was August and much too hot for such food, but the chops were all there'd been in the fridge, and even before the cramps started, she hadn't had the energy to shop. She'd been exhausted for months, pouring all her strength into the child, and this was the way it ended.

Beer can in hand, Denia looked out the window and watched rain splash onto the concrete patio, collect in her whisky-barrel planters. The geraniums were going to drown.

She got a frying pan out of the cupboard and set it on the stove. It was an old pan, dented and discolored, which her mother had given her along with other discarded kitchen equipment five years ago, just before her wedding. Clueless little eighteen-year-old bride, who barely knew what a frying pan was for.

Marty had been thirty when they got married. Now his gums left pink on his toothbrush, and there were hairs on his pillow in the morning and clogging the shower drain. Corns on the soles of his smelly feet. In the beginning she'd been attracted to him in a crazy kind of way that was all mixed up with feeling sorry for him. He was clumsy and gentle, like a big old horse. She was pleased with herself for catching an older man, gratified she had that much power. He said, in the backseat of his car, he wasn't going to do it unless they meant a lot to each other, and she swore to him that he meant everything to her. Was it a lie? Denia couldn't really remember.

She'd never had sex with anyone before Marty, and she liked it: "giving herself to him" was the way she'd thought of it, as though she were making a sacrifice. Like a saint.

She threw the empty can in the trash and got another beer out of the fridge. Jesus, she felt wired, as if a zillion imps were jumping up and down inside her skin. The screaming meemies, her mother used to call it. In the vegetable compartment she found a bunch of broccoli, yellowing and wilted, but she didn't care. Marty would eat anything she served without complaint, and she had no appetite herself. She scrubbed a couple of big new potatoes, put them in the potato baker on top of a burner, and turned the dial to medium.

Cutting the woody stalks off the broccoli, she thought about how in high school she devoured *Bride Magazine* and *House Beautiful*, imagining herself walking down the aisle in an ivory satin dress and, after a honeymoon cruise to Bermuda, entertaining in a sunroom with chintz-covered wicker furniture and pots of tulips on the coffee table.

She and Marty set a date, the Saturday after graduation. Then she began to wonder if she was doing the right thing. Marty only worked in a hardware store—assistant manager, big deal—and wasn't all that good-looking. But the satin dress was half paid for, and everyone in school envied her diamond, and her best friend threw a surprise shower for her. She was afraid of the consequences if she broke it off, not quite sure what those consequences might be. Maybe she'd accepted too much love from Marty, owed him too much, to back out now. She still was a little in awe of him then, because of the twelve-year age difference. Why hadn't it occurred to her to wonder what kind of thirty-year-old man marries an eighteen-year-old kid?

Denia put down the knife and dropped the stalks into the trash on top of the beer can.

She hadn't known she'd stop liking the sex as soon as they were doing it on a mattress they'd bought at Merrill Furniture instead of in the backseat of his car, as soon as they could do it anytime they wanted and it was legal and expected and inevitable and her goddamn duty. And then she got pregnant, and the baby wound up flushed down the toilet, to be followed by four more bloody little disasters.

When she'd drained the second beer and opened another one, she heard him stamping his feet outside on the mat. "Hallooo," he said, poking his head inside the door, greeting her in that cheerful clownish voice he liked to put on, too dumb to realize she'd stopped being amused by it years ago. She wanted him to see that something terrible had happened, something final, but instead he shut the door behind him and bent over to take off his rubbers.

What kind of man wears *rubbers*, for Crissake?

Still struggling with the left one, he said, "Did you hear? Elvis died. Poor old guy. Forty-five years old."

"What do I care about Elvis? That's your generation, not mine."

Finally he looked up at her, his thin hair wet and sticking out at absurd angles, his raincoat dripping onto the rag rug by the door. "What's wrong?" he asked.

"I lost the baby."

He crossed the kitchen and tried to put his arms around her, but she backed away.

"That was the last. I'm not going to try again."

"I understand you feel that way now, but—"

"No, you *don't* understand." She was so itchy with nerves she could hardly see straight, and the beer was no help at all. "You never have understood one thing."

"Denia," he began, then closed his mouth. He returned to the kitchen door and hung his wet raincoat on a hook. His seersucker jacket, which he wore to work day in and day out all summer long, had become damp and wrinkled under the raincoat, making him look even nerdier than usual. "Did you call the doctor?" he asked.

"I did not call the doctor. This time around I'm going to deal with it myself."

"If something's left inside . . . Couldn't it cause problems?"

Some obscure "problems" down the road were the least of her worries. She didn't know how she was going to get through this week, this month, without going nuts. Why enrich some doctor for pretending to clear out what was already good and gone? "I'll take my chances, thank you."

Marty stood there awkwardly, watching her switch on the burner under the frying pan and pour Wesson oil into it. She pressed the chops into the paper towel, and when the oil was smoking, dropped the chops in. Oil spattered over the stovetop and sizzled on the potato baker. She saw him glance into the trash bin, notice the beer cans and rotting broccoli stalks. "Listen, Denia," he said, "things will work out. You'll see."

Denia turned away from the stove, leaving the pan for him to tend to, if he chose. She didn't give a shit one way or the other. Let the chops burn to a crisp, for all she cared. Let the whole house go up in smoke. As she strode by the counter on her way out of the room, her elbow knocked the handle of the knife she'd been using to cut broccoli. The knife went clattering to the floor, barely missing her as it fell. She didn't stop to pick it up.

BUTTON, NEEDLE, THREAD

QUARTER TO SIX, time for a glass of wine, not a moment too soon. Anne lit the lamp just inside her apartment door and turned the deadbolt. Since early this morning she'd been meeting with students in individual conferences crammed between her classes, no time even to catch her breath. Lamb chop tonight? she wondered. She hung her raincoat in the closet. Or maybe she'd better have linguine instead. The sauce she'd fixed on Monday wasn't getting any younger.

So comforting, after a rough day, to be home. Anne always felt thankful for the calm white walls, the *fin de siècle* fixtures with their frosted glass shades, the understated fluted moldings. On her way across the living room she noticed something lying on the carpet. A button. She bent to pick it up. Mother of pearl, shallowly concave, somewhat larger than a man's shirt button, two small holes in the center. If she'd happened to step on it, the delicate object would have been crushed. Strange, she thought. She owned no clothing with buttons like that, and no one had visited here for days. Definitely not since she vacuumed last weekend.

Slightly puzzled, Anne left the button on the coffee table and went down the hall to the kitchen. The chop, she decided. She deserved it, after a day like this. Too many fragile psyches needing to be propped up, not nearly enough of her to go around. At the beginning of every semester she scheduled the conferences because she wanted to establish a bond with each student, in a warm climate of mutual trust. She'd never been willing to treat students as mere names on a list or bodies in a classroom. The opportunity to make personal connections with them and to nurture them in their work was what made teaching a pleasure. But maybe the conferences, and the clinging attachments they often engendered, weren't really worth the emotional toll. The university did not pay her to be a therapist or a nanny.

No, she was just tired. In the morning she'd feel differently.

From an open bottle Anne poured herself a glass of cabernet, then surveyed the contents of the refrigerator. Maybe she'd have a cucumber salad with the lamb, and a baked potato. As she switched on the toaster oven, her cell phone on the counter began to trill.

"Hey," he said heartily, too heartily.

Terry. Anne was not happy to hear from him. She'd broken off with him the month before, feeling defeated, finally, by the morass of his life—always late for appointments, forever in arrears on debts, chronically fifteen or twenty pounds overweight. Terry was a good person. Intelligent, patient, caring, attentive. But not, she'd come to believe, good for her.

"How are your students this semester?" he asked. "Any incipient Faulkners among them?"

"Not that I've noticed so far. Terry, I thought we agreed . . . "

He coughed, and she pictured his dank basement apartment in Veazie. Everywhere piles of books with ruptured spines and musty, yellowing newspapers stacked on bare floorboards. His voice dropped. "I can't help thinking about you," he said.

"We've been all through—"

"Listen, you were absolutely right, I recognize that." He sounded a little hoarse. "I just wanted to check in, find out how things are with you."

She carried the phone to the window and looked out at the

slate roof of the building next door. A pigeon landed on the gutter, mournful in the drizzle. "Do you have a cold?"

"I don't know, I might be coming down with something. Anne, could we meet for a drink sometime . . . no obligation or anything . . . it seems a shame to act like strangers after all—"

"I'm really sorry," she said gently. "I don't think it's a good idea." It had been wrenching enough to extricate herself from his life once. She couldn't face doing it again.

"You're sure?"

"I'm sure, Terry."

Anne hung up and turned off the cell. She felt exhausted. In her distraction she cooked the lamb chop at too high a temperature, setting the smoke alarm to shrieking.

~

Several weeks later, a Sunday, Anne and her friend Myra ate lunch at Siam Garden and afterward, because it was such a perfect fall day, drove out to an orchard in Winterport where you could pick your own apples. Anne didn't arrive back at her apartment until late afternoon. At her desk she annotated half a dozen student stories. When she noticed she was hungry, she fixed herself a grilled cheese sandwich. Around nine she decided to watch a David Mamet film she'd recorded from cable earlier in the week. While the introductory credits were rolling she laid her hand on the sofa arm, and something sharp bit into her wrist.

Anne turned on the floor lamp. What she discovered poking out of the upholstery was an ordinary sewing needle, such as you'd buy at Walmart. She stared at the needle for a moment, then went into the bathroom to examine her wound in better light. A prick only, barely visible.

The movie, when Anne returned to it, quickly annoyed her. The two characters, professor and student, noisily projected at each other as if they were on a stage rather than alone in a classroom after hours. The situation seemed contrived, the direction overwrought.

In her bedroom she tuned in a choral music program on the radio, but wasn't able to concentrate on it.

She could scarcely remember when she'd last mended something. Might the needle have been stuck in the sofa arm all that time without her noticing? It didn't seem possible.

Anne closed the blinds, undressed, got into bed.

So she'd found a button of uncertain provenance on the Bokhara and a needle in the sofa arm. Not exactly earth-shaking events, she told herself, hoping to lull herself into sleep.

~

A minor infection developed in the needle prick, but healed within a few days. The following Saturday, during her weekly once-over-lightly with the Dust Devil, Anne sucked the button and the needle from the glass-topped coffee table into the machine. Yet another of life's unsolved mysteries, she thought, in the same category as her mother's case of the disappearing teaspoons and the ephemeral odd sound in the front end of Anne's '02 Volvo, which none of the mechanics at the garage believed in.

That fall Anne served on several time-consuming committees in the department—these, plus the usual preparation and paper-grading for four courses, kept her busy enough. The leaves fell from the trees; she had to scrape frozen dew from her windshield before starting out for the campus; she began wearing her winter coat. Terry called once more, and she got off the phone as soon as she could.

She went out on a couple of dates. One was with an assistant professor of economics whose passion, she learned, was tuberous begonias—the other with a friend-of-a-friend, a urologist, whose notion of conversation was a blow-by-blow account of his custody battles. Neither connection would go anywhere, of course. Anne wasted no time grieving over the loss. Her loneliness she viewed as similar to a mild case of arthritis, an affliction you simply live with and do your best to ignore.

~

On a Friday in late October, as Anne was getting ready to leave her office after a long day, a student from her freshman lit course waylaid her, distressed over a low grade. Anne knew that Randi had recently, to her fundamentalist parents' dismay, aborted a pregnancy. "Everything's such a *mess,*" Randi wailed, shredding a Kleenex from the box on Anne's desk. Anne spent half an hour soothing and encouraging the girl. Thick fog on the interstate made the trip home to Bangor slow going.

When she'd stowed her coat, Anne's eye was caught by something on the otherwise-bare, glass-topped coffee table: a tangle of black cotton thread. She set down her book bag and took a look. Close up, the tangle seemed almost to have a pattern to it, as though the thread had been loosely woven into a circle.

This was getting too weird. Since the landlord's office closed at five, she left a message on his home answering machine and went to the kitchen to see about her dinner.

Mr. Peyzer returned her call as she was finishing up the dishes. "What's the problem?" he asked briskly.

"I guess it's not really an emergency. I just . . . I have the suspicion that someone's been in my apartment."

"What makes you think so?" She could hear the exaggerated patience in Mr. Peyzer's voice, the tone with which men deal with hysterical females to whom they are required to be polite.

"I keep finding things, like a button on the living room floor—not my button. A needle in the sofa arm." She knew how ridiculous this sounded. He was going to conclude that she was becoming one of those nuisance tenants who drive landlords insane. "I was wondering," she went on, "if you happened to let anybody into my place today."

In the background a dog barked, a television set shrilly yammered. Finally Mr. Peyzer said, "I think the fire inspector was by your building this week. I remember the girl mentioning something about giving him the keys."

When Anne hung up she felt better. She couldn't see what a snarl of thread had to do with investigating smoke detectors and fire escapes, but at least there was a halfway plausible explanation for the presence of an unknown person in her apartment. Anne threw the thread in the wastebasket next to her desk and decided to forget about it. She settled down on the sofa with the current issue of *The Atlantic.*

However, her mind kept straying from the words on the page. She went into her bedroom at the far end of the apartment and opened the wicker basket in which she kept her sewing things. Nothing seemed out of place or tampered with. But how, she asked herself, would she be able to tell if it had been?

~

A month went by, during which no further alien objects appeared in the apartment. When she came home to find the kitchen tap dripping, however, she could not be sure whether she'd turned the faucet handle tightly before leaving. Had she left the curtains in the living room drawn? Her closet door half open? Had the crumbs of dried mud on the mat fallen off her own boot or someone else's? Anne felt unsettled, unable to focus on her work, troubled by the idea that her apartment might not be the safe nest she'd always assumed.

On a Sunday morning in November she telephoned Myra, hoping they could have lunch together, but reached only her answering machine. Another friend's phone rang and rang. A third was on her way out the door, late to church.

By afternoon Anne badly needed to get out of the apartment. She put on her boots and coat. The weather outside was gray and cheerless, and downtown Bangor would be dead. However, the Blue Moon Café, the little coffee shop–cum–bookstore, might be open. Maybe she'd treat herself to the new novel one of her colleagues was excited about.

On Main Street, ahead of her, she noticed Terry's bulky figure. His thin hair wafted in the breeze as he peered into the window of the Surplus Store. From a distance he looked good to her, familiar and comforting as shepherd's pie. Anne found herself hurrying to catch up with him.

He turned away from the window and spotted her. "Anne," he said.

For a moment they took each other in. "What are you doing downtown on a Sunday?" she asked.

"Delivering a bike," he said. "To a guy around the corner, on Cross Street. Mongoose. Lovely machine."

The bike shop had been one of the things she and Terry fought over. The patchwork hours—never being able to plan this week what he'd be doing next week—the insulting pay and zero benefits. How, she'd demand, in the heat of argument, could somebody as smart and well educated as Terry be content, year after year, with such a go-nowhere job? Why didn't he take control of his life, *do* something? Now Anne regretted that she'd harangued him. People don't change simply because you want them to.

Awkwardly they stood gazing at heaps of Day-Glo orange knit caps and nylon hunting vests in the window of the Surplus Store. In spite of her innate reticence, she felt a strong need to talk to somebody about the odd things that had been happening in her apartment. Terry was a good listener. She'd always given him credit for that, at least. "How about a cup of coffee?" she suggested.

"Why not?"

She felt a twinge of guilt for taking advantage of him. Still, he went along willingly enough.

In the Blue Moon, most of the tables were unoccupied. They chose one near a window, and after the waitress brought their cups of espresso, Terry said, "I wasn't expecting this. To run into you, on the street."

"It's not as though I live very far away."

He shed his down parka and she saw that his shirt was wrinkled, his tweed jacket in need of pressing and starting to fray in one elbow. Still, he seemed his usual cheerful self. Surprisingly cheerful, considering. He rubbed his plump hands together and said, "Cold out."

"True."

"Going to be a hard winter."

"How can you tell?"

"Caterpillars," he said, launching into an explanation of what it meant that a particular kind of striped brown caterpillar, which his grandmother had called woolly-bears, was fuzzier than usual this year.

Just like Terry, to depend on the wisdom of caterpillars for information about the future. Terry hated winter. He'd moan about the relentless cold, the miserly short days. Anne didn't mind winter the way he did, and her indifference to it had perplexed and even aggrieved him. "You could live somewhere else," she'd say. "California, Florida. There are bike shops everywhere." "Come with me," he'd plead. But how could she? Not many job options for lecturers in English these days.

"Are you going to eat something?" he asked.

"I don't think so. But don't let me stop you."

He picked up the menu and read out the list of lunch offerings. "Veggie pita with sprouts. Barley-and-carrot soup. Zucchini quiche." He made a face. "Do you have to be a vegetarian to read books?"

"Here I guess you do."

Folding the menu he said, "So Anne. How are you?"

She stirred her coffee. "Actually, I haven't been sleeping too well."

"Oh?"

She thought she detected a note of hope in his voice. "I have the feeling someone's been getting into my apartment."

"What do you mean? Breaking in?"

"No, no sign of that."

She told him about the button, the needle in the arm of the sofa, the web of black thread. Terry didn't look alarmed, but wasn't dismissive, either. "Who has a key to the place?" he asked.

"The landlord, of course. My sister. Remember when she visited me? She never gave the key back—typical. You, I suppose, come to think of it."

Terry took his bike-shop-logo keychain out of his pocket and, smiling, removed a Kwikset key. "Time to get on with our lives," he said. He placed it on the table between them. "I believe those are the words you used."

Yes, she had, on that August day when they'd sat in her Volvo at Schoodic Point, looking out to sea, and she'd told him it was over. Embarrassing to have let such a hackneyed expression escape her lips, even in that stressful situation. She picked up the key and dropped it into her handbag.

"Who else has one?" he asked.

She pondered a few moments. "I can't think of a soul."

"Does your sister have some score to settle?"

"She may well, but she's out in Santa Cruz, three thousand miles away."

A couple at another table got up and left, and Anne watched the waitress load dirty dishes onto a tray. "Actually," she said, "there was a student I lent the key to two or three times. But that was last spring."

"A student? Why'd you do a thing like that?"

Anne finished her espresso, although the caffeine, on an empty stomach, was beginning to work on her nerves. "He needed a quiet place to write. He was having problems."

"What sort of problems?"

"Family stuff."

"You let those kids take advantage of you."

"Nonsense," she said, though maybe there was some truth in his accusation. "Anyway, Derek would always be gone by the time I got home. I'd find the key on the coffee table."

"You never heard of copying a key? He could've strolled down to that hardware store next to Dunnett's and had a new key made for the price of a cup of coffee. Less. Take him twenty minutes, max."

"But why would he?"

Terry shrugged. "You tell me."

She remained silent, examining the grit in her cup. She wondered if it could be Terry himself, playing these tricks. The key-copying scenario rolled off his tongue with suspicious ease. Maybe he hadn't been delivering a bike at all, but instead loitering in the vicinity of her apartment. When it came down to it, however, she couldn't picture him stalking her. Terry was too bumbling, too let-it-all-hang-out to be that devious.

"Out of curiosity," Terry said, "what became of this student?"

"He was a senior. I assume he graduated." Derek had not, however, turned in his final portfolio, had not bothered to do the required revision. He'd simply disappeared at the end of the course, and she'd been forced to give him a far lower grade than she would have otherwise. Anne didn't mention that to Terry.

"Living alone," he said, "you're vulnerable."

Translation: "Let me take care of you, Anne." But if he couldn't take care of himself, she thought, how in heaven's name could he take care of her? What he really wanted was for *her* to nurture *him.* Rescue him from the dumpy apartment, cook his meals, patch his elbows, iron his shirts. She wasn't going to cave in to his neediness, she just wasn't.

~

At first it seemed beyond credibility, the idea of Derek Millet harboring a copy of her key for half a year, then secretly re-entering her apartment to plant a button, unwind a spool of thread.

But Derek's major work of the semester had been a long, intense story about a private detective hired to tail a client's wife. Carefully, lovingly, the story had explored the detective's growing obsession with his prey, ending after a hundred pages in the wife's ambiguous death in a blood-soaked motel room. Derek's particular skill was in verisimilitude—meticulous accuracy of detail—which had made what amounted to genre melodrama believable, and even moving. She recalled the banal settings in coffee shops and bus stations and strip malls that Derek had rendered with precision. The taut, slangy dialogue. The sly use of metaphor—so much hidden, or half-hidden, beneath the surface.

Anne reflected on the detective's subtlety and inventiveness. His determination.

Now that Terry had put the idea in her head, she couldn't entirely dismiss it. What if a clever writer were to confuse the line between fiction and reality?

In her apartment Derek would have been surrounded by her possessions: the framed snapshots of her parents and sister; her collection of glass, stone, and ceramic eggs; the Undset first English editions among her books; the prescription container of Atenolol in the bathroom cabinet; the old beaver coat deep in the back of her closet. He might have begun to ruminate about her, using the details of her life to turn her into a character of his own contriving. A character that he, in the guise of detective, eventually felt driven to hunt down.

No. Not possible. What was she thinking? Derek was an ordinary kid—from Lewiston, she remembered his telling her. Straight out of working-class stock, but touched by random luck with a talent for fictive invention.

Yet there had been something a little strange, a little exotic about Derek Millet. Older than the typical senior, but hard to say how much older. Thick dark hair that looked as though it had been chopped off with a hatchet. Sallow complexion, lips bleached of color, sharply bony facial structure that suggested the steppes by way of a dirty mill town. Knowing, faraway smile. In her office, bent with her over his manuscript, his chair pulled close to hers, he'd given off a pungent odor of wood smoke and cigarettes.

When she first started teaching, an ancient professor of medieval literature had cornered her and, with no clear provocation, begun to lecture her about the number of certifiables wandering the halls of the English Department. "Freaks who can't even tie their own shoelaces fit right in here," he'd muttered. "Place should have bars on the windows and a high brick wall around it. Take my advice. Keep your distance from the crazy bastards." Of course she'd paid no attention to him, but maybe what the old goat said wasn't just blather.

Pound, Woolf, Lowell, Styron, Plath, Berryman . . . The line between brilliance and lunacy could be thin.

All right, admit it. She'd lent the key to Derek, an unprofessional act she hadn't committed before or since, because she'd felt some special attachment to his creative gifts. To him. Admit also that she'd been bitterly disappointed over his casual failure to turn in his portfolio. She'd given him the C-minus not because she couldn't in conscience do otherwise, which is what she told herself at the time, but in revenge for her hurt. Anne's sleep that night was ragged, invaded by disturbing dreams.

The next morning, having dropped off a bundle of clothes at the laundromat on State Street, Anne took the back route to the university. As she drove along the river in Veazie, not far from Terry's apartment, she considered again whether he might be the one playing these mind games with her. The rejected suitor, she'd heard, is always the first suspect in situations like this.

Anne shook her head at the thought. She and Terry had been lovers for more than two years and had talked seriously of marriage. He still cared about her. She felt sure he would never hurt her if he could help it. In any case, she couldn't imagine him organizing himself sufficiently to plan and execute a scheme of harassment—or whatever this was.

When she reached her office, she phoned down to the department secretary. Yes, Rose confirmed, Derek Millet had indeed graduated the previous May. The address in his file was a post office box in Old Town. "Probably gone by now, though," Rose said. "Most of them vanish in a nanosecond once they've got that diploma."

"What about a home or family address?" Anne asked. "Lewiston?"

"None listed here on the form."

"Isn't that kind of unusual?"

"If you pay your own bills, you don't have to tell the university who your people are—not if you don't want to."

"Is there a telephone number?"

Rose read it off, an Old Town exchange.

Before she could think better of the idea, or decide what she'd say to Derek if he answered, Anne called the number. A recorded voice announced that it had been disconnected, "no further information available." Almost certainly Rose was right, and the post office box would be defunct, too.

Next she called the Careers Center. He might have left a résumé with a current address on file there. Apparently, however, Derek had not been eager to let the university in on his future plans.

Nor did the Alumni Association have any idea where Derek Millet had landed after graduation, or demonstrate much interest. Perhaps they sensed, in their practiced bureaucratic intuition, that this alumnus was not among those likely to make millions and gratefully donate hockey arenas.

She tried the Bangor phonebook. No Derek Millets, or even D. Millets. She turned on her computer, logged onto the internet, and searched three different telephone directories. No matches in any of them. In the city of Lewiston no Millets at all, not a single one. Had Derek Millet and his kin disappeared off the face of the earth?

He wouldn't necessarily have a landline, she reminded herself. Or if he did, he wouldn't necessarily have a listed number.

Anne pictured Derek returning to the seedy, shadowy life from which he'd emerged. He might be working as a night clerk in a rundown motel, a security guard in a warehouse, a truck driver, a bartender. He could be anywhere. He could be right around the corner.

She met her freshman lit course, only part of her mind focused on the material; absently graded some late papers from the lit course; stumbled through her creative writing class; attended a department meeting without making a single contribution to the discussion.

At the end of the afternoon she sat in her office with the door closed, considering what metaphorical meaning objects from a sewing basket might have for Derek Millet.

A tangle of thread: web, fairly obviously. Needle: sting perhaps, or bite. Button? Anne thought about the button's smooth, pearly surface, its fragility. In memory she saw the two tiny holes drilled into its center. She recalled reading somewhere that the bite of a spider is differentiated from the bite of insects by a double, two-fanged puncture wound. The button could represent the victim.

Anne wheeled her desk chair around and took from a shelf Biedermann's *Dictionary of Symbolism.* Spider: "a creature capable of spinning a web and lying in wait to paralyze flies and gnats and suck them dry"; "the sinful urges that suck the blood from humanity."

A few minutes past five she left the building and headed for the faculty parking lot where she'd left her car. Dark already. Overcast. A wind had picked up and a few flakes of snow skipped on frozen ground. Unaccountably, she felt a shivery rush of something akin to joy.

Anne poured herself a glass of Chablis. As she was heating a portion of braised chicken she listened to the forecast on the radio. Arctic front approaching, accompanied by high winds. Gale warning along the coast with seas of fifty to sixty knots. Temperatures statewide expected to drop below zero or into the single numbers by morning. "Keep your pets inside tonight," the weatherman advised. "Bundle up if you have to go out."

After her meal she washed the few dishes in the sink, looked at the newspaper, turned the pages of an Ondaatje novel without absorbing a word. The wind groaned, flinging freezing rain against the window glass. She felt restless, excited by the knowledge of the cold front moving in, bringing with it a dangerously low wind chill—enough to congeal your blood, stop your heart.

Just before eleven, when she was preparing for bed, her cell rang, startling her. She went down the hall into the kitchen and, without turning on the light, picked it up from the counter.

"Sorry to call so late," Terry said.

She pictured him in his stingily heated basement apartment, missing her. She never should have had coffee with him, never mind confided in him. Absolutely she could not let him back into her life.

"I was out," he said, "but I wanted to be sure to reach you tonight."

Out? Where would he have gone, in weather like this?

"Remember what we talked about in the Blue Moon yesterday?" He paused, and she saw his plump hand moist on the receiver. "Anne, I was your intruder."

She almost didn't believe him.

"The first time," he went on, "was a spur-of-the-moment type of thing. I happened to be near your place—I was picking up my laptop from the computer repair place on Hammond—and I remembered I still had your key. I missed you. I wanted to be close to you. Without giving it any more thought, I pulled into your parking lot and ran up the stairs and turned the key in the lock."

So that's the way it was, she thought.

"Once I was there, in your apartment, I had this urge to leave something behind for you," he said, his voice earnest and a little breathless in confession. "Some little treasure. I searched through my pockets and found a button that I'd picked up from the sidewalk or somewhere. I left it on your red rug, where you'd be sure to notice it."

She'd noticed, all right.

"Button made me think of needle," Terry continued, "so the next time, I took a needle out of my emergency sewing kit. Remember the one I keep in my glove compartment? I think it was a prize in a cereal box."

The puncture in her finger, how painful for such a small wound.

"With needle goes thread. *Old Mother Twitchett had but one eye, and a long tail which she let fly . . .* "

"What?"

"The third time, I unwound the black thread from the card in the kit and left that on your table. I kept expecting you to call me up and yell at me. To be honest, I hoped you would call me up and yell at me."

Phone in hand, Anne walked to the window. Outside, a loose cable slapped insistently against metal siding. The panes in their old frames rattled with the wind.

"But you didn't," Terry was saying, "and anyhow, since then things have changed." He coughed meaningfully. "For the better."

She understood at once. *Sincere, college-educated, gainfully employed WSM wishes to meet . . .* Of course someone would bite. She might have bitten herself.

"Yesterday, when I realized how upset you were, I felt kind of sheepish, and like a coward I kept my mouth shut."

After a long moment she asked, "Out of curiosity, what prompts you to unburden yourself now?"

The question seemed to surprise him. "Guilt. I didn't want you worrying for nothing."

For nothing. Anne pulled the cord to close the blind and moved away from the window. Steam had begun to burble and spit into the tall iron radiator. She told Terry it wasn't important, forget it. Without saying goodbye she hung up and plugged her cell back into the charger.

How, she asked herself, could she have been such an imbecile? How could she have supposed that Derek Millet, or any of them, for that matter, would give her a single thought after departing her class—let alone turn her, a fortyish old-maid lecturer in English, into the object of passionate obsession? "Get a grip," Derek would say. "Get a life."

The wind died down during the night, and the Volvo started right up in the morning.

FIRE ESCAPE

WALLY IS AT the kitchen table eating his evening meal, reheated veal stew that he cooked on Sunday, watching a cat squeeze through a partly opened window in the building across the alley. Wally has never noticed this cat before. It's shorthaired and dirty white. Seated outside on the window ledge, the cat gives its coat a few casual licks. Suddenly, without bothering to consider the consequences, the animal springs from the ledge and lands on a step of the building's fire escape. Wally stops chewing. What if the cat had misjudged the distance and tumbled down three stories? He winces, almost feeling his own spine twist to right itself, his feet sting as they hit the concrete, his bones shudder with the impact. Oblivious to Wally's concern, the cat settles down to take a nap.

The fire escape, the cat's perch, is made of perforated segments of rusty iron attached to one another at forty-five- or ninety-degree angles and bolted onto painted brick about the same color as the cat. The building was once a private home, Wally has learned, a mansion built in the early nineteenth century by a man who made a pile of money in the lumber trade. Later on, in leaner times, at least a half dozen apartments were crammed into its spaces, a rabbit's warren electrified with hazardous improvisation within and around the old walls. The apartments would have been divided by partitions made of some flimsy material like particleboard. Possibly some of them still retain their original fireplaces, from which drafts seep into the rooms, any warmth doomed to depart.

By contrast, Wally's own building is plain but efficient: three floors of nearly identical one- or two-bedroom apartments, each opening off a carpeted central corridor. Often he blesses his luck that his is at the far end of the top floor, on the south side. He doesn't have to listen to the elevator whine up and down in the shaft, or the footsteps of other tenants passing his door, or anyone stomping about above his head, or car doors slamming in the parking lot.

Wally wonders whether he should cut himself a slice of the rhubarb pie he bought on sale at the Mini-mart. Or instead save it for later, when he watches his video.

~

A week or so later, a face appears in the same window out of which the cat climbed. Wally pauses, his fork halfway to his mouth. He's never seen this woman before, either. Although her light hair is pulled back from her forehead, perhaps into a braid, he gets the idea that the hair is fuzzy rather than smooth. Her face is oval, her lips full. She stares in his direction, her head level with his. Then she brings the window down and draws a curtain across the opening. The material hangs limply—cheap fabric, by the look of it, hastily hemmed and strung up on a wire, more to keep out prying eyes than to decorate the room. Wally finishes his meal and washes the dishes, feeling oddly disturbed. He's not sure whether it's the woman's abrupt invasion of his solitude that troubles him or the dismissive gesture that followed it.

Although occasionally he sees the cat coiled on the fire escape, he doesn't lay eyes on its owner again for quite some time. By now it's late October, and dead leaves stick to his shoes as he starts down the hill from his apartment building. A drizzle is falling. The air feels raw. First he sees an open umbrella heading toward him, an ugly streaked and faded shrimp color, and then he realizes it's the woman from across the alley who grips the handle.

Not really wishing to become involved with any of his neighbors, he intends to pass her without speaking. However, she stops him. Rain drips from her umbrella spokes. He's close enough to see that freckles lightly fleck her sallow, shiny cheekbones, close enough to smell smoke on her breath. There's an unusual cast to her features that he can't identify, perhaps the result of a mixture of races somewhere in her ancestry. The word *octoroon* comes to him.

For a moment her fingertips touch the back of his hand. They feel warm and slightly oily. "I wonder if you might have seen a gray knapsack," she says. "In the parking lot." The lot is a paved area behind their apartment houses, which the tenants of both buildings share. Yesterday, she tells him, she was unloading things from her car and somehow the knapsack hadn't made it inside with the rest of her belongings.

He denies any knowledge of the knapsack but for the sake of politeness asks, "What was in it?"

"Oh," she says in a slow, low-pitched voice, "nothing of much value to anyone else . . . Some books . . . Those guys must have taken it."

"What guys?"

"You know . . . The guys that hang out back there, by the Dumpster."

Wally hasn't observed any loiterers in the parking lot, but since he can walk to work and doesn't own a car, he has no reason to linger there. Damp is seeping through the soles of his shoes. She's not properly dressed for the weather, either—over her loose cotton dress she wears only a cardigan that is missing a button or two. But both of them seem stuck here on the sidewalk, the missing knapsack hanging between them like a dull gray cloud.

He begins to be aware of a peculiar sensation of guilt. It's as though he himself snatched the knapsack when she wasn't looking, removed the books and spirited them to the secondhand bookseller on Central Street, stowed the knapsack in the back of his closet and blocked it from his memory until her question brought back his crime with a rush.

Finally she says, "Well thanks, anyway," and walks past him. From one of her umbrella spokes rain water trickles onto the sleeve of his topcoat.

The following morning, on his way to work, Wally carries down to the Dumpster his weekly accumulation of garbage. Because he is a recycler, his contribution to the Dumpster generally amounts to no more than a pound of detritus in the bottom of a sack from the Mini-mart. Before he deposits the knotted bag, he peers into the Dumpster in case the knapsack might be there, tossed away by a thief. A frustrated thief, angry that his haul turned out to be worthless to him. All Wally sees are the legs and spines of broken furniture, and huge black trash bags, foul-smelling, some of them pecked or ripped open by foraging animals.

~

In November, Wally is offered a promotion at his job. If he accepts, it will mean transferring from Bangor south to the Portland area, becoming assistant manager of a newer and busier store. The small chain he works for sells business supplies at discount, office furniture, computers in the low-to-moderate price range. He thinks it's probably time for a move. Since his girlfriend broke up with him, two years ago, he hasn't had much of a social life. Everyone he and Roberta knew in common drifted into her camp after the split. That's the way it usually goes, Wally has observed—the woman in question is accorded most of the sympathy, never mind whose fault the parting. Back in the summer, when Wally ran into the Burketts on the street and invited them up for a drink, Peggy giggled nervously and Ron mumbled an obvious lie about an engagement they were already late for. Wally refuses to feel bitter. Resentment gets you nowhere.

It's true that things here seem stale, repetitious, the dreary season dragging him down. Somehow, though, he can't make up his mind about the transfer. More pay, of course, but more hassle, too. He'd have to find a new apartment. It's more expensive to live in Portland than in Bangor. If he couldn't walk to work he'd have to acquire a car and renew his driver's license, which has lapsed, and probably pay to park the car in some garage.

The next week, without giving Wally sufficient opportunity to consider fully all the implications of the transfer, the district manager offers the job to one of Wally's coworkers, who is off to Portland like a shot.

The first snowfall comes, and the cat has long since given up sunning itself on the fire escape. Sometimes Wally observes it resting behind the closed window, on the sill. As if sensing Wally's attention, the cat raises its head and meets his glance with squinty eyes. Wally finds himself thinking about the young woman who lives behind the dirty-white brick wall. *Octoroon*. A musical word, like ocarina or Cameroon. He invents names for her, foreign names, appropriate to her vaguely exotic appearance. Thibedi. Stazi. Aïsa.

He speculates on where she's gone during those times when no light glows in her apartment. She must have a job, he decides, but nothing very much, not with that shabby, unkempt air about her. One day during his lunch hour he wanders into an import shop on the sudden hunch that she works in this place. For some reason he wants to see her behind the counter, taking people's money, flattening the bills between her oily palms before tucking them into the cash register drawer. Maybe she pierces people's ears and fits their lobes with those tiny gold wires. The shop, which is jammed full of colorful merchandise, reeks of incense. Wally looks at a rack of hand-sewn blouses and at strings of beads. He examines stone boxes carved in Africa and decides on impulse to buy one. Not that he is much for table ornaments and there's no one to whom he owes a gift. Although he takes his time over the purchase, weighing the merits of black versus red and deliberating over which of the etched designs is the most attractive, she does not appear. If she does work here, she must be on her lunch hour, too.

Now, instead of packing a sandwich, he eats his noontime meal in one or another of the little cafés that dot the downtown area. Sooner or later she'll come in and sit at one of the round tables and order thick lentil soup, or flatbread filled with sprouting bean seeds and that garlicky substance that looks like damp putty. Neither will presume on the acquaintance—she values privacy, just as he does. She'll sit at one of the round metal tables and take a book out of her new knapsack and read while she eats.

Although Wally spends more time at his kitchen table in the winter months, paging through the newspaper or listening to a news program on public radio while his dinner bakes in the oven, he rarely sees her face. Just a hand moving the frayed curtain along the wire, or a distant shape passing between him and the light in the depths of her apartment, momentarily blotting it out.

She keeps the window shut tight—to hoard the heat, he supposes, atavistically craving warmth. He watches vapor steam the inside of the glass. She must have plug-in heaters to supplement the building's ancient radiators. In that temperature, fruit put out in a bowl to ripen would rot before she could eat it all.

Outside, snow layers the iron steps of the fire escape.

~

Early in the new year Wally begins to have troubling dreams. He awakens at two or three in the morning with his heart banging explosively in his chest. Scraps of memory remain with him: his teeth coming loose and falling out of his gums, his feet mired in an underground passageway flowing with sewage. Couldn't the physical effects of dreams like those kill you? When you don't show up for work for a week, they call the police who break in and discover you in bed with a burst aorta.

At his memorial service his former friends are shamed and overcome with grief. Deaf to their laments, Wally is now nothing but ashes in his black African box with an ibex etched on the lid.

~

Late one afternoon, as Wally is returning from work, he comes upon two young men leaning against a graffiti-covered fence within a block of his apartment building. One of the men is scrawny, eyes small and bright as a weasel's. The other has hair so short Wally can see scrapes and lumps on his skull. "Hey, man, got a light?" the weasel-eyed one says. He's amused by some joke Wally isn't in on. Wally shakes his head and goes on by, holding his apartment keys in his pocket.

It occurs to him that they might be the men she mentioned, the ones she saw lounging by the Dumpster. They certainly looked up to no good. In his kitchen, he stares across the alley at her window. He wonders what she'd do if she encountered them by the fence. Would she pause when they spoke to her, grope in her bag for a matchbook, offer it to them when she found it?

Just before going to bed, he realizes that his bathroom sink has begun to drain sluggishly. He digs into the hole first with a pair of tweezers, then with a long-handled fork, then with a coat hanger he unbends and bends again so that it has a hook on the end. The quantity of metallic-smelling, gelatinous black sludge he is able to extract both repels and fascinates him. With a wad of tissues he wipes out the sink bowl, flushes the mess away down the toilet. But water still dribbles only reluctantly down the drain.

It must be the soap he's been using, he decides, that created the blockage. He remembers that Roberta gave him half a dozen bars of the stuff one Christmas. Oatmeal soap, densely medicinal, uncompromisingly good for you. Prized for its natural exfoliating qualities, according to the promotional material on the box.

Roberta is behind him as he wipes his hands on a towel. If he turned quickly, she'd be close enough to bump into. "Why can't you ever tell me what you're thinking?" she demands. "Am I your enemy, or what? Why does everything have to be such a big secret?" If only just once it had occurred to Roberta to have a secret or to keep one.

He decides to eat a piece of coconut cream pie before turning in.

In the kitchen, setting out a fork for himself, he sees a ghost of a light burning behind the curtain across the alley.

~

One morning on his way to work he notices the shrimp-colored umbrella ahead of him on the sidewalk. It's February, giant clots of wet snow dropping from the sky.

He takes pleasure in watching the octoroon negotiate the steep downhill pavement on Middle Street, umbrella lifted high above her head. The hem of her dress skims the slush. Stumbling behind her in bald rubbers, he realizes that as she has neared the bottom of the hill she has begun to walk more rapidly. She's serenely confident of her ability to stay on her feet. She rounds the corner onto Main Street, and he follows. As far as the Army-Navy store he is able to keep sight of the umbrella floating over the heads of pedestrians.

Then, without warning, she steps off the curb and moves into the street, cutting through traffic as if she's indifferent to the possibility of being run down and killed. Wally sucks in his breath. Apparently she's heading for the entrance to the building that occupies the whole of the opposite block. But that building, once Freese's department store, has been vacant for years. A bus trundles by, obscuring Wally's view. When he manages to make it across the street himself, she has vanished. A rusty chain, padlocked, is looped through the department store's door handles. Where in the world can she have gone? No sign of the umbrella anywhere up and down the sidewalk.

Wally picks his way through dirty slush, around to the rear of the building. Dark back here. Heaps of abandoned junk that may well harbor vermin. Strange fishy smell, whiff of rotten eggs. To one side of a loading ramp he sees a door that has a peeling coat of brown paint on it. No chain or padlock. The door is stiff in the frame, but grudgingly it opens.

Inside, as his eyes adjust to the dimness, Wally makes out a narrow staircase, and faintly, above his head, he hears out-of-tune piano music. At the top of the steps, in a dusty room the size of a warehouse loft, an old woman sits hunched at the piano. She has a dowager's hump so pronounced it seems to wrench her entire body sideways. Her hands curl arthritically over the keys, bony wrists poking out of her sleeves. Feverish swipes of rouge inflame her cheeks.

The room is lined with mirrors. Wally almost doesn't recognize his reflection, because some distortion in the glass makes him look humpbacked, too. He has no neck, and his legs have buckled and shrunk. But it's definitely his own topcoat, his own thin hair damped down with melting snow.

Where can she be? Perhaps changing out of her clothes in a room elsewhere in the building. The pianist's fingers twitch upward from the keys. "What do you want?" she croaks.

Of course he can't say who he's looking for. He doesn't know her true name.

"You made a mistake," the old woman says. "You came to the wrong place."

No one at work notices he's late. In fact, it's only four minutes past nine when Wally boots up his computer in the office at the back of the store. He considers returning to the dance studio another time—perhaps he'll have better luck—but in the end never does.

~

He falls into a spell of insomnia. Even his sleep doesn't feel like real sleep, but more like an uneasy and partial letting-go of consciousness. He dreams that he is awake and unable to sleep.

Wally decides to unplug the phone, so a call can't disturb him. Not that he receives many these days. However, you never know when some fool is going to ring the wrong number at three in the morning, or a deranged person dial at random and commence to harass you. The next morning he neglects to plug the phone back in, and he discovers that being without a phone makes little difference in his life. After that he leaves the plastic connector dangling aimlessly from its cord.

~

As spring approaches, he becomes afflicted with a constant itchy ache in his muscles that makes it impossible to concentrate on a book or video. Is this the opening round of some chronic incurable disease? In an attempt to deal with his agitation, he takes to walking around the city every moment he's not at work or in bed struggling with sleeplessness. He passes the boarded-up department store and thinks of the octoroon dancing in bare feet, her hair plaited with beads and ribbons and tiny brass bells that smell of tarnish.

One night, as he's heading up the hill back to his apartment, the wail of sirens breaks into his thoughts. He can see, blurry in the fine mist that's now falling, fire engines on the crest of the hill, in his street. Wally begins to run. He stumbles on the uneven sidewalk and nearly falls, by some miracle righting himself just in time.

At the summit he finds a knot of gawkers gathered in the street, shards of broken glass in the alley, water dripping down the steps of the white brick building and pooling on the sidewalk. He pictures her climbing through the window and leaping onto the fire escape, the terrified cat clawing her arms. But the firemen are already leaving the building, winding up their fat gray hoses. To the disappointment of the bystanders, the fire caused little damage, and that to a side entryway on the ground floor only. The tenants must have huddled outside in the mist no longer than the time it took him to run up the hill. He never even got a glimpse of her.

Next morning, a Saturday, the curtain still is drawn across the opening, frame to frame, the only gap near the top where the wire it's strung on sags a little. At quarter past eleven Wally takes his shopping bag from its hook by his front door and sets out for the Mini-mart. Next door, carpenters are busy nailing sheets of plywood to the frames of the ground-floor windows that the firemen busted through. As Wally passes by, he hears one of them tell a scruffy woman in ragged parka and baseball cap, probably one of the mental cases from the nearby halfway house, that the fire was set.

"By who?" asks the crazy woman.

"What they think is, some character stalking one of the tenants."

Wally's heart jerks in his chest.

"But they didn't catch him yet. Lucky the super found it before it got going good."

"Lucky," she says, grinning happily, slack-jawed.

"The old place would go up like a tinderbox."

"Pitiful pile of soggy newspapers," the other carpenter says. "A little kerosene poured on 'em, smoldering in the entryway. Dumb asshole. You gonna do it, do it right."

"Luckee luckee luckee . . . " Wally watches the lunatic hokey-pokey down the sidewalk, careen around the corner onto Union

Street, and vanish into the ether. Carrying his empty shopping bag, he returns to his apartment.

Across the alley the curtain is closed. He thinks about Weasel-eyes and Scar-scalp hanging out by the Dumpster, by the graffiti-sprayed fence. Maybe they're not casual loiterers, but people she knows.

What would be the harm in ringing her buzzer, asking if she's all right? He could sit with her for a while.

But it wouldn't be easy to work out which apartment is hers, inside the complex maze of the partitioned mansion, with multiple dark staircases, winding and windowless corridors, double locks on oddly placed doors. He could lose his sense of direction. People could notice him wandering about, suspect him of being the arsonist.

Wally decides to fix himself a sandwich, and when it's made, he sits at the table to eat it with an eye on the rag of a curtain. Suddenly he notices that her window is open a few inches. Has it been that way all morning, or did she raise it as he cut his bread, layered it with leftover meat? He wonders at himself for not being certain one way or the other. The hem of the curtain fidgets, sucked in and out by shifts in air currents, nervously dragging on the frame. He toys with the idea of calling across the alley, but soon abandons that notion. She wouldn't hear, or if she did, would assume it's the men stalking her, and retreat to the farthest reaches of her apartment.

Then it comes to him. He'll take the elevator down as he does every day on his way to work, calmly, casually, and then equally calmly and casually walk around the side of the building, enter the alley, mount the fire escape, and slip his fingers between window and sill. No one pays any attention to someone who looks as if he knows what he's doing and has every right to be doing it.

Of course she'll be frightened at first, hearing the heavy old window scrape up in its frame, but once she understands, she'll be glad.

To calm her nerves he'll offer to brew her a cup of tea. She owns very few cups, of course, two at the most, one of them chipped. She has only a dented aluminum saucepan to heat the water in, no proper kettle. He'll find real tea, though, black and smelling like smoke and prickly as twigs in the palm of his hand, and a china teapot, its spout stained from all the tea that has passed through it.

He'll steep the tea for six minutes before pouring it into one of the cups, the one without the chip, and adding milk from a carton in the refrigerator. *Shall I bring it in to you?* he'll call.

Please, she'll answer.

Her bedroom is in the innards of the apartment, dimly lit by an oil lamp that sits on the mantelpiece amid tissue-paper roses and heaps of yellowed letters in some illegible foreign script. Used books sprawl open, half read, on the couch and the floor. Her bedclothes are rumpled. On her dressing table is an unstoppered bottle, from which emerges the odor of musk.

He'll set the cup on the dressing table and wait while she takes a sip.

Seated there at the dressing table, she'll begin to unbutton the back of her loose, thrift-shop dress. He'll see one shoulder emerge, then the other, and the dress will fall to her waist. Her back is the color of wax, or egg white, no color at all.

She'll take another sip of the cooling milky tea. One by one he'll count the knobs of her spinal column and, in the mirror, watch her breasts leap up as she unbraids her pale kinky hair.

The dirty-white cat will watch, too, with its lazy, slitty eyes, from atop the marble mantel.

Later, while she lies sleeping, for safety's sake he'll walk through the apartment, double-locking the door and hooking the chain, turning the latches on all the windows. Then he'll stretch out beside her on the couch.

In the night, the cat, aroused from its sleep by some unusual noise, will spring to its haunches and tip the lamp over.

DRAGON PALACES

Nicola appears on the beach dressed in a pearl-gray silk shirt and crimson trousers, her long black hair still damp from the shower. She's been in the cottage all afternoon, writing. Laurie watches her take from a canvas bag a corkscrew, a bottle of chilled Muscadet, and two wineglasses, each wrapped in a dishtowel.

"What a good idea," Laurie says, though it's illegal to drink alcohol on the beach, of course, and she feels a little nervous that someone's going to say something to them.

Smiling, Nicola uses the tip of the corkscrew to remove the metal wrapping and then winds the tool into the cork. She pours wine into the glasses and hands one to Laurie. The wine is not a present, exactly—the bottle is from a case that Steve bought in the wine shop in town. Nicola's hostess gift was three bars of almond-scented soap, purchased, Laurie guesses, in an airport terminal shop.

Laurie takes a sip of wine, her eyes never leaving the kids. Cameron is loading stones and shells into a bucket and dumping them out again, his waterlogged disposable diaper sagging around his hips. Now and then the tide slithers higher up the beach than the boy expects, momentarily unsteadying him or knocking him down. He doesn't cry or look to his mother for reassurance. Helen's with a group of children younger than she, who are packing damp sand into pails and then upending them, constructing an extensive, monotonous city. With one hand Helen keeps yanking the bottom edge of her swimsuit down over her rump, and with the other she swipes at her nose. Helen seems to be allergic to beach grass. Helen is allergic to almost everything. She's not an attractive child, and to her own shame, Laurie feels embarrassed about her daughter in front of sleek, together Nicola.

Nicola has composed herself on the beach blanket, avoiding the wet places where the kids have recently perched. "When will Steve be back from Boston?" Nicola asks.

"In time for dinner. I bought some mussels this morning. We can steam them."

"Oh, let's make a rémoulade."

The suggestion tires Laurie. Next thing you know she'll be driving into town in search of fresh tarragon and capers and imported mustard that costs nine dollars a crock and God knows what else.

"Cameron takes after his father," Nicola observes. "Not just the dark coloring. He projects the same intensity."

"So everyone says."

"Something about the set of the jaw, I think." With a manicured fingernail Nicola flicks away a yellow jacket that has discovered her wine. "There must be, what, five or six years between him and his sister?"

"Almost six."

Casually Nicola asks, "An afterthought?"

"Not really."

Between her two living children, four summers ago, Laurie gave birth to a child with genetic anomalies so devastating that it could not survive. Steve insisted they not name the baby or bury it, arguing that it would be useless to prolong the attachment with ceremonies. Laurie wept at his cool rationality, his stubborn refusal to acknowledge grief or perhaps even to feel it. Both exhausted, they agreed that he move out of the house for a few months, and they came close to separating permanently. Laurie is all but certain that Nicola has heard about that wretched time in their lives and is probing to learn more. Inquisitive beasts, writers. All she says, however, is, "Helen was so happy to have a baby brother. She didn't want to be an only child."

"She was lucky, then."

A big brown dog heads their way, running in and out of the surf, chasing a stick thrown by a man in a sun visor. The dog barks a guttural *wuh-wuh-wuh-wuh-wuh*. Helen looks up from her play and becomes perfectly still. But Laurie knows how the child's heart is hammering, how desperately she's trying not to bawl, because if she does, the other children will make fun of her. Laurie rises and moves between the advancing dog and the sand city. "Get away!" she yells. The animal feints and dances with the stick in its mouth, teasing her, then hurtles past and within moments is a quarter mile down the beach.

When Laurie returns to the blanket, Nicola says, "She's afraid of dogs?"

"Always has been, I don't know why."

"She'll have to learn to deal with them sooner or later. You won't always be around to chase them off."

Laurie knows Nicola is right. For her daughter's own good, Laurie must harden her heart. Nevertheless, she feels an aching tenderness for Helen's sharp shoulder blades, wispy hair, sunburn-prone skin.

For a while Laurie and Nicola sit in silence, watching the tide that is swirling with froth like soapsuds. The sky has become overcast; the forecast is for rain. Laurie calls the children and begins to pack up.

Out in the kitchen, cupboard doors bang, the girl whines, a radio jabbers mindlessly. The noxious smell of hotdog sizzling in a pan drifts into every corner of the cottage. Nicola plucks her cell out of her bag and takes it out to the screened porch. Having settled herself in a rattan chair, she has to wait nine rings for him to pick up. "It's me," she says.

"Are you coming home soon?" Pertek asks in his gasping, croaky voice. Home is the East Village, where she lives with Pertek when she's not away on reading or lecture tours.

Nicola leans back against the chair frame and crosses her legs. "Something surprising has happened. I've started a new long poem. All of a sudden the idea hit me, like a punch in the gut."

"That's splendid, Nicola."

"It may be my best stuff since *Dragon*. To be honest, I feel superstitious about interrupting it."

"I understand," Pertek says reluctantly.

She's sure he's fumbling with a match, the phone jammed between shoulder and ear. He won't ask her to tell him about the poem, because she's made plain her scorn for writers who talk their work away. That's what he's done in his declining years, Nicola believes, holding court in bars and dissipating his creative energies in a haze of smoke and alcohol fumes. "I wouldn't have predicted it," she says, "but I'm absolutely knocked out by Maine."

From behind a muffled receiver she hears spasms of coughing and throat-clearing. Pertek will be in his grave in five years, probably sooner, with no one to blame but himself.

"The sea, the tides, the centrality of nature in people's lives . . . " She pauses. "I'm thinking that before I can move forward, I need to go back."

"Back where?"

"Back to essentials."

"It's hot as blazes here," he says irrelevantly—self-centered, as always.

Finally, having made a kissy sound into the iPhone, she clicks it off and walks out onto the deck. The tide is receding, leaving an expanse of dully shining pebbles. A few drops of rain blotch her silk blouse.

~

The kitchen in this rented cottage is cramped, inconvenient, equipped for minimal cooking only—and that's fine with Laurie. Her enthusiasm for preparing complex dishes disappeared after the stillbirth. Her taste buds dulled. She lost confidence that a hollandaise would thicken or popovers rise.

She's slicing bananas and a chicken hotdog and putting the chunks on the tray of Cameron's highchair. Helen eats her supper in the glassed-in, shed-like room next to the kitchen, which serves as a dining room. From day one Helen has been a poor eater, and now her meals are virtually limited to pasta and whatever sweets she can wheedle out of her mother or father. Laurie doesn't understand her daughter's obstinately conservative habits, although she worries that in some way she's to blame. A few weeks ago Helen played the part of a faerie in the end-of-term pageant at school. The role called for her to frolic, with several other pink-Spandexed faeries, in a sylvan glade. "Egregious miscasting," Steve said to Laurie after the performance. "Helen doesn't frolic, she plods. She'd have been more convincing as a tree."

"That's cruel," Laurie replied. But she recognized the uneasy disappointment he felt. And she'd have to admit, if pressed, that neither of her children is turning out the way she expected. Unfair to imagine that the critically damaged baby, the one too fragile to draw a single breath, was the child who would have done so. Yet Laurie dreams often about the lost child and never, ever, about the living ones.

Having grown bored with tossing banana onto the floor, Cameron is wrestling with his harness and demanding to be let down. She wipes his fingers and unhitches him, then holds him against her and kisses the soft skin under his ear. But this is not a cuddly child.

Released, Cameron steams off toward the opposite end of the cottage. Ten past six by the flyspecked clock over the sink. Steve will be on Route 1 by now, cursing the slow summer traffic. Someone else at CK could have handled these negotiations, Laurie thinks, big deal though they may be. She mashes cloves of garlic into butter that's been softening in the humid air. It's not in Steve's nature, however, to detach himself lightly from something he has a stake in.

Laurie removes a baguette from its paper bag, cuts the bread across as far as the opposite crust, and spreads the slices with garlic butter. She takes a sip from her wine glass, then approaches the second baguette. With any luck, Nicola has forgotten about making a rémoulade.

~

Nicola is turning the pages of an old Sarah Orne Jewett novel that she found in the bookcase when Steve crosses the deck and enters the porch. He has a long face that has improved in the fifteen-odd years she's known him, hardening at the jaw line. His fine straight nose is more pronounced, and it gives his expression authority. You can see that he's become accustomed to making crucial decisions and profiting from them. His dark hair has only a touch of gray in it.

"Where's Laurie?" he asks.

"In the kitchen. Feeding the kids, I guess."

Briefcase in hand, he moves to the rattan chair and grasps Nicola's shoulder, his fingers pinching into her flesh.

"Cut it out, Steve. That hurts."

"Why did I let you invite yourself here? What in hell was I thinking?"

"Do you want me to leave?"

"Goddamn it, Nicola."

"How did the meeting go?"

Without replying he walks across the porch, the heels of his polished Oxfords firm on the splintery floorboards, and enters the house.

~

The kids are tucked in bed, at long last. Steve and Nicola, well into a third bottle of the good French Muscadet, sit out on the porch. They chip thin fragments from a wedge of Stilton and converse on literary topics. In the kitchen, Laurie stands at the sink scrubbing grit and barnacles from a pail full of mussels.

Before Laurie knew him, in college, Steve was an editor of a little magazine called *Quadrat.* Between its sober buff covers appeared his reviews and essays; he likes to joke that one day the stacks of unsold copies moldering in their basement will be collector's items, worth a fortune. When Laurie moved East with him, back to his former haunts, they'd often have his *Quadrat* friends over to their Cambridge apartment. Although Steve still read *The New York Review of Books* and considered himself up on literary matters, by then he was working at Channing Kittredge and putting in ridiculously long hours. He enjoyed mastering skills that don't come naturally to English majors. Laurie sensed his genial contempt for the kinds of jobs his old friends took to keep body and soul together: Staples employee; computer repairer; used bookstore clerk. Even worse off were the PhD candidates, who'd get their degrees years hence, loaded with debt, and *then* customize other people's party invitations or install their software.

Early the following year Nicola Delepine came to Boston to confer with someone at Little, Brown. She'd also been a Quad Rat, as that select group referred to themselves, a poet and interviewer of writers in the literary limelight. Steve invited her for dinner; Laurie remembers cooking a veal ragout with morels. Over dessert Steve talked about the satisfactions of prospering in a climate of risk and competition—the real world.

"Ah yes, the *real* world," Nicola said.

"Don't mock. One of these days you'll have to cave in and find a proper job," Steve told her. Nicola was at the time manuscript reader cum copy editor cum cocktail-party caterer for an obscure poetry journal in New York. "Or a husband."

She just smiled.

In June Steve and Laurie were married in Appleton Chapel. Her parents drove out from Indiana and his up from Greenwich; Laurie baked her own wedding cake. That same month Steve heard from another Quad Rat that Nicola had taken off for Beijing with an activist Chinese writer she'd somehow hooked up with. In spite of Nicola's knowing not one word of the language, she traveled all over China with him, meeting with dissidents in places like the back rooms of noodle shops.

The week Nicola's book-length poem about the dissident movement was nominated for a National Book Award, Laurie happened to catch her on the *Today* show. Nicola told the interviewer about passing as a native so as not to attract the suspicion of the authorities. In a public toilet, she'd chopped her hair to just below her ears using somebody's penknife. "What a fantastic story!" the interviewer exclaimed. *Fang of the Dragon* sold fifty thousand copies. Prominent on the jacket cover was a photo of Nicola, with her delicate, vaguely exotic features and that striking black hair, which luckily had grown back in. As it turned out, Nicola Delepine did just fine in the real world.

Laurie rinses the mussels under the tap and dumps them into a kettle. Time to mix a salad dressing and light the oven for the garlic bread.

Last month Steve ran into Nicola on the street in Manhattan, where he'd gone on business. They had a drink together, and on the spur of the moment it was decided that Nicola would join them here. Odd, Laurie thought when she heard about the pending visit: Steve had been out of touch with his *Quadrat* friends for years, ever since he got his first promotion and they bought the house in Newton Corner.

But maybe not so odd, after all, that he'd want to see an old Quad Rat. It occurs to Laurie that the energy and excitement with which he used to speak of his work on the magazine has been missing from his voice for some time. And maybe not so odd that Nicola would want to see him. The sweetest joy in making it must be gathering tribute from those who knew you when.

Five days ago Nicola arrived at the airport in Portland with a leather carry-on bag, the modest size of which rather relieved Laurie—but like a magician, Nicola has since pulled numerous silky outfits from the bag's interior. Who can tell how long she plans to stay?

~

By morning steady rain has settled in. Laurie's been up a couple of hours, playing Parcheesi with Helen and trying to divert Cameron from dismantling the cottage. The damp brings out the smell of the ancient straw matting and the musty sofa cushions.

Shortly past nine, looking somewhat hung over, Steve emerges. Last night, as they have every night since her arrival, he and Nicola stayed up drinking wine after Laurie went to bed. Even with earplugs in, she could hear their voices murmuring through the balsa-thin wall that separates the living room from their bedroom. Grumbling about the shitty weather, Steve leaves for town to buy newspapers and bagels. Laurie starts a second pot of coffee brewing.

Nicola appears wearing peach silk trousers and a loose top with a mandarin collar. She takes her cell phone and a mug of coffee out to the screened porch, shutting the door behind her. She's going to call her lover, the famous poet Emil Pertek. According to an article in *People* that Laurie happened to see in the dentist's office, Nicola is "utterly devoted to Pertek, her mentor, the Pulitzer Prize–winning author almost twice her age."

When Steve returns from town, he and Laurie sit in the dining room off the kitchen. On a decent day they'd eat breakfast on the front deck while Helen and Cameron played in the sand. Today the kids are watching a noisy rerun, tuned in by Laurie, on the vintage TV in the living room.

"They say in town it's going to be a three-day blow." Between glances at the front page of *The Wall Street Journal,* Steve spreads cream cheese on a pumpernickel bagel.

"Terrific. Cameron's worn me to a frazzle already."

"Renting a beach cottage was your idea."

"I forgot about rain." After a silence Laurie says, "Just before dawn I woke from a weird dream. It's very vivid still."

He lifts his eyes from the newspaper. "Tell me about it."

From the beginning, back when Steve was in business school and she was working as a graphic designer, he's been interested in Laurie's dreams. Sometimes she suspects he takes her unconscious self more seriously than her conscious self. Remarkably, he claims never to dream himself.

"I was in a large flower garden," Laurie says, "blooming with perennials. A man was locked inside the house, behind French doors. I knew there was something malignant about him—deranged. Doctors had put him on a psychedelic drug to control his behavior."

"Psychedelic?"

"In the dream it made sense. I couldn't see him through the glass, only my own reflection."

"Who was this man?"

"I don't know. As I walked in the garden I began to realize that the irises were opening with crumbling black spots that had ruined the blossoms. I pulled a bud apart and saw tiny maggots chewing away its insides."

Steve stirs his coffee but doesn't drink it.

"Then the man was in the garden, and I turned away, not knowing how to deal with him. He grabbed me from behind. I realized he'd gotten hold of the needle with the drug in it and was going to stick it into the back of my neck. I struggled, expecting at any instant to feel the puncture."

"Sorry," Nicola says. "I called Pertek to check on him, and he went on and on." She slides onto the bench next to Steve. "Puncture? What are you talking about?"

"Just a dream Laurie had."

Nicola slices a plain bagel in half and breaks off a piece. "Scientists say dreams are no more than random electrical firings in the brain. Freud and Jung were wasting their time."

Laurie expects Steve to dispute this—how can dreams not have meaning?—but instead he turns to Nicola and asks, "How's Pertek?"

She shrugs. "He can't write if he doesn't smoke. If he smokes he can't breathe."

~

Even though puddles have collected on the floorboards and mist clings to every surface, Nicola has retreated to the porch with her laptop to escape the racket of the TV and the kids. The truth is that she works extremely well in distracting, uncomfortable situations. Much of the first draft of *Fang of the Dragon* was composed in trains, railway stations, tiny apartments crammed with people chattering in some Chinese dialect.

Finally, in the afternoon, the rain stops falling and Steve comes out to put on his sneakers. He's going for a walk, he says.

"I'll go with you."

The shoelace snaps. He ties the broken end to the other with a knot he'll later have to cut off. "I think it would be better if you didn't."

But she lifts an army-surplus poncho from its nail by the screen door and slips out with him. They walk as far as the jetty without speaking. "I don't know how she stands it," Nicola says at last.

"She's a good mother."

"Of course she is. That's not the point."

"Nicola. If the ambience around here annoys you, you can always go home to your famous prize-winning poet."

The water is roiling. The last high tide, swollen with the storm, left stinking heaps of junk on the sand: yellow plastic rope, decomposing parts of sea creatures, seaweed yanked from the bottom, chunks of Styrofoam. Sappho said that if you don't want to find something rotten, don't go poking into beach debris.

"You sound jealous of him," she says.

"I'm not jealous of him. As a matter of fact, I don't think you treat him very well."

"*Sor*ry."

They pass a dozen beach houses, each of which looks desolate and hunkered down, the inhabitants having abandoned them for cineplexes or outlet malls. Swimsuits and towels flap dismally on outdoor lines. She knows how conscious he is of her body: that's why he won't look at her. Her nipples, under silk, chafe against the heavy rubberized cloth of the poncho.

She touches his thigh. "I'm not married to Pertek, you know."

"I'm aware of that."

"I owe him only so much."

"If you say so."

"Why are you giving me such a hard time?"

He laughs bitterly. "Because what we're about to do scares the shit out of me."

"I've never known you to be a fearful man, Steve."

They leave the sandy cove now and climb over heaped round boulders, which shift disconcertingly under their feet. Beyond a weathered sign lies land owned by the Nature Conservancy. From there they cut inland, across scrubby juniper and wild cranberry, to a grove of jack pine. They use the poncho to lie on, and when they get up, it's covered with brown pine needles and bits of lichen.

~

At 2:34 a.m., according to the clock on the dresser, Steve drags himself out of their damp, lumpy bed to go pee. When he returns, Laurie whispers, "I'm awake."

"Go back to sleep."

"No, I've *been* awake. For hours."

"It's the bed. Next time we rent one of these places I'm going to check out the bed before I sign a thing."

"It's not the bed, Steve."

He won't roll over and go to sleep until she has aired whatever is troubling her. He's a responsible husband.

"What is it, then?"

"Were you and Nicola involved when you worked together on the magazine?"

He grunts. "We were all *involved*, Laurie. We were trying to do something new, with zero funding, in the face of a lot of establishment bullshit."

"You know what I mean."

It's too far from the water's edge to hear the tide lapping on the beach. The only sounds are the refrigerator rumbling at the back end of the cottage and Steve's sinusy breathing. Abruptly the fridge kicks off. He says, "I wasn't even under consideration."

"Did you want to be?"

"Why are you asking these questions?"

"What about now? Are you under consideration now?"

"Nicola's a friend. You have no reason to upset yourself."

Steve often says that the most valuable commodity investment bankers trade in isn't stocks and bonds. It's confidence. Distortions of fact, if not outright lies, might well be used to bolster that confidence, she figures. That's the way it works in the *real* world.

Next door, Helen moans softly in her sleep. The fridge starts up again. Steve's breathing has become regular.

Laurie never managed to shed the extra ten pounds after the dead baby's birth. Her pale hair won't take a perm and it sticks to her skull in the cold, dry, staticky Massachusetts winter. She doesn't have reliable clothes sense; she's not quick on the conversational uptake; her children are difficult and either too much like her or too little. Once she had some talent as an artist—professors whose opinion she respected thought so. Steve thought so. She isn't sure where that talent has gone or whether it really existed in the first place.

She thinks about the novel Steve wrote, the summer between college and business school. He mentioned it to Laurie several times when they were dating, back in Ann Arbor, but wouldn't show it to her. "A juvenile effort," he said dismissively. Years later, during the move from Cambridge to Newton Corner, she came upon a stack of yellowing pages in a box that also contained balled-up underwear, perhaps hastily stuffed in as packing material. Feeling like a voyeur, hoping for insights into his secret emotional life, Laurie began to read the manuscript while Helen napped. But all that happened in the novel were endless discussions on philosophical questions between characters named Krebs and Widmer. She replaced the novel in its box, confused and disappointed—yet also somehow relieved.

When he came back to her after their months of separation, Steve said, "You are the only woman I could ever live with." She has remembered his words many times and found comfort in them. But what, exactly, had he been telling her?

In the morning she's surprised to find that she must have gone back to sleep, and in the meantime the weather has cleared.

⁓

They've been eating lunch on the deck: an impromptu salade niçoise. Laurie feels dazed by the heat of the sun and a glass of beer. There's talk of going for a swim to cool off, but no one moves.

Nicola says languidly, "Do you know that dragons live down under the sea?"

Steve chews away the flesh from an olive, palms the pit, and tosses it over the railing.

" . . . in palaces."

Looking out at the sparkly band of sea, Laurie wonders what dragon palaces might be like. She imagines structures made from the intricate skeletons of marine animals, watery passageways shimmering with phosphorescence.

"Chinese dragons," Nicola says.

Steve scowls. Having taken the cottage's rowboat out this morning to go fishing, and fought with the balky outboard, and wasted eight dollars worth of bloodworms, and caught no fish, he's in an irritable mood. "So tell us, Nicola, how does a Chinese dragon differ from your common garden-variety dragon?"

Serenely Nicola replies, "Chinese dragons are benign. They represent the rhythms of nature, change and transformation. Dragons are shape-shifters. They can make themselves visible or invisible, as they please."

With belligerent sound effects Cameron is driving a fleet of Tonka backhoes and steam shovels up and down a grassy mound of sand.

"If they're so fucking benign, why do they have fangs?" Steve says.

Laurie sees a look pass between them.

"Dragons take a variety of forms. The *Mang*, the temporal dragon, symbolizes the power of the State. As such, it needs to be able to bite."

"And what," he asks, "do dragons do in their palaces under the sea?"

Nicola smiles, showing small, even, white teeth. "You have to go there to find out."

Steve pours more beer into their glasses. Three or four yellow jackets circle the salad bowl. Their nests seem to be in the grass between the cottage and the road behind it.

"I don't *want* to." Helen's querulous words reach them from the pebble-strewn beach, where she's playing with another little girl. "You can't *make* me."

"She's a whiner," Nicola remarks, as if making an objective observation. She pulls back an apricot-colored sleeve and lifts her glass.

Laurie feels she should defend Helen, who is only sticking up for her own rights, after all, but she can't deny the plaintive shrillness in the child's voice. Anyway, the conversation between Nicola and

Steve has moved on to an anecdote about an eccentric novelist and a fistfight on a flight to Paris. Somewhere inside the cottage, Nicola's phone begins to sound its quasi-musical trill. Possibly it's her poet. As it rings Laurie pictures the old man in extremis, on the verge of strangulation, turning purple down in the East Village. Nicola ignores the phone. After a few more rings it stops.

Steve and Nicola have organized a plan to drive up the coast to an art museum this afternoon. Unthinkable to bring Cameron on such an expedition: he doesn't travel well and is a menace to any institution. "You go," Laurie says.

~

The woman in the painting wears a white wimple, linen. Underneath it, her head is shaved. Her face is smooth as an egg and her eyes are empty ovals.

Nicola and Steve are standing side by side, not touching. At the far end of the gallery, a guard looks at them with mild curiosity, perhaps making a guess as to their relationship. You'd have to play games like that in order to endure the tedium of the job, Nicola supposes. The guard glances at his watch. Must be about twenty minutes until closing. Other than the guard, she and Steve are alone in the room.

"I need to have time with you," Steve says in a low, urgent voice.

She says nothing.

When they left the cottage he assumed their destination was a motel in a nearby town. Swiftly she let him know he could forget that idea. They would visit the museum, just as they'd told his wife: Nicola has no intention of handing her body over to him in some tacky motel room. Under the jack pines she set the hook. Make him wait now.

"Come up to Boston," he says. "Get a writer-in-residence gig somewhere."

She pauses, as if contemplating the idea for the first time. "What about Pertek?" she asks, moving on to the next painting.

"Screw Pertek," he replies, loud enough for the guard to hear.

Inwardly she smiles.

~

In the kitchen, Laurie opens the last bottle of Muscadet, which she has chilled in the freezer compartment of the refrigerator. A dragon palace, she thinks, would be so deep under the sea that it's immeasurably cold. A cold beyond pain, beyond any feeling at all.

She hears a car on the dirt road, but it drives on past.

Dragons are kindly, and welcome your presence in their domain. Their palace is so beautiful you have no wish ever to leave it.

~

During the night Cameron came down with an earache, and Nicola got very little sleep. Skipping the chaotic family breakfast—Cameron squalling, toast mashed into the kitchen floor, Laurie in bathrobed disarray—Nicola goes for a swim.

As she performs her calm, competent breaststroke, she thinks about the conversation in the museum. She's not yet certain what she wants to do, but is enjoying the various possibilities in the situation. In a way, this thing with Steve is unfinished business: going backward before she can go forward, as she told Pertek. She was always attracted to Steve, sexually as well as intellectually. In the *Quadrat* days, however, she couldn't let herself be drawn into entanglements, with Steve or any other neophyte, that would lead nowhere and only drag her down. Now her reputation is firmly established; her ability to earn a comfortable living is not in doubt. She's free to do as she pleases. The conventional wisdom is that the older you become, the narrower your choices. Nicola will not allow herself to be bound by that rule.

She rides the breakers to shore, dries herself with the bath towel she left on the sand, and walks up to the cottage. She has no interest in destroying Steve's marriage, not for her own benefit. However, if she happened to rescue him from his dim and frantic wife, she might be doing him a favor.

While Nicola's been gone, Laurie has managed to locate a doctor willing to see Cameron in his office this morning, although it's a Saturday. Steve's insisting on going along. He takes his parental role seriously, and Nicola finds his decisiveness appealing, in contrast to Pertek's fumbling frailties.

"Will you keep an eye on Helen?" Steve asks Nicola.

"I guess so. Sure."

"I want to go," Helen complains.

Laurie begins to waver and then says, "No, you stay here with Nicola. We won't be long."

"But I want—"

"I don't *care* what you want."

Helen is astonished into silence; the brat clearly is used to having her whims indulged.

"Pay attention to what Nicola tells you," Laurie says. "And stay far away from the water."

They leave by the screen door to the deck, Steve carrying Cameron wrapped in a blanket taken from one of the beds. Nicola sees that Helen has been playing with a set of Princess Di paper dolls: spread out over the porch floorboards are clumsily cutout ball gowns and riding clothes and dresses to wear while pecking the cheeks of AIDS victims and disaster survivors. They smell musty and are curling with damp; a kid from some previous summer must have left the set behind. Helen stares rabbit-like at Nicola, her eyes not quite in focus. For some reason the timid, snot-nosed stupidity in Helen's expression makes Nicola say, "I suppose you know she's dead. Killed in a car crash, a long time ago. The princess didn't live happily ever after."

In her bedroom Nicola strips out of her suit, then goes to the bathroom to shower. When she returns, Helen is no longer on the porch, and the paper outfits are fluttering about in the breeze. Nicola glances through the screen and sees the child wandering aimlessly in the sand, licking a bright red Popsicle. Must have helped herself from the freezer, the sly little creep. Nicola flips up the cover of her laptop and opens the file that contains her new long poem, begun here a week ago.

Images begin to leap into her mind with almost alarming ease and rapidity: strange and illuminating juxtapositions. It's sexual excitement that's punching her into gear, in spite of the lost sleep. She'll show the work to Steve this afternoon, Nicola decides, even in this early, very rough draft. It will be like their time together at *Quadrat,* when they examined each other's writing word by word, provoking, goading, exulting in hard-earned, shared epiphanies.

Suddenly she hears screams.

~

Obeying her mother, Helen walked not toward the water but in the direction of the low grassy dunes behind the cottage. Yellow jackets lit on her mouth and chin and hands, sticky with cherry-red juice. She began to run and stumbled in the coarse grass. Dozens of yellow jackets rose out of their nest to sting her.

The emergency crew that Nicola summoned restarted the child's heart, shot her full of epinephrine, cut a hole in her throat, spirited her away to a hospital.

"I'm sorry," Nicola said to Laurie and Steve when they returned with Cameron. "I really am. But it wasn't my fault. Surely you can see that it wasn't my fault."

This morning Steve arranged for a taxi to collect Nicola and take her to the airport in Portland. It's the last they'll see of her, Laurie is certain, but that will make no difference in their lives, one way or the other.

Helen lies on a hospital bed, her body grotesquely mottled and swollen. The child's ribs are taped; an IV runs into her armpit. Her thin hair looks dark against the sheet. Its strands feel stiff to Laurie's fingers, and smell of salt and beach decay. Doctors have stitched together the wound in her throat and hidden it beneath white gauze. Laurie can tell by the blankness in her daughter's eyes that she has gone somewhere far away, to a place so remote that scary things can't find her ever again. Laurie hopes she is frolicking with dragons, in their palace under the sea.

WHY MEN LOVE TO CUT THINGS DOWN

NANCY COMES OUT to the deck with a colander and a mixing bowl full of pea pods. She stands for a moment, watching her husband and son-in-law attack the new growth that has burgeoned in the past year. Don is felling branches with a lopper, Brock yanking up spruce and fir seedlings with work-gloved hands. "Why is it that men love to cut things down?" Nancy asks.

Her daughter lifts her eyes from her book, a mildewed novel she checked out of the little town library earlier in the week. "If they didn't thin out the woods every now and then, soon you'd hardly be able to see the water."

"That's not why they do it, though. Look at the joy they take in the work. Whack! Whack! Whack!"

Gina smiles. "I have to admit, neither one of them spends much time in soulful contemplation of the view."

Nancy pulls a molded plastic lawn chair into the sun and sits, the colander in her lap. With her thumbnail she slits a pod and scoops the tender peas into the colander. The empty pods drop onto the deck planks, next to the bowl. "You're worried about something, aren't you?" she asks.

"What makes you think that?"

"You seem distracted. A little edgy."

Gina crosses and re-crosses her long denim-clad legs before answering. "Shit, Mom. I've never been able to hide things from you."

"You don't have to tell me, if you'd rather not."

Shelled peas ping steadily into the colander.

"No, it's not that. I just don't know how to say it."

Out on the bay, a sailboat bounces along on choppy water. Somewhere in the distance a chainsaw whines. The smell of crushed needles and wounded bark reaches them, carried on the breeze.

"All right," Gina says, "here's the story. I want to have a baby."

Well, good. But . . . ? Nancy imagines opposition on Brock's part. Or some dysfunction like a disastrously low sperm count. Frustrating trips to specialists. "I've wondered if you and Brock were thinking about a family. I didn't like to ask."

"The thing is, I'm not sure I want to have a baby with Brock."

Nancy looks at her daughter. Leaner now that she's into her thirties, brown hair longer, almost stringy on her shoulders. In the sunlight gleam a few gray hairs you'd never notice otherwise. Shallow breasts, bra-less, under a faded T-shirt. Good bones, a facial structure inherited from a Lithuanian great-grandmother on Nancy's side. Gina also inherited Don's long legs and something of his shyness. "I don't understand," Nancy says.

Gina closes the library book and sets it on the bench beside her chair. "It's not that our marriage is so awful. After eight years you get used to things the way they are, you find ways to accommodate."

Nancy bends forward for a handful of peas and notices that her thumbnail is now green. Her own marriage evolved that way, too: accommodation, resignation. She's long since made her peace with Don's reluctance to take risks, his penny-pinching, his maddening aphorisms. Measure three times, cut once.

"But," Gina continues, "for a long time I've thought that someday I might want to move on. Brock and I are so different, in so many ways."

Moving on. Divorce. The word is tawdry, has a dismal air of defeat. Used goods. And yet Nancy isn't nearly as taken aback as Gina must expect her to be, or as shocked. Yes, Gina and Brock are different from one another. He's a lot older, for one thing, an established partner in a Wall Street law firm even before he met her daughter and married her. Gina wouldn't need to keep her job as a designer for a small publishing house if she didn't want to; in fact, Brock claims half-jokingly that tax-wise, Gina's job costs him a bundle. A show-off, too, is her son-in-law, constantly dropping into the conversation references to Latin-American novelists or particle physics or medieval theological disputes. The first day or so of the annual visit to Maine Brock demonstrates elaborate interest in Nancy's garden and Don's latest workshop project. Then patronizing his in-laws becomes a bore, and he turns his energies elsewhere: running timed miles up and down their dirt road while complaining about the dust and potholes, fighting with the ancient Evinrude so he can take the leaky old skiff onto the water only to get stuck at low tide fifty yards out and have to wade home in muck up to his ankles.

"A baby connects you in ways that aren't easily undone," Gina says. "With a baby there's not the same possibility of moving on."

The men are now dragging felled vegetation into preliminary piles, from which stick out slender trunks with fist-sized clumps of roots on their ends.

"How does Brock feel about a child?" Nancy asks.

"He's all for it. Has been right from the beginning. I'm the one who's been procrastinating." Gina turns toward her mother. "He'd probably be a very good father. He'd insist on religious training—Episcopal, of course—music lessons, the best schools. I can just hear him bragging about little Tristan's prize in violin, little Isolde's prowess in the swimming pool."

"Tristan? Isolde?"

Gina laughs. "No common ordinary names for him."

"No, I suppose not." Nancy gets up from her chair, leaving the colander on the seat. She stoops to gather empty pea pods into the bowl.

"So what do you think I should do, Mom?"

What Nancy wants to say is: Dump the arrogant creep! Find somebody gentle and unpretentious, like yourself, while there's still time. Age thirty-five becomes fifty in the blink of an eye. But of course she can't say that. What mother advises her daughter to break up a comfortable marriage, to leave a good provider? To venture into the unknown for no demonstrably good reason? "Oh, dear," she says. "I'm afraid I can't help you on this one." She carries the bowl down the deck steps and dumps the pods into the compost bin.

~

They parked in Don's falling-apart old Catalina behind a factory that made spark plugs. On the radio was a Petula Clark song she'd heard a million times. *Downtown . . .* Don let his arm drop from the back of the seat and rest on her shoulder. Then he pulled her close and kissed her, his mouth tasting of onions and catsup from their meal at McDonald's. He groped inside her coat to unbutton her blouse, and she asked him not to.

"Why not, what's the matter?"

"I'd just rather not tonight."

"All right," he said, letting go of her.

Nancy knew he wouldn't force himself on her. He wasn't that kind of person.

The disk jockey, reading the AP news, announced that Malcolm X had been shot dead in Harlem. "Wasn't he the guy who said Kennedy's assassination was chickens coming home to roost?" Don asked.

Nancy was eighteen years old, taking courses for an A.A. at the community college, working part time in a gift shop, living with her parents. She had barely heard of Malcolm X.

"I think more chickens just flew home," Don said.

She'd met Don at the college on her first day, in the line in the cafeteria. He carried her tray for her, sat with her while she ate her American chop suey. She found out he was soon to graduate with a degree in business, and that he was quite a bit older than she was. Right out of high school he'd gone to work in his dad's company, a modest operation that manufactured plastic placemats with scenes like the Grand Canyon and Old Faithful printed on them. After six years his father died of a heart attack, and Don decided to sell the faltering business and go to school. The sale had brought just enough money to allow his mother to stay in the family bungalow in Bergenfield. Don didn't want to make placemats his whole life, he'd confessed to Nancy that first day in the cafeteria.

"Ranger 8 ended its life last night in the Sea of Tranquility," she heard the disk jockey say. "Before crashing, the spaceship sent back to earth seven thousand pictures of the moon. And now the weather. A cold front will move in overnight, temperatures falling to around the freezing mark, sleet or freezing rain before dawn. Take care, all you commuters out there." The music resumed, a new Beatles tune. *I don't want to. Spoil the pa-ar-ty.*

"I have something to tell you," Nancy said. "I'm pregnant."

At first he didn't seem to have heard over the noise of the radio, and she reached to turn the knob. "Don, I said—"

"You can't be."

"I saw a doctor. Friday they called to give me the results of the urine test."

He stared straight ahead and she knew that he was thinking about the unreasonableness of it. Just the one time, and he never even managed to get all the way inside her before he came, and then all weepy she'd made him take her home.

Their breaths had fogged the windows. The factory's security lights were fuzzy blurs. "Don't worry," he said. "I'll figure out something."

~

Don shut the door of the Catalina, leaving his pregnant wife inside. Crammed into the backseat were practically all their possessions. A floor lamp that Nancy's mother had pressed on her at the last minute poked crazily out of a mess of supermarket bags full of secondhand house furnishings, wedding presents still in their boxes, clothes on hangers. Through the passenger window Nancy gave him an encouraging wave.

The sign attached to brick at 33A Main Street said "Ellsworth Business & Tax Services. Second floor." It featured the outline of a hand with a finger pointing upward.

They'd picked Maine because he'd heard somewhere that it was a cheap place to live, a bargain. Nancy liked the idea of living near the ocean, away from congestion and traffic and, Don suspected, from people who would know or guess why they had to get married. Ellsworth was the town from which he'd received the one reply to the dozens of letters of inquiry he'd sent out.

Don climbed the dark, narrow steps, which smelled of rubber

from the treads, dust, and something vaguely ether-like. The stairs reminded him of those leading to the doctor's office in Bergenfield where his mother used to take him as a child. What he felt in the depths of his stomach now was the same as knowing he'd have to undress with his mother watching and be prodded by the doctor in places he didn't want to be prodded and then get a shot.

Behind the glass door there wasn't a secretary, just a balding fellow in a none-too-clean shirt seated at a big old oak desk. The room reeked of cigar smoke. On the desk and stacked on top of file cabinets and on the floor were ledgers, thick wads of paper in manila folders, mottled black and white cardboard boxes. The man—Al Pitkin—offered Don a plump hand. "Sit," he ordered. Gingerly Don moved a pile of papers from his chair to the corner of the desk and obeyed.

Without preamble, Al Pitkin launched into his speech. "Like I said in my letter, I'm looking to ease off a tad. Want to do some fishing, play with my grandkids. Could use somebody to lighten the load. Think you can handle it?"

Don gazed at the chaos surrounding him and assured Al Pitkin that he'd be on top of the job in no time.

"I'll be honest with you. Won't be able to pay you a whole lot, seeing as you haven't much experience, just out of school and all. One-thirty-five a week's the best I can do."

Don reminded him that he'd helped his father run a business, knew firsthand something about how books were kept.

"Fine, that's fine," Al Pitkin said enthusiastically, plucking a cigar stub out of an ashtray half-buried on the desk. "Give you a good leg up. Of course, certain things they do different down in Jersey than we do here in Maine. Take you a while to learn the ropes.

How-some-ever, if things work out, we'll talk about giving you a little raise, maybe in a year or two."

Don thought about the baby in Nancy's belly, how he'd have to find a place for them to live and pay for it, plus the doctor and hospital, plus the myriad other expenses of maintaining a family, not to mention the payments on his student loans and helping his mother out from time to time. He felt responsibilities cropping up around him like enormous weeds. Would it be possible to manage everything on a hundred thirty-five dollars a week? He doubted it, even if Maine actually was the bargain it was cracked up to be. Still, he couldn't go back downstairs to Nancy and tell her he wasn't going to take the job, after all. Gypsy-like, they'd have to roam the state or maybe all up and down the Eastern seaboard in the Catalina packed to the gunnels until he found something else. The car, ten years old and beginning to signal transmission problems, might not even make it to the next town. Well, he could always begin here and be looking for a better opportunity at the same time. "Sounds good to me," he told Al Pitkin.

~

The men stow lopper, sickle, saw, and work gloves in the shed and start back to the house. Over by the gravel parking area is a mound of foliage the size of a minor hill, which will be burned come fall. The smell of sap is strong in the air, an aroma that has delighted Don ever since they moved to Maine all those years ago. It pleases him to see the results of a day's work all in a palpable mass like that. So many efforts that a person makes can't be quantified so readily or even observed at all. Don's also pleased that there's one thing—a tradition now—that he and his son-in-law can do together in a companionable way. You have to hand it to Brock, he's a hard worker once he sets his mind on a task. All that energy.

"Wonder what Nancy's cooking for supper," Don says, to make conversation, though he knows Nancy was planning on lobsters—a treat for Gina and Brock's last night in Maine.

Brock doesn't bother to answer, just runs up the steps and into the house.

Don sits on the top porch step to take off his work boots and then stays there awhile, the boots beside him. He'll let Brock shower and the water heat up again before he goes inside.

His daughter opens the screen door and pokes her head out. "Mosquitoes acting up yet?" she asks.

"Not yet."

"Want a beer?"

"Sure."

Gina reappears with two cold Heinekens—Brock imported them from New York, on the theory, apparently, that Maine is devoid of all forms of civilization—moves the boots to one side, and sits next to him. "Impressive," she says, gesturing with her bottle toward the mountainous heap by the parking area. She takes a sip and then says, "Mom says men love to whack things down."

"Hm." Don mulls this over. It kind of surprises him that Nancy would say such a thing, or even think it. Why doesn't she understand how fast things get out of hand if you aren't paying attention? For reasons he can't specify, what she's said makes him feel bad. But then, Nancy has often surprised and wounded him without intending to. Women are confusing, even Gina, whom he loves dearly. Sometimes Don wishes he'd had a son, but after Gina's miraculous conception in the backseat of the old Catalina they'd never been able to start another baby, almost as if God was punishing them for their sin. Well no, not God. Don's not much of a believer. The fates, then.

Gina tells him a little about the book she'll be working on starting Monday—a collection of travel essays by a man whose name means nothing to Don—but soon the mosquitoes do start to bite, and they go inside. When Don comes down from his shower the lobsters are already on the table, pound and a halfers, hard-shells. There's Nancy's special potato salad with hardboiled eggs, too, and peas right out of the garden, and melted butter in little cups, and homemade bread, and the bottle of white wine he splurged on at the Shop 'n Save. No meal could give Don more pleasure than this one.

"Come eat," Nancy says, and everybody takes their places, Gina to Don's left because she's a lefty, her husband across from her, and Nancy across from Don. Nancy's gray hair, worn short now, is curling around her face, which is flushed from the heat of the boiling lobster water. She has never in her life looked better to him. Happy in his role as head of the family, Don uncorks the wine and fills their glasses.

"Ah," Brock exclaims grandly, rubbing his hands, "how splendid. Giant red bugs."

There's a brief silence. Then Gina says, her voice so soft that Don can barely make out the words, "Is it really necessary to be so obnoxious?"

Brock smiles. He has a ruddy Anglo-Saxon complexion, thinning blow-dried hair, large white orthodontically straight teeth, and a nose that's sort of squashed at the tip. Not especially good-looking. When Gina first brought him to Maine, before they were married, Don wondered what she saw in him. Now, however, Don understands the steadiness underneath the bluster and appreciates it. "I'm sorry if I offended anyone," Brock says, "but in point of fact that's what a lobster is. An arthropod. Nothing more than an oversized wood louse."

"Have some peas, Gina," Nancy says, trying to pass her the bowl catty-corner above the food.

Gina ignores her mother. "And what you are," Gina says, smiling sweetly at her husband, "is an asshole."

Brock again shows his white teeth. "Perhaps, my dear, you've had too much to drink."

"Or perhaps, my dear, you haven't had enough." Gina lifts her glass, rises from her chair, and upends the glass over her husband's head. As they watch, wine drenches him and his clean lime-colored Lacoste shirt, pours into the lap of his L. L. Bean khakis. He doesn't move. Liquid drips from his chin and from the squashed tip of his nose onto the carapace of his lobster.

Nobody says a word. Don reaches across the table to hand him his own napkin, and Brock mops his head, ineffectually pats his shirt front and trousers. Then he leaves the table, walks across the room, opens the screen door leading to the deck and lets it fall shut behind him. Not with a bang. More of a wheeze.

Don looks down at his cooling lobster. He has lost his appetite entirely. The two women dig in, however, wrenching claws off bodies and cracking them open. Beside him, Gina dips a chunk of meat into melted butter and pops it into her mouth. "Yum," she says. "Giant red wood louse. Me eat giant wed rood louse." She and Nancy begin to laugh. The two of them laugh until tears run down their faces.

Well, Don thinks. His son-in-law might from time to time display certain asshole tendencies, but he didn't deserve to be humiliated that way. He was only trying to be entertaining.

Outside, Don finds Brock sitting hunched on the edge of the deck, dangling his legs over the side, gazing out at the water. His formerly blow-dried hair, swabbed with Don's napkin, is mussed all to hell and the poor guy looks generally bedraggled. Don sits beside him.

After a while Brock asks, "Do you think she's still angry?"

Don contemplates the scene of hilarity from which he has recently departed. "Hard to tell." That's the truth. He hasn't a clue.

"It was meant to be a joke. A lame one, I guess." After another long pause Brock says, "We accomplished a lot today."

"Yes. We did."

"Now you have a pretty good view."

Tide's up. Soon the moon will rise and between the trees they will see it reflected on the glimmering bay. Two moons for the price of one, definitely a bargain.

" . . . until next year, anyway," Brock adds. "Downright scary the way the weeds grow back."

"Sure is," Don says. "Downright scary."

JUNK

TODAY IS GARBAGE day. Lyle slips out of bed without waking Frances and is out on the street by five a.m. You have to get to the cans before the truck rolls by, and as the days lengthen that seems to be earlier and earlier.

The trouble with this town is that everybody's either a pack rat or a pinchpenny, or both. Nobody ever throws anything away that they might possibly be able to sell or barter or that could, by some wild stretch of the imagination, come in handy some day. The summer people are different, of course, but they don't start flitting back into town until after mud season.

Still, you never know, and all Lyle has to lose is a couple hours sleep. It's true he might be spotted digging into a garbage can and held up to ridicule by some, but it's not his fault Mildred Flowers decided she had to live in Florida. It's not his fault she made Billy shut down Flowers Insurance so now Lyle's about to be out on his ear. Let people blame Mid if they want to blame someone. He's only doing what he has to.

Nothing so all-fired freakish about this idea anyhow, or even original; half the people on Main Street empty out their attics onto their lawns every Memorial Day and don't pack the junk up again until the leaves drop. Only thing is, Frances isn't going to be happy about tourists trampling her dahlias and asking to use the bathroom. She's a moody person, Frances. Wiser not to let her in on the yard sale plan until absolutely necessary.

In the Caprice he cruises slowly down Cottage Street, keeping his eyes peeled for any clue that might announce a treasure. An unusually large heap of trash probably means somebody's either moving or else swamping out their attic or their cellar. What you can hope for is that the size of the job at some point overwhelms them, especially when they're old and there's no relations close by, and that they'll lose heart and give the whole lot the heave. Last Tuesday after Milford Potter went to the nursing home, Lyle found a carton of ancient kitchenware—egg beater, soap cage, masher, flatiron—just sitting there in the gutter, waiting for Lyle to pick up and haul away. It's hard to believe, but people pay money for those things.

The shed's getting kind of full, in fact. And worse, Frances is suspicious. She wanted to know why the padlock is kept clamped shut now, instead of just hanging from the hasp to keep the door from sagging open.

"I heard in the office kids have been vandalizing outbuildings," he told her. "Dumping out cans of paint. Smashing Mason jars. Setting little fires."

"What kids?"

"I don't know. Just kids."

"I haven't heard anything like that."

"Maybe if you got out more, you'd hear things."

"I get out all I care to, thank you."

"All right, all right."

"And I need my potting soil from the shed."

He carried the plastic sack of soil inside for her and left it by the kitchen door, and he's noticed it hasn't been touched since. Also, she wanted to know where he went at the crack of dawn last Tuesday morning. He said he'd had a sudden craving for eggs and home fries at the Brass Lantern.

"I've never in my life known you to do such a thing."

"You haven't known me all your life."

"I have, too. I remember when you were a little twerp in the fourth grade and you cried because a big boy took your milk money."

He remembers her from those days, too. Eighth-grade Milk Monitor, fat and bossy, with a heart like a lump of coal. But he only said, with dignity, "You haven't known how I felt about home fries."

That made her even more suspicious, unfortunately. He could see right into her head: Frances was sure that Marilla, his first wife, used to cook home fries for him every day of the week. Queer the way she resents Marilla; if Marilla hadn't left him, Frances wouldn't even be here. Anyway, breakfast is the meal Marilla never fixes for anyone but herself. He doubts that's changed, even if she is living with that shiftless worm digger over on Monkey Bay Road, and supporting him too. Serves her right.

On Flat Bay Road Lyle finds an amber glass whiskey bottle lying in a scrap of leftover snow. The bottle might look old, he thinks, if he soaked the label off and incinerated it for a while. A little farther on he spots a three-legged kitchen chair on top of a heap of trash by the drainage ditch. Under those chipped layers of paint the chair's solid maple, he guesses. He hunts around in the frozen dried weeds near the trash pile, but can't find the fourth leg. How did it come to be detached and lost? he wonders. In a domestic dispute, maybe. Or under a very fat person. Without warning she crashed to the floor, and in the ensuing confusion the leg rolled under the stove or behind the refrigerator.

He looks up the slope at the house whose occupants have put out this pile of debris. It's a rackety farmhouse, half covered in tarpaper. The rest is unpainted board, weathered to a splintery gray. No TV antenna, which definitely means no refrigerator, either. He gives up any hope of recovering the leg and leaves the chair in the ditch. Tourists may be crazy, but probably not crazy enough to buy a three-legged chair, even if it is solid maple.

He doesn't stop at the heap in front of the trailer around the next curve, although something's sticking out of one of the cans, an old floor lamp minus the glass shade. Outside chance it's brass. Even if it's only iron, you could spray it with gold paint. But the trash pile is near enough to the trailer that whoever inhabits the place might hear him rattling around in the can, and besides, it's getting late. He wants to hit the Dumpsters at the boat launch down the road before turning back.

The Dumpsters turn out to be a disappointment, though. The only thing worth mentioning is a doll without a wig. Its eyes flicker open as he lifts it out. His daughter Hannah had a doll something like this once, he recalls. The grayish cloth body smells musty, and the rubber fingers of one hand are gone, chewed off it looks like. By a dog, maybe. Probably cost more to fix up than he could ever sell it for.

But he hates to have come this far with so little to show for it, so he lays the doll on the backseat of the Caprice and heads for home.

~

"I hate to break this to you, Frances, but I think there's something wrong with Lyle." Frances's girlfriend Bev shakes the crumbs from her fingers into the sandwich wrapper and taps her own skull. "Upstairs."

The vinyl pad sticks to her bottom as Frances shifts uneasily on the bench in the breakfast nook. She's afraid to hear what's coming next, but she wants to give Bev the impression she's one step ahead of her. "A man's bound to be upset when he's going to lose his job," she says. "The truth is, he's been better lately. More cheerful."

Bev's mouth had been open to bite into her cream cheese and sardine sandwich, but instead she puts the sandwich down. "You know what they say about a depressed person who suddenly becomes cheerful, don't you?"

"Of course I do."

Bev's long experience as a teacher makes her alert to equivocation. Without pausing for breath she pounces. "All right, what do they say?"

"Why, that the person is coming out of the depression."

"No, dear. He's cheerful because he's made a decision to escape his misery and he's figured out how to do it."

"Lyle?"

"Well, you can't entirely rule it out, I suppose."

"Oh, my lord. That's what the suitcase must be for."

"Suitcase?" Bev asks with her mouth half full. "What suitcase is that?"

"The other day I was dusting the blinds in the front room, and I glanced out the window and saw Lyle coming down the street with a suitcase in his hand. Around the corner of the house he went, and I ran out to the kitchen, and out this very window I saw him hiding the suitcase in the shed. It was plaid, the cheap cloth kind that zips instead of buckles. I wouldn't put any clothes of mine in it, but men don't care about such things."

Bev looks confused. "What's a suitcase got to do with anything?"

"What you said about deciding to escape, of course. He must be planning to escape with the suitcase."

"I'm afraid that wasn't the kind of escape I had in mind, Frances."

"Why are you being so mysterious, Bev? Are you deliberately trying to provoke me?"

"Calm down, Frances. How are you going to help Lyle if you work yourself into a worse state than he's in?"

Frances slams her coffee cup onto the saucer, and a chip flies off the saucer rim. "Now see what you made me do."

"You're talking exactly like a second grader."

Frances squeezes out from between the bench and the table and moves heavily to the window. Across an expanse of fresh snow, she can see the shed, with the closed padlock dangling from the hasp. "What kind of escape, then?" she hears herself ask in a weak, high-pitched voice.

"Suicide," Bev says briskly.

Home fries with eggs and sausage flash before Frances's eyes. He wanted to taste home fries once more before . . .

"But we're getting off the track here," Bev continues. "I said there was something wrong with him. I did not say he's about to do himself in. Quite the contrary."

"But—"

"People contemplating suicide get rid of things. They give their gold watches and bowling trophies to their loved ones. They might take trips to the dump with their old love letters. They do not make trips to the dump to collect more junk than they already own and haul it away with them."

Under the snow near the shed are some lumps, unharvested cabbages. Frances watches a tree sparrow land on one of the lumps and then flit away. "Please do tell me what you're talking about," she says wearily.

Bev takes a deep breath, the way she does when she's about to explain the Pythagorean theorem or the causes of the French and Indian War. "Well, in case you've forgotten, the happy day of my retirement from Stony Harbor Elementary is a mere three months away."

No, Frances hasn't forgotten. At one time, before Lyle talked her into marrying him, she and Bev were going to go off to the condo in North Carolina together. Leave the ice and mud behind for good and all. She'd contributed her share of the down payment on the condo and everything.

"And you know," Bev goes on, "how I've been going from room to room, deciding what I want to take with me to North Carolina and what I'd just as soon leave behind. Like that mahogany parlor suite I've always hated, but Mother would rise from the dead and smite me if I sold it or gave it to the Salvation Army."

"Yes," Frances says with a pang, both because of the thought of Bev's leaving and because she'd once looked forward to living with that furniture, especially the marble-topped occasional tables and the footstool with the Scottie dog done in needlepoint. She'd had no idea Bev hated it.

"Well, it's not going. Cost a fortune to move it, and Mother will have a hard time finding me in North Carolina."

Frances thinks about putting in a bid for it, but that wouldn't be appropriate right now, considering how worried she is about Lyle. And anyway, she's not sure she'd enjoy the tables and the Scottie dog without Bev. They'd only make her sad.

"So," Bev says, unwrapping a date square from its waxed paper, "one way and another I'm finding a good deal of rubbish to give the heave to, and I'm hauling it out to those Dumpsters on Flat Bay Road, because you never know what the trash men will be so kind as to pick up and what they won't. Considering the taxes we pay—"

"Bev, not the parlor suite. You're not putting the parlor suite in the Dumpster."

"Of course not. Some fool will give me good money for it. But as I was saying, I drive out there early in the morning, before school. After school I'm too bushed to lift a pincushion. Yesterday around six a.m. I was pulling into the spot where the Dumpsters are, you know, where the clamdiggers park their vehicles, but there was only one car there because the tide was in. And guess whose car it was."

"I don't want to guess, Bev."

"It was *your* car, Frances. And there was Lyle, big as life, hanging over the side of the Dumpster. At first I thought he was being sick into it. I was so flabbergasted I just sat there, smack in the middle of the road. Anyone could have come along and rammed right into me. Then I realized he wasn't being sick at all, he was rooting around in there. And do you know what he came up with, finally?"

"No, Bev."

"A doll. A stark naked bald old doll. I couldn't believe it. He looked at it for a while, turning it over and over in his hands. And then he put it in the back of the Caprice and started the engine. He had to drive around my car to get into the road, but he never even saw me. Now what do you think of that?"

Frances turns away from the window and stares at Bev. "I don't know what to think. What can be happening to him?"

"Beats me," Bev says, zipping up her galoshes. "I'm going to be late for fifth period hygiene if I don't get a move on."

Lyle told Billy he couldn't work this afternoon. No excuses, he's beyond that. What's Billy going to do, fire him? Anyway, there's not much to do around the office now, just sit at his desk amid the taped cartons and drink instant coffee and listen to talk that's like flies buzzing on a ceiling, like the hum of a distant highway.

He's been waiting impatiently for this day, the third Monday in the month, when Frances goes to her Current Events Club meeting. At half past one he rounds the side of the house and sees, to his frustration, the Caprice still parked in the driveway. It's not like her to skip the club meetings, and he worries that maybe the arthritis has kept her from going, or the fear that her enemy Mid Flowers, all set to loll on a beach in Florida, will be the current event topic of the afternoon. Cautiously he opens the kitchen door and calls her name. But there's no sound except for the furnace kicking on in response to the blast of chill air from the open door, and then he remembers Frances mentioning that one of the other members was going to pick her up, something about a tray of cupcakes. He shuts the door again and slogs out through the mud to the shed. The glacier of drifted snow there is retreating. He sees the yellowed tops of cabbages, the spine of the stone wall, the cross-plank of his sawhorse.

He has two hours, maybe two and a half if the girls linger to gab, but he can't count on that. He unlocks the padlock and swings the shed door wide open, forcing it over a crust of ice. He needs the wheelbarrow, but there's such a jumble in the shed that it takes him a while to shift things enough so he can extricate it. He scrapes his knuckles on the underbody of a Royal portable typewriter, which has long ago been separated from its case, and a splinter from the wheelbarrow handle jabs into his palm. When he has loaded the wheelbarrow as full as is practical, he trundles toward the house. It's slow going through the bog, and an alligator handbag bounces off the top of the heap and lands in the mud. He'll be able to wipe it off, though; luckily, it's simulated, not the real thing.

Damned tricky getting everything into the house. He doesn't want to take time to pull on or pry off his rubbers every time he crosses the threshold, and Frances would surely notice an accumulation of mud in the rag rug by the kitchen door. So he kicks the rug out of the way and resolves to scrub the linoleum when he's done. Two more wheelbarrow trips, and he's ready to haul the whole hodgepodge to the attic.

But his heart is beating uncomfortably with the exertion and with the possibility that Frances might come home early with a sick headache or some other complaint. He pours himself some water out of the glass jar in the refrigerator and makes himself sip it, slowly, until his pulse is under control. He thinks about taking his blood pressure and then rejects the idea. He can't stop now, with the kitchen floor piled high with rubbish: even if his b.p. is out of sight, he'd just as soon not know about it.

He unzips the moldy old suitcase and begins to cram whatever will fit into it. The battered unabridged Funk and Wagnalls dictionary and the stone doorstop painted to look like a sleeping cat make it weigh half a ton, never mind all the other trash he wedges in there, but at least he'll have to make fewer trips upstairs. He's had the foresight to filch the suitcase from the cellar under the insurance building way back when he first got his idea. Billy was up to something with that suitcase fifteen years ago, but then whatever it was came to an end, and Billy stowed the suitcase in the cellar and forgot about it. At the time, Lyle had felt sorry for Mid—getting cheated on—little knowing that Marilla was going to do the same thing to him, and worse, and that one day Mid would triumph at everybody's expense, including his own. Thinking about the worm turning that way gives him a perverse sort of pleasure, and the strength to lug the suitcase up the two flights with only a brief pause on the landing.

They don't heat the attic stairway, or the attic, and as he opens the top door the cold, close, dusty attic pinches his nostrils. It's dim under the rafters and the windows at the gable ends are covered with cobwebs. He sits on the sheet-covered couch to rest a minute before unpacking the suitcase. Gradually he finds his eyes adjusting to the gloom.

Lyle hasn't been up here since he and Bramley Johnson, who he hired for ten dollars, moved all of Marilla's things up here the week before he and Frances were married. Frances wasn't going to live with Marilla's odds and ends of furniture, she wanted matching. When Frances said she wanted to get rid of the stuff he'd thought she must mean burn it. He got a bonfire permit from the town office and bought a quart of charcoal lighter to douse the upholstery with, and he and Bramley were just struggling out the kitchen door with the old brown couch, when Frances dropped by to see how they were coming with the move, and yelled bloody murder, and made them haul the couch back through the kitchen and up to the attic. And all the other furniture with it. She was shocked he was planning to burn the stuff, and he was shocked she wanted to save it. You might call that their first quarrel, with half-witted old Bram Johnson standing there on the back stoop grinning like a maniac.

That couch they had in the trailer on Seal Neck Road, he and Marilla. He lifts the sheet, and puts his nose down close to the coarse wool material, and imagines it still smells the way the trailer smelled all those years ago—of kerosene, and cooking oil, and the soap Marilla used. He remembers making love to her on the couch soon after Hannah was born, and they had to snatch a few moments between feeds. He remembers the milk in her breasts, how swollen they were, how the milk would leak out on its own when she was in his arms. Now he wonders whether Marilla was happy with him, even then. He'd believed she was, she never said otherwise, but with women, how are you going to know for sure?

He wishes to hell Frances hadn't come by that day and he'd burned the whole caboodle once and for all.

He doesn't bother to unzip the suitcase and empty out its contents. He knows now he couldn't possibly stand on his front lawn and bargain with tourists over Marilla's things, or Hannah's, or even the sticks and oddments belonging to strangers. They're too private, it would be too painful. He's amazed that he ever thought he could make a living that way.

He lugs the suitcase down the two flights and loads it, as well as all the accumulated trash from the shed, into the car. When he returns from his trip to the Dumpster he sees that the wheelbarrow has made six slithery ruts, like the trails of snakes, in the mud. Carefully he smears them over with his rubber. He's just replacing the rag rug over the clean linoleum by the kitchen door when Frances unlocks the front door and cries, "Halloo, I'm home."

MILLENNIUM FEVER

THE LADIES ARE talking about RVs. The Maine winter builds character: they have long taken this on faith. But as they age, they're more and more tempted by temporary escape. Mordina's been campaigning to buy one of those cute motorhomes so she and her hubby can drive down to Florida and have a place to stay once they get there. So far, Ed has put up a resistance on account of the expense, Mordina reports, but she senses that she's wearing him down. The other ladies cheer her on.

"What about you, Carlene?" Mordina asks. "Fancy spending the winter under palm trees?"

Carlene laughs. "Chalkie thinks a day trip to Ellsworth is a big deal." She's placing baskets of hot bread at either end of the four long tables, which have been set up with checkered tablecloths, forks and spoons, and paper plates to go under the soup bowls. Behind her a gaggle of crockpots are plugged into a multi-outlet extension cord on the counter. Today, for their monthly public luncheon, the church ladies are offering a choice of fish chowder, minestrone, split pea, or chili. Five dollars a head, and that includes coffee and a slice of homemade pie. The minestrone is Carlene's, made of vegetables she canned herself.

Their first customer of the day comes down the steps and opens the door to the church basement, bringing with him a gust of snowy wind. He's alone, a lanky grizzled fellow wearing a watch cap. Because she doesn't exactly recognize the man, Carlene wonders whether he's a member of the crew installing the new furnace in the town hall. But he looks familiar, somehow. She watches him hand a twenty-dollar bill to the money-taker and pocket the change. Casually he hangs his parka over a folding chair, walks to the counter to select his soup. As he's lifting the glass lids, contemplating the possibilities, Carlene realizes that this is a person she once knew very well.

She slips into the kitchen, her back to the counter, and plunges her hands into the dishwater. She doesn't want him to notice her, rack his brain to remember who she is, stumble over her name, ask what she's been up to for the past forty-odd years. She scrubs some utensils and holds them under the tap, drops them clattering into the drainer. What is he doing here?

Carlene whispers to Mordina that she's got a wretched headache. Startled, Mordina says, "You better go on home then." Carlene grabs her coat and runs up the steps.

~

Chalkie pushes aside his dessert plate and lights a cigarette. The doc says if he doesn't quit smoking it's going to kill him, but Chalkie's not one to listen to doctors. "How'd the lunch go?" he asks.

Carlene finishes the coffee in her cup, rises to clear. Hoping for leftovers, Bob, the old yellow tiger cat, plummets from the radiator. "I didn't stay long. I had a headache."

"A headache?" Like Mordina, he looks at her as if she's sprouted a sausage at the end of her nose. "You don't get headaches."

"Today I did."

"You aren't coming down with something, are you?"

"By the time I got home it was gone," she says, evading Bob, who is endeavoring to wind himself around her legs. She carries dishes to the sink. "I doubt there was much of a crowd, anyway, on account of the weather."

Limping, Chalkie takes his cigarette to his easy chair in the next room. Years ago, before they were married, even, a chunk of the innards of some vehicle fell on his foot and it didn't heal right. A few pieces of mail await him on the side table. "Letter from Jill, I see. What's it say?"

She refrains from telling him to read the letter himself: she's not his interpreter. "They hope to come up for Thanksgiving, if Ron can take the time off work."

Chalkie grunts. It's a sore subject, how both his sons left town the minute they graduated high school, neither having any interest in a partnership in their dad's garage. Them boys never liked to get their hands dirty, Chalkie would say. He'd think they were pansies if they hadn't married, and sometimes he wonders even so. Chalkie's narrow-mindedness irks Carlene, but on the other hand she can see his point. He worked so hard to make a go of the business, and he can't help taking his sons' indifference as a slap in the face.

~

On Sunday Dana Cox comes to church. He strolls in after the choir has already sung the introit, sits in a rear pew, doesn't take communion. The Coxes were never churchgoers; Carlene wonders if Dana has experienced some kind of conversion along the way. However, he doesn't know the words to the responses, appears more curious than devout as the service unfolds. She knows he's observing her up in the choir, because their eyes meet for a second when she happens to glance his way. It's strange and unsettling to see how he has aged: the gray beard and thinning hair, the slight stoop of his tall frame.

As she starts the walk home, he eases into step beside her. Sunlight reflects brilliantly from a fresh layer of snow and the air is so cold it tightens her throat. Without saying anything, they pass the library, the Masonic Hall, Chipman's boatyard. Damned if she's going to be the first to speak.

Finally he says, "Here's what I imagined about you. You taught school for three or four years, then got married. You had two children, a boy and a girl."

She doesn't tell him there wasn't a daughter, though she keenly feels the lack. *A son is a son till he takes him a wife; a daughter's a daughter all of her life.* Nor does she explain that she went back to teaching when Matthew started kindergarten, first to make ends meet, then to be somebody other than Chalkie's wife and the boys' mother. She taught for thirty years altogether, until Chalkie insisted that she retire.

"Am I right?" Dana asks.

Now they're on the bridge, their boots clanging on the iron grate. She always thinks she's going to catch her heel and go flying. Below them, visible through the grate, the tide pours upriver. To their right sea smoke boils off the bay.

"Near enough."

A van enters the bridge, and they move against the rail to let it pass. The bridge trembles under the van's weight.

"They tell me you married Chalkie Hutchins."

They? Who's Dana been talking to? "That's right," she says, walking on. She knows what he's thinking. An ordinary person, nothing very remarkable about Chalkie Hutchins.

They've left the bridge now and turned onto Bay Road. Her house, the white farmhouse, is at the top of a rise. "Here's what I imagine about you," she says. "You stayed in the navy for a hitch or two. Then you got restless. Worked one job after another. Picked up some education in night school, maybe. Moved around a lot. Every place you lived you had a girlfriend, a waitress or a schoolteacher or a clerk in a department store. You were good to her, and she thought sure you'd settle down, but that never happened. Am I right?"

"Carlene—"

"Goodbye, Dana." No, she is not going to invite him to stay for Sunday lunch, eat her pie, chew the fat with Chalkie, as if nothing had ever happened. She hurries up the driveway, her boots unsteady on slick, hard-packed snow.

~

The next day, three days before Thanksgiving, Carlene is in Spinney's Hardware for flashlight batteries, and Fran Spinney tells her that their old classmate was in the store. "You just missed him," Fran says. "Bought tarpaper, caulking compound, plastic window insulation, you name it. He's fixing up some old cabin used to be his cousins', way in back of beyond. Nobody but a crazy person would live out there this time of year." Carlene watches Fran load D batteries into a paper bag. She doesn't need to ask, "Out where?" She sees the threadbare pink quilt, feels the plank floor hard against the bumps of her spine.

~

After boot camp, in October of '57, Dana came home for two weeks' leave. They'd both graduated high school in June, and Carlene was attending teachers' college in Machias, commuting the thirty miles each way, working odd hours in Bradbury's Pharmacy to help pay her tuition.

On his first Saturday morning home Dana stopped by Bradbury's to pick up his mother's prescription for heart pills. They got to talking about this and that, and since it was a nice day, unseasonably warm, he invited her to go for a ride. "I don't get off till noon," she said, but he hung around, thumbing through magazines from the rack, until old Mrs. Bradbury told her she could go. In his mother's two-tone green Oldsmobile he took Carlene out to Fiddlers Point, going fast on the rough road, the two of them laughing as the tires jounced over the ruts and spat gravel in their wake.

They sat on granite ledge, talking, watching sea water flood the rocks below them and then be sucked away. Or anyway Dana talked, mostly about his adventures at boot camp, and Carlene listened. They'd been classmates since first grade, but she'd never before been alone with him: Dana Cox, basketball wizard, clever if not very ambitious student, class president. They stayed on the rocks so long that the breeze turned chilly, and she shivered. Dana reached out to touch her long, thick brown hair, gently winding a lock of it around his finger. He looked at her in a way that no one had ever looked at her before, and in that instant Carlene knew she'd fallen in love with him.

The next day he led her to an old cabin in the woods near the Point. Over the plank floor he spread a quilt he'd brought with him in the trunk of the Olds, a ragged quilt smelling of mildew. He was sweetly and comically awkward, fumbling with the rubber.

They returned to the cabin nine times. She cut classes, called in sick, lied to her parents to be with him. And then he was on the bus, off to Norfolk, Virginia, where his ship awaited.

Dana's letters were full of funny stories about his life on board—he was doing something with electronic navigation, and he joked about plotting the ship's course off the end of the earth—but not one word about any future for them. She knew her letters were dull compared to his, though she did her best to make entertaining her ed classes and Mrs. Bradbury's crotchets and the tame town gossip. When she signed her name "with love," she hoped he realized how much she meant it. He sent a snapshot of himself taken in the Grand Bazaar in Istanbul, which she studied for insight into his feelings for her. As she stared his face would drift out of focus, and she'd be left with the sensation that what she held was the photo of a tall, good-looking stranger in a sailor suit. Gradually his letters grew shorter, less frequent. The last was a picture postcard of a camel in front of a palm tree, dated March 11, 1958, with the scrawled message: "No time to write. Take care of yourself."

With Dana away in the navy, his mother lived alone. Her husband had been killed in the Battle of the Coral Sea shortly before Dana's third birthday, and she didn't remarry. Mrs. Cox would drive into town in the Olds and come into Bradbury's for a tube of zinc ointment or a bottle of rubbing alcohol or to have her prescription refilled. She was a slight woman, with blurry eyes and graying hair. She'd smile vaguely at Carlene, having no idea who she was. Carlene longed to ask, "What do you hear from Dana?" but never dared, in case she'd find out something she didn't want to know.

The day before Thanksgiving, Carlene's daughter-in-law telephones and announces that something has come up with Ron's job, an emergency having to do with upgrading his firm's computer system in advance of something called Millennium Fever. That's what Carlene thinks Jill said, anyhow. Something to do with the advent of the new century fouling up computers. Carlene doesn't understand a word of it. Anyhow, the point is that Ron has to work on Friday, and they won't be making the trip up from Massachusetts after all. "I hope you aren't too disappointed," Jill says. "I know you've gone to a lot of trouble."

"No, no trouble." Carlene has a twenty-pound turkey defrosting in the sink, three kinds of pies cooling on the sideboard. "How are the kids? Danny still enjoying kindergarten?"

"The kids are great. Hey, I have to run, I'm late for my yoga class," Jill says, hanging up.

Carlene goes upstairs and strips the sheets off the beds in the two front bedrooms, folds them, stows them in the linen closet. Chalkie will have to dismantle the crib and lug the parts back up to the attic. He'll be crushed, though he'll try to keep that to himself, and she feels bad for him, but there isn't a thing she can do about it.

~

She and Chalkie started going out in the summer of 1960. Nobody had thought he'd amount to much, but he'd done well enough. He'd taken over his uncle's failing garage in town and installed gas pumps out front, overhauled the accounting system, erected a big new sign. "Grease monkey" were the words that came to Carlene's mind when she thought of him, his hands always stained black. He was wiry in those days, before he began to put on the pounds.

The next spring, teaching certificate almost in hand, she applied for a job down in Brunswick, just north of Portland. She thought getting out of town would be good for her; she imagined herself going to concerts, art museums. The school invited her down for an interview, and everything seemed set. But then her father collapsed on the carpet of Quirk Insurance, where he worked, knocking over a vase of dried hydrangeas as he fell. The doctors' tests were inconclusive, and her father suffered no more strange attacks. However, her mother asked Carlene if she—the only child—could put off her plans for a while, well, just in case.

She'd found herself going to one friend's wedding after another, and Chalkie began to sound as though he assumed they'd get married, too, and she never got around to saying otherwise. He was good-hearted and reliable, and her parents liked him. Carlene had come to understand that Dana Cox was gone from her life for good.

She taught English for two years before the June day when she and Chalkie stood up in church and promised themselves to each other. What she'd pictured was a place of their own, two or three rooms, starting out simply. In April the apartment above Leighton's General Store became vacant, and she thought it would be fun to see what she could do with it. However, over a Sunday lunch her father proposed an arrangement—Chalkie would do handyman jobs around the house and the newlyweds could live rent-free—and the bargain was sealed in a moment. After the wedding Chalkie moved into the house Carlene had grown up in, the big old Stanley farmhouse on Bay Road stuffed to the gunnels with five generations' worth of shabby furniture, mismatched china, and dust-catchers. Of course the plan made good economic sense, so how could Carlene object? Chalkie was turning the money he earned back into the business, didn't have any extra to throw around.

In the spring he dug up the weed-choked field next to the house, worked a truckload of cow manure into the soil, planted a garden. Every waking moment that he wasn't at the garage he'd spend grubbing in the dirt; he grew sweet corn, tomatoes, spinach, several varieties of potatoes, pole beans, bush beans. At harvest time he cradled squash and melons in his arms as tenderly as babies. Carlene's mother told everybody in town her son-in-law was bringing the farm back to life—though of course, it could never be a real farm again, most of the land sold off long ago.

Carlene's life was not an unhappy one. However, something kept her from throwing away the black and white snapshot of Dana. If Chalkie ever opened the Bible she'd been given for Confirmation he'd find it, but she knew he was about as likely to do that as march down Bridge Street in his birthday suit.

Ron was born in 1965 and Matthew in 1967. That same fall, when Matthew was a newborn, Carleen heard that Dana's mother had succumbed to the heart trouble that long plagued her. What a shame, people said, that she passed with no kin at her bedside. Carlene was sure Dana would come home for the funeral, but he never showed.

~

Back downstairs, in the kitchen, Carlene finds Bob perched on the edge of the sink eyeing the turkey. Its grayish goosebumpy skin is punctured with holes where feathers once grew. "I'm going out for a bit," she tells him. "Don't you dare touch that bird while I'm gone."

Carlene climbs into the pickup and heads out Fiddlers Point Road. "It's only the neighborly, Christian thing to do," she tells herself. The

Point is at the end of a six-mile-long peninsula that elbows out into the sea northeast of town. The last two miles of the road are unpaved, since it's mostly summer people who have houses out that far.

Carlene yanks the lever into four-wheel drive and lurches along through muddy slush, bouncing from pothole to pothole, branches slapping the windshield. A queasiness in her gut tells her this is not a good idea and there's nothing Christian about it. If there were a good place to turn around she'd do so, but she's not very expert at driving the big old pickup. Projects that need to be done in four-wheel drive are Chalkie's bailiwick, and she's afraid of getting stuck.

Near the Point the road divides. She takes the left-hand fork, the road no more than a path now. Around a bend is a ramshackle building with smoke wafting out of the chimney pipe and a tinny little car, rusted-out red, South Carolina plates, parked next to it. No four-by-four in that baby, Carleen thinks. He's going to have fun when it really snows. Not to mention mud season. She leaves the pickup behind his car and wades through the snow to the door, which is already opening.

The place is hot and smells of wood smoke and snow melt, damp wool, kerosene. There's a camp cot piled with blankets, an ancient wood stove, a lantern hanging from a rafter and casting a reddish glow on the walls. "I came to invite you to . . . "

Dana closes the door behind her, reaches forward and unzips her coat, as if she were a child coming in from playing in the snow. He hangs the coat on a nail by the door. "I knew you'd remember the way," he says, kneeling and unlacing her boots. His hands are large, with neatly trimmed fingernails. There are brown splotches of freckles on his bald spot. She doesn't ask why he seems to have been expecting her.

"Your hair," he whispers. "You never wore it braided then." He unpins it from the crown of her head and lays the fat gray braid on her shoulder. Softly he brushes her cheek with his beard. His eye sockets, now in shadow, are deep in his skull—the irises, she knows, are a very dark blue, like the sea on certain fine days in winter.

She feels dizzy from the heat, thinks she's going to faint. He's unbuttoning her cardigan. She closes her eyes. Soon he will see the empty breasts slung low on her ribcage, the too-soft belly, the stringy thighs and gnarls of her joints.

Naked, they lie together on the camp cot, under a heap of blankets. Their bodies are slippery with sweat. Her heart beats frantically. She has not felt like this in more than forty years.

~

"Henry saw you on Fiddlers Point Road yesterday. In the pickup."

"Things must be slow at the garage these days," Carlene says, "if the boys have time to talk about who saw whose wife going about her daily rounds."

"He just happened to mention it." Chalkie spoons some creamed onions onto his plate, which is already heaped with mounds of vegetables and slabs of turkey in a sea of giblet gravy. Grew them little pearl onions himself, he'd brag to Ron and Jill, if Ron and Jill were here to hear it. Nothing tastier than home grown. "Problem with the Escort?" he asks.

The lie unwinds itself from her tongue as smoothly as if she'd been keeping secrets from Chalkie all her life. "I was delivering Thanksgiving boxes for the church," she says. "One of the families on my list was those Mexicans, I think they are, in a trailer out past Kennedys'. I thought their driveway might not be plowed, so I took the pickup."

"Why do the Mexicans get a Thanksgiving box?" A forkful of mashed butternut squash goes into his mouth. "They don't even have Thanksgiving in Mexico."

"Because it's the neighborly, Christian thing to do." Carlene wonders whether the Mexicans, who work in the sea cucumber plant and may or may not possess immigration papers, actually received a box. She wonders also what lie she can concoct for next time. But of course there isn't going to be a next time, because God might be asked to overlook one moment of weakness but not a whole string of them.

Chalkie picks a biscuit out of the electric bread warmer that Matthew sent for her birthday—the cord dangles treacherously from a wall outlet to the kitchen table—and breaks it open. "People ought to stay put," he mutters, "where they belong."

~

A few days later Carlene sits amid a heap of bedclothes on the camp cot, braiding her thick gray hair. Dana, wearing only his unbuttoned shirt, opens the wood stove door and shoves in a couple more logs. Sparks shower into the air.

As in his youth, Dana's legs are long and lean. His buttocks have lost some of their flesh, and the skin is faintly wrinkled, reminding her of an apple that's hung onto the tree over the winter. Yet she likes his body even better than she did all those years ago. The mysterious, oddly shaped scars, the ropy veins, the butterfly tattoo on his left biceps, the flat brown patches suggesting exposure to the sun. He has not been shut up in a garage from one end of his life to the other. He has not run to fat.

Dana clangs the door shut and sits next to her, wrapping a blanket around them. Outside, the wind howls. "Sounds like a pack of wolves," she says.

He takes her hand, the one bearing the gold band that nowadays wobbles loose as far as the knuckle.

"Dana," she says softly, "I need to know why you came back."

Inside the stove the logs shift. Steam rises from a pan of melted snow on the surface.

"Oh . . . I had some things to attend to."

If only he'd come right out with it, *I love you, Carlene, I've always loved you*, but she guesses that would be too much to ask. She unfolds her hand from his and pulls an elastic from her wrist, wrapping the band three or four times around the tail of the braid. "You hurt me, you know."

"Seems you got over it."

She never did. Never never did.

His spine against the plank wall, he says, "I started a million letters, Carlene. I didn't know how to find the right words back then."

"You were always so good with words."

He smiles. "Not the hard ones."

"Okay, then, tell me now."

"I just couldn't see myself settling down here, scrounging up some lame way to make a living."

"Chalkie managed."

"I wasn't Chalkie."

She listens to the cabin's windows, loose in their frames, rattle violently in the wind.

His voice gentle, he says, "How could I have dragged you around the world with me? You wouldn't have wanted that kind of life."

"You never gave me the choice."

"I thought the kindest thing was just to leave you be."

"You left us be, all right. You didn't even come home for your mother's funeral." That fall she'd sat up in the night nursing her voracious newborn, glad of the soreness in her nipples, glad because the pain of cracked nipples almost killed the pain of longing for a man who was not her baby's father.

"I was out on the West Coast. By the time I heard, she was a week under ground."

Carlene gets up from the bed and retrieves her clothes from the floor. "I have to go."

As she's backing the pickup around, her eyes fall on some boards stacked against the woodpile. They are pale, raw, newly-planed. He must be intending major renovation, she thinks, her heart swelling.

~

No, she thinks, no. She's not going back there.

Five o'clock and the dark closing in already. In the next room Chalkie, in his easy chair, turns the pages of the weekly newspaper, patiently awaiting his dinner.

That ratty old chair, the threadbare upholstery stinking of cigarette smoke and decades of cooking smells and body sweat and cat hair and engine grease soaked out of Chalkie's pores. She'd dearly love to haul the chair and all the rest of the junk in that room straight to the dump. No such luck. He's wedded to that chair.

Lumps in the milk gravy, she sees, poking at them dismally with a wooden spoon.

~

Forty-odd years ago, or even twenty years ago, Carlene realizes, she would have been planning curtains for the cabin's windows, rugs for the floors. She'd have wanted to make the place homey for Dana and herself, a nest. Now the emptiness there is what she craves, the stripping away of the burden of possessions. It seems important to her to find out how simply one can live, how little one needs to survive. The pleasure is in the rubbing of joint against joint, bone on bone.

Three days a week she drives the pickup out to the end of Fiddlers Point Road. Her recklessness amazes her. She tells Chalkie she's tutoring the Mexican children who live in the trailer beyond Kennedys', so they can catch up with their appropriate grade levels by September. Although this is a lie of breathtaking proportions, since she knows no Spanish beyond *Si, Señor*, Chalkie doesn't ask the kids' names or anything about them. As long as his dinner's on the table at 5 p.m. sharp and there are clean socks in his drawer and a full tank in the pickup when he wants to use it, that's all he cares about, she figures.

In the cabin Dana tells her stories about his travels, his various jobs. For the past few years he's been constructing miniature golf courses, mostly down South. "Each course has its own theme," he explains. "Treasure Island. Destination Moon. Twenty Thousand Leagues Under the Sea." She imagines him directing, with the artistry of a symphony conductor, a fleet of backhoes—his arms and chest bare to the sun, dirt and trees and boulders yielding to his will.

She packs picnic lunches to bring with her to the cabin, sandwiches made from her own homemade bread, containers of different kinds of salads. Dana eats sparingly. He doesn't care for meat. On the road he got used to doing without it, since it spoiled so fast, and now it's too rich for him. Too much bread bloats him, he says. After their meals she tosses the leftovers onto the snow for the birds.

Though he seldom drives into town, he talks about coming to church. But it would be too painful for her to sit in the choir, her face aflame under his gaze, and she asks him not to. "Don't you fear for my soul?" he asks, kidding, and Carlene says his soul is his own problem. If he feels himself in danger of hellfire he can always go pray with the holy rollers in their Quonset hut on Back Bay Road—the Church of the Open Culvert, as he refers to it.

When she's not with him, Dana repairs the cabin and the outhouse, tramps in the woods. He tells her he longs for her when she's gone. "Come live with me," he says, and she's not certain whether he's serious. *Come live with me and be my love.* She imagines the gossip at the next soup luncheon if she were to tell Chalkie she's going away for a while, hop in the pickup, and barrel off down the road to shack up with Dana Cox.

Christmas passes quietly, without visits from their children, who are both spending the holiday with their in-laws. Carlene and Chalkie don't stay up to welcome in the new century, but go to bed at their usual 10 p.m. "The world will still be there in the morning," Chalkie says. "Or if it ain't, we won't be around to care."

There's a blizzard in January that keeps her away from the cabin for a whole terrible week. Lent begins, and she makes love to Dana with a smudge of ash on her forehead. "Oh penitent one," he says drowsily, his scratchy beard against her breast.

"Not very penitent, I'm afraid."

He sags into sleep, his mouth agape. She studies his sinewy body, lightly traces the design of the tattooed butterfly. She thinks: I will care for you, Dana Cox. I will sustain you. It's not like years ago, when you didn't need me or anyone else.

~

One afternoon she stops by the garage to speak to Chalkie. He's in the cramped, messy little front office where they ring up gas sales and make out work orders and invoices, talking to Lucille Jarvis. Lucille is wearing a faded jacket that looks like it came from the extra-large rack in the Second Chance Thrift Shop. "Bad news," she hears him tell her. "You got a stuck brake caliper. Left front wheel ain't hardly turning, even on the lift."

"Oh, geez," Lucille says. "Can you fix that?"

"Sure I can fix it, but it's gonna cost you." Behind him, in the garage, some electric tool begins to shriek. He looks kindly at Lucille. "You want me to go ahead and order the parts?"

Lucille shifts her weight from one foot to another, contemplating life without her car. She lives a mile from town, thirty miles from her job as a supermarket checkout clerk. "What choice do I have?"

Carlene knows Chalkie's going to let Lucille pay it off at a rate of fifteen or twenty dollars a month, without charging a dime of interest. Lucille's old man is one of Chalkie's Lodge brothers. Still, easy payments or no, Lucille will notice that twenty bucks. When she has gone, waddling down Main Street, Carlene says, "Jill called this morning. She's going to have another baby. Due in August."

"Well, that's fine." Chalkie grins, more cheerful than he's been in a while. The coverall zipped over his beachball-shaped middle has *Chalkie* embroidered in yellow thread on the pocket. As if there's a single soul in western Washington County who doesn't know who he is, Carlene thinks, who hasn't at one time or another hauled in some crippled wreck for him to resuscitate.

~

The days lengthen. When she turns off the pickup's engine she can hear chickadees whistling their monotonous mating call in the woods. After lovemaking she and Dana walk to the granite ledge, now free of ice, and watch the waves slosh on the rock and smell the salt air. Sometimes they see a ship way off in the Gulf of Maine and guess where it might be heading. The Maritimes, the Azores, anywhere.

One day early in April she drives into the clearing and sees all the blankets airing on lines stretched between trees. Dana's sitting on the cinderblock stoop and she joins him. Sunlight finding its way between the spruce branches makes her squint.

They talk about one thing and another and then he says, "So here's the story, Carlene. I'm about through my stash."

She's surprised. She'd assumed he had savings in a bank somewhere, at least enough to retire on in a modest way.

"I'm going to have to find work," he says.

Carlene thinks about this. There's the sea cucumber plant, but the task of extracting the edible parts from those disgusting creatures is so grubby and poorly paid only Mexicans and Hondurans will do it. She doubts the boats will be taking on many new hands this spring, and anyway, Dana doesn't know a thing about fishing. Plus, he's over sixty years old. She says, "I'm not sure any towns around here are ready for miniature golf."

He laughs. "True enough. I have to go where the work is. I think you should come with me."

Suddenly it's not an idle romantic notion anymore: *Come live with me and be my love.* She can actually picture herself doing it, getting into his rusty red Honda and driving through town—past the library, the church, the Citgo station, the Clip 'n' Curl, the pharmacy—for the last time. She wouldn't take a thing with her besides the clothes on her back.

"What about Chalkie?" she asks.

"There must be any number of widows in town who'd be more than happy to take care of him. He might not even notice the difference."

Well, that's a little hard on Chalkie, she thinks. He'd notice.

Carlene feels the damp of the cinderblock seeping through her pants. A red squirrel chitters menacingly in a nearby tree. "When will you be going?" she asks.

"Soon."

~

The next morning Carlene borrows the key from a cup hook on the sexton's screened porch and goes into the church to pray. The sanctuary is unheated, empty. A few petals from last Sunday's altar arrangement lie shriveled on the carpet. Absentmindedly she picks them up and puts them in her pocket.

She sits in one of the rear pews and looks up at the altar. For some reason she remembers the evening a disheveled black man burst into the church when the choir was getting ready to rehearse. He'd planted himself there on the altar steps, haranguing them in the choir stall, referring to Scripture in a garbled way. "I'm passing through," he told them. "People have reasons for why they leave places, many reasons, but they don't know their destinations. Lot didn't know. Noah didn't know. Moses didn't know. Nossir." One of the tenors slipped a five-dollar bill into the man's palm and escorted him to the door. Carlene wonders if he's still wandering up and down the seacoast looking for handouts, or whatever it was he was looking for.

She notices that the Pentecost banner with its dove cut out of felt, a Sunday School project a few years ago, hangs a little crookedly on the wall. Somebody ought to get out a stepladder and straighten that, she thinks. The ceiling has begun to peel, too. Soon the church ladies will be raising money to have the sanctuary repainted. Rummage sales, soup luncheons, quilt raffles, baked bean suppers . . .

The clock in the steeple strikes nine, then quarter past, then nine-thirty. Rain begins to spatter the tall, half-shuttered windows.

My last crack at true happiness, Lord. What shall I do?

~

The weather turns raw, as raw as February, and the rain persists. Slicing vegetables for supper, she cuts her finger and bleeds in large bright drops on the linoleum. When he sees the bandage Chalkie asks what happened and she shrugs and says, "Nothing." He doesn't question her further. At night she lies beside him and doesn't sleep. He's so still she wonders if he isn't sleeping, either. Maybe he's begun to suffer from insomnia and never mentioned it, the way he doesn't talk about aches and pains, in case she'll say, "You better see the doc about that." During the days Carlene's eyes burn with fatigue. Two weeks drag by. She doesn't go out to see Dana. She hopes he'll leave without her, is terrified that he will.

After supper one night Carlene is patching the elbow of an old pullover of Chalkie's that really belongs in the ragbag, but he refuses to part with it. Just breaking that in, he says, though the sweater must date from the Carter administration. The phone rings and Chalkie gets up to answer it. "I'll tell her," she hears him say out in the kitchen.

He appears in the living-room doorway. "That was Mae Pomeroy. She wanted to know why you weren't at the Fourth of July Cod Race Committee meeting."

"Oh, Lord. I completely forgot about that meeting."

"Carlene got another one of them headaches? she wanted to know."

Carlene removes some pins from the tomato-shaped pincushion that used to be her mother's and begins to fit a patch over the hole. Bob aims himself at the sofa and leaps cautiously, his joints too creaky for high-flying maneuvers these days.

"Do you?" Chalkie asks. "Do you have a headache?"

"No. I don't."

He sits in the easy chair and picks up his cigarette pack, then puts it down again. "You're close as a clam with your words, Carlene."

"I'm sorry. I really don't have anything to say."

He clears his throat. "Well, I have something."

"I'm listening."

"It's been preying on my mind."

"Go ahead," she says, imagining that he's discovered carpenter ants in the woodwork or a leak in the attic roof. As if she'd care if the whole house fell to pieces around them.

"End of November," he begins, "Linwood Spinney brought his truck in for the state inspection."

Linwood Spinney? What's he got to do with anything?

"Thirtieth, must've been," Chalkie says, "because I recall it was the last day he was legal. Not that that would've made a scrap of difference to ole Linwood. He does things when he's good and ready."

"Like you," she says, cutting off a length of thread and putting a knot in it.

"I damn well care whether I'm legal or not."

Yes, she'll grant him that. He may not enter a church from one end of the year to the other, except for weddings and funerals, but nobody in town is more respected for probity than Chalkie Hutchins.

"Linwood's truck passed inspection," Chalkie continues, "and when I was filling in the form for the state, Linwood commenced to tell me about how a day or two previous he drove out to a cabin on Fiddlers Point, deliverin' a load of lumber." Chalkie pauses, fingering his pack of Luckies. "Saw the pickup parked there."

Carlene stares at him, the sweater limp in her lap.

"Linwood figured I had some business with that Cox fella, didn't want to barge in. Left the boards leaning against the woodpile and went back to town. A course, he was kinda curious to know what Dana Cox and Yours Truly were cooking up."

Numbly she asks, "What did you tell him?"

"Well, Carlene, since it wasn't me out there, I couldn't tell him a thing."

For a long time she listens to rain tapping on the window, Bob licking his tough yellow coat. Suddenly, in her mind, she sees the wood stove, left to go cold, its door hanging open. She smells the acrid sodden ashes remaining inside. At last she says, "All these months. Why didn't you say something?"

He takes a cigarette out of the pack but doesn't light it. "Seemed to me I'd better just let you get whatever it was out of your system. I couldn't keep you here anyways, not if you wanted to go."

"Oh, Chalkie. You thought I might?"

"I've always understood that, Carlene. I'm not quite as dim as you think."

He gets up and limps to the kitchen. She hears him take a match out of the canister by the stove, strike it, open the kitchen door and shut it again. Just as he's done for the best part of four decades, he'll lift his plaid wool jacket from a peg in the back hall and go out into the drizzle. Standing by the compost heap, smoking, he'll ponder what seeds he'll plant when the soil is dry enough to work.

ORIGINAL BRASSES, FINE PATINA

A BIT CHILLY in the air-conditioning, Helen sits on a bench in the American wing and waits for Cal to arrive. She imagines he selected this particular gallery because it would be lightly visited on a Monday afternoon, not like the Hopper show, for which you have to pay an extra fee on top of the already expensive regular admission for the museum. Helen remembers when the museum was free, and she'd take the MTA here on Sunday afternoons to study objects covered in her art history survey or just to absorb the grace imparted by beautiful things. But nothing is ever really free. That year, and the next, had their costs in spite of her scholarship.

When choosing the museum for a meeting place, Cal couldn't have guessed that as a scared college freshman she'd lurked in these halls eyeing Greek and Roman sculptures, trying to figure out if Cal's male member was within some kind of normal range, or if he was in fact the freak she feared. She hadn't understood erections, that's how naïve and uneducated—about things that actually counted—she'd been then. Daughter of a small-town schoolteacher, granddaughter of a potato farmer, the first in her family to go to a real college, far away from home. Before Cal, she'd never seen a man without his pants on.

Freak or no, he'd succeeded in getting inside her stubborn little hole, and that's why she'd given birth at Mt. Auburn Hospital the summer following her sophomore year.

A young Asian couple pause in front of a portrait of a bewigged gentleman, clasp hands, move on to gaze at a mahogany tea table set with Staffordshire and silver, preserved behind glass.

He's late, but she might have expected that. Reluctant to meet her at all, not even very curious about her mission. With a name like Calvin Turnipseed he'd been a cinch to research on the internet; his email address took her but a few minutes to locate. She learned that he'd used his degree in chemical engineering to secure a career in industry, was now retired and serving on the boards of several charities, a Boston-based chamber music ensemble, and a hospital—not Mt. Auburn. Google turned up a group photo that included Mrs. Dolores Turnipseed, smirking for the camera at a benefit dinner. "I'll be in town soon," Helen had written Cal, "and wonder if you and I might get together." No reply for more than two weeks. She assumed her message had been zapped in his electronic trash basket, but then he did write, apologizing for not answering right away. He'd been in Europe, he claimed. Yes, he could find time to meet and suggested the Museum of Fine Arts, the eighteenth-century gallery down at the far end of the American collection. Perhaps he's had rendezvous here with other women, escaping Dolores, Helen thinks, and has already scouted out the territory. Dark rooms, sleepy guard.

An old lady pushes another old lady in a wheelchair from one painting to the next, the women murmuring to one another. Is that how I'll look to him? she wonders, aware of her own gray hair and creaky knees.

When he appears in the doorway she's taken aback; if the forty-seven years since they last saw each other haven't been particularly kind to her, they've been even less kind to him. Liver spots splotch his bare scalp and cheeks. His face has a distinct pallor. The paunch he carries on his beanpole frame is of the approximate size and placement of a six-months pregnancy. She squelches a laugh. "Helen," he says, moving toward her on the bench. Will he kiss her? A peck on the cheek, maybe? But no, he sits beside her and lays an oversized black umbrella between them. "Sorry to keep you waiting. My meeting ran late."

"I'm not in any great hurry."

"In Boston on vacation, did you say? Where do you live now, still Maine?"

"I haven't lived in Maine since I was a girl."

Cal nods but asks no further questions. He was never good at small talk, and anyway, he's certainly no more interested in exchanging details about spouses and children and grandchildren, illustrated with wallet photos, than she is. The guard strolls past them, affording them hardly a glance. For all he knows they're an old married couple: in any case, no obvious threat to the collection or to public decorum. Deciding she might as well come right to the point, Helen says, "I've heard from him. Our son."

"I don't understand."

"Or from the agency, rather. He wants to find his birth parents, and the agency contacted me, to see if I was willing."

"But the records were sealed."

"Things have changed, Cal. Adoptees have rights, and they exercise them. What planet have you been living on?"

After a pause he asks, "What are you going to do?"

Although there's no doubt in her mind that she'll see her son—she's already given the agency her go-ahead—something makes her wary now about revealing this to Cal, so soon in the conversation. "Some days I'm inclined one way, some days another."

Beside her Cal removes his glasses and digs at the inner corners of his eyes with his thumbs, a nervous gesture Helen remembers from all those years ago. Like her, he had an uncertain, vulnerable side then. Otherwise, she probably wouldn't have fallen in love with him or let him do the things to her that he was bent on doing. But then what? No abortions other than the coat-hanger variety in those days. No marriage in the cards, either, not without money, not without love on his part—or more love than he could spare, anyhow. He had too many other fish to fry to consider acquiring a wife, raising a brat. To give him credit he did hang around in town that summer while she waited out the nine months, finding a shabby little sublet in Somerville for them to stay in. He'd go out in the middle of the night to buy her pints of peanut brickle ice cream, if that's what she was craving.

The steamy August morning she was released from Mt. Auburn he picked her up and drove her downtown to the bus terminal, his Beetle bouncing painfully over potholes. Without saying anything directly, both of them understood this would be the end of it. Impossible to go on as if nothing had happened. After he shoved her suitcase onto the rack above her seat he muttered something unintelligible; she willed herself not to watch him leave the platform. All the way to Portland, Bangor, and at last Caribou, she wept quietly, secretly, her bottom sore from the stitches, her breasts aching with milk that was just coming in. How was she going to hide from her mother these dismaying changes in her body, which nobody had told her about and which she'd never anticipated? How was she going to live without Cal, even if he was a rat who'd forsaken her? On the bright side, Helen thought, doing her best to console herself, she and the child wouldn't have to go through life called Turnipseed.

"So what do you want from me?" Cal asks now.

"Aren't you curious about him? Don't you ever wonder how he turned out?"

The glasses go back onto his nose. "Helen, let me tell you something," he says under his breath. "When we agreed to give him up I made a deliberate decision not to think about him, and I've stuck to that resolve. In no way did that baby belong to me, legally or otherwise."

"You made damn sure of that."

"*We* made damn sure of that. You were the one who signed the papers, don't forget."

"What choice did I have?"

"You had choices, Helen. You opted for the sensible way out of the mess, just as I did."

"Sensible. As euphemisms go, that takes the cake."

"What word would you use?"

"Craven," she says, tears sharp in her eyes.

His voice tight, he says, "Have it your way," and she thinks absurdly of all the times they ate at Hayes-Bickford's in the Square and he'd invariably have the ninety-nine-cent special, no matter what it was that day, because if the meal cost more than ninety-nine cents the state of Massachusetts charged a tax, but she'd order the hamburg plate, so delicious with fried onions and a scoop of mashed potatoes under mushroom gravy and a side dish of baby pickled beets swimming in their red juice, and he'd pay for the meal of her choice without grumbling, even if he had to pony up the tax.

For the first time this afternoon they look one another in the face. Can this old man whom she scarcely knows anymore and doesn't even like have been that generous ice cream and hamburger-provider and the father of her firstborn child? His anger shows in the pinched white area around his mouth. She remembers the one time he hit her, during an argument over a book he'd borrowed from her and carelessly lost, an argument that was actually about far bigger issues—sexual pressure and mutual obligation and heedfulness and moral responsibility—but she was too shy and muddled to articulate them. She almost thinks he'd be capable of hitting her now, if not for the guard ghosting the periphery of the room and the pair of suburban matrons who have materialized and are inspecting a Philadelphia highboy. "Fabulous," one of them says. "I'd give my eye teeth to own that."

"Original brasses, obviously."

"And just look at the patina. My God, it takes centuries to get a patina like that."

"Don't touch, or the alarm will go off."

Cal reaches for his umbrella as if he's going to get up and walk out. Good riddance, she thinks. But then, apparently changing his mind, he places the umbrella between his knees and, leaning forward, grips the bentwood handle. She guesses that, like hers, his spine is bothering him, sitting without back support. He stares straight ahead, perhaps at a portrait of a dark-browed young woman in silk, perhaps at nothing. Amid freckles and liver spots on his left hand is a small sore with a yellowing bruise around it. From her own fibroids surgery she recognizes the wound: an IV tube ran into that vein a short time ago. Europe, indeed.

After a while the matrons from Brookline or Newton move out of earshot and their calm chatter at the far end of the gallery seems to dissipate the tension. A cell phone rings; someone laughs out in the corridor. Cal extracts a handkerchief from his trousers pocket and mops his forehead.

Wearily he says, "I didn't come here to fight."

"Nor I."

"When I read your email," he continues, stuffing the crumpled cloth back into his pocket, "it didn't occur to me that the boy was the subject of this meeting. It never dawned on me that he'd popped up out of nowhere, after all this time. He's not a boy, for Chrissake. He's pushing fifty."

"What else could I have wanted to talk about?"

He hesitates. "People our age sometimes have an impulse to tidy up loose ends before it's too late. They might have health problems—a bad heart, say. Or cancer."

"I don't have either. I'm not about to croak."

"I'm happy to hear it, and that's the truth."

"And what about you?"

"I'm fine," he says shortly. "Fine."

Well, okay, she's just as glad to take him at his word. "So you figured you were one of my loose ends?"

"I assumed the idea was for us to wish each other Godspeed, or something of the sort."

Helen mulls this over. Godspeed. Maybe he has something there. Maybe a gentle farewell is precisely what she's wanted all along, and the letter from the agency was the excuse she needed to go hunting for him on the internet. In spite of a mostly compatible (if ho-hum) marriage and three dear (if at times disappointing) children, she never quite got over the crushing loss of her firstborn child and her first love. Not that she and Cal could ever have made a go of it, even if he'd been as willing to spring for a wedding ring as he was for a meal at the Bick. If she didn't know that then, she does now.

"I'll be frank," he says. "It's always been like a pebble in my shoe that we parted the way we did."

That's as close to an apology as she's going to get, but she'll take it. "Never mind, Cal. We were too young, too clumsy to know any better." Buttoning her jacket, she says, "I gather I'm on my own in this situation."

He shrugs.

"So be it."

"I have a request. If you do establish contact with him, I'd rather you didn't mention me. At this point I can't afford . . . " He stops himself there, but she's pretty sure he isn't referring to money.

She lays her hand on his, just for a second. "Don't worry. I won't betray you. Our son will never know who you are."

Briefly she wonders if she should suggest tea in the museum café, now that they have achieved détente. Instead, though, she makes a show of consulting her watch and tells him that she's meeting a friend at five and must be on her way. She leaves him meandering among the Copleys and Peales, a tall balding man, rather oddly shaped, somewhat stooped, a big black umbrella hooked over his arm.

FROM AWAY

STAN'S TRUCK, PULLING into Clara's drive, scatters the mourning doves that are pecking for seeds in the gravel. They flutter onto the lawn or up into the maple tree, from which dangle clusters of pale green polynoses. Stan takes the cooler from her and sets it in the back of the pickup, taking care to tuck it under a tarp. Beneath his suspenders he wears a shirt that's faded and soft with many washings, frayed at the collar.

"Something different about you," he says, opening the passenger door for her.

"I got my hair cut."

"Looks good."

He helps Clara into the cab and goes around to climb in on the other side. His legs are so long he has the seat pushed way back. Clara feels somewhat insecure, so far from the dashboard, and would buckle the seat belt if there was one. However, this pickup predates the advent of seat belts. She settles her sunhat on her lap and tries to compose herself, though she feels self-conscious about the haircut. To have her shoulder-length gray hair cut boyishly short was a decision made on impulse. Three days ago, on Thursday, she was walking past the Clip 'n' Curl on Main Street and thought, what the heck. She's still not used to it. Her head feels so light, as if it might spin off her neck if she moves suddenly. The haircut has given her a sense of quivering on the brink of some sort of transformation, a moth breaking out of its brittle old wrapping. Or it could be the season. May is a flighty month.

Stan starts the truck and backs expertly down the drive, then takes a left onto Bridge Street in the direction of town.

"Can't you tell me where we're going?" Clara asks.

"Not yet. Like I said, this is a mystery tour."

She didn't know how to dress. Stan told her only that they'd be having a picnic outside somewhere. But there are picnics and picnics. She surveyed her limited wardrobe and settled on a pair of hopsack trousers and a blue linen blouse her daughter Janet gave her for a birthday present. That was in September, a few months after Henry died. Clara hasn't worn it before today, hasn't found just the right occasion.

After crossing the bridge and passing the Congregational Church on the right, Stan makes another left onto Route 1, which is also Main Street. Downtown consists of a motel and restaurant next door, a gas station, some shops, and about a dozen houses, mostly of nineteenth-century vintage. At the bottle redemption place Stan leaves Main Street and veers left, taking the road that skirts the bay. They pass a cannery, the town dock, and several small weathered buildings with metal roofs. Lobstermen stow their gear in those shacks, he tells her. Beyond them are a boarded-up store and a Wesleyan chapel, which has fallen into considerable disrepair. The paving worsens, and Clara is bounced around quite a bit. Clinging to the door handle, she hopes the door won't suddenly open and pitch her onto the road. Also she hopes the cooler and its contents are secure under the tarp.

She bought the cooler at the general store in town because her wicker hamper, the one her family took on many a picnic when the girls were young, is still in her house in Massachusetts. This bright red plastic one is fine—better, even. Easier to clean and has some kind of insulating quality. Bigger than she needed, but the only size the store carried. When, a week ago, Stan knocked on her door and invited her on this expedition, he said he'd furnish the lunch. Don't bother, she told him, it would be no trouble at all for her to throw a few sandwiches together. Since he'd charged her only five dollars for the work he did, she felt she owed him something. Besides, she rather feared what Stan might come up with in the way of food. What do men know about picnics? Henry never concocted a picnic in his life, would have been flummoxed at the very notion of doing so. After pondering the menu for some days, Clara made a number of neat little sandwiches with a variety of fillings. Even if Stan has some health problem that restricts his diet, he'll surely find one or two he can eat.

As he drives, Stan talks about the old days in town. At first he went to school in a one-room schoolhouse, which has since been moved from its original location and is now part of a summer person's house. He graduated from the brick school building that the town built after the war, on filled-in marsh. It's been derelict for years, most of its windows broken. Periodically there's talk of making it over into apartments, low-income housing, but nothing ever comes of that. Now the kids attend an ugly cinderblock district school two towns away, transported there in yellow buses.

"That's why you see so many overweight youngsters," Clara remarks. "They never have to use the good legs God gave them."

"That and the dad-blamed TV."

Smiling, she says, "We sound like a pair of old fogies."

The road narrows, turns to dirt, and begins to climb above sea level, the truck's engine mildly protesting the ascent. At the top of the rise Stan reveals their destination, the town park. "Haven't been here before, have you?"

"I didn't even know it existed."

"They hide it well." He grins. "From the tourists."

He turns off the road and the truck jounces between two fieldstone pillars.

"Property was deeded to the town in the thirties," he tells her. "Owner went bankrupt, couldn't pay his back taxes. He was from away and didn't come to town much, anyhow. It's a nice spot. You'll see."

The access road, though, is in wretched condition. So big and deep are the potholes, Stan can go no more than four or five miles an hour. The drive meanders through scrubby woods and granite ledge, stands of jack pine, some wild azalea just coming into bloom. Clara holds onto the door handle for dear life, expecting momentarily to be knocked senseless by striking her head on the roof of the cab or to crash headlong through the windshield. At last Stan brings the truck to a halt in a small parking area and turns off the engine. He leaves the key in the ignition. And why not? Who'd want to steal this old rattletrap? How far would the thief be likely to get when everybody for miles around knows this truck? *Stan the Fix-it Man* it says right there on the driver's door.

He carries the cooler as they weave their way between shallow boulders and low scrub: lambkill and creeping juniper, mountain cranberry and sweetfern. Other plants Clara doesn't recognize—they must be native only to Maine. Blackflies zoom around them. Though she can't perceive it with her eyes, the strain in her calves hints that the terrain is gradually sloping upward. Then Clara and Stan come to a place on flat ledge where the landscape opens. Like a fantastic vision, the bay, the wooded offshore islands, and a wide expanse of open ocean appear before them.

"My goodness," she exclaims. "If it weren't for the mist on the horizon, we'd be able to see all the way to Portugal!"

Her late husband, God bless him, would have pointed out that because of the curvature of the earth, you wouldn't see Portugal, mist or no mist. Stan says simply, "From time to time cork bark washes up on the beach."

All the way from Portugal. Think of that.

For a moment they admire the panorama. Then Stan starts down the treacherous pink granite cliff, Clara gingerly following behind in the trail he picks out between patches of ledge and the bushes in the cracks between them. She feels a breeze off the water. Her cotton sunhat flaps in her hand, threatening to take off for distant shores, but she hangs on tight.

Before long they reach a nearly level spot, sheltered on three sides by rock formations, where they have a fine view of the sea. Stan sets down the cooler. Clara dons her sunhat and seats herself on the granite. So what if her hopsack trousers get a little dirty? She removes the cooler's cover and unpacks little crustless sandwiches, each cling-wrapped, with a stick-on label. "Egg salad?" she asks. "Tuna fish? Deviled ham? Chicken salad? What suits you?"

Above them, herring gulls swoop and cry out to one another. The outgoing tide crashes against the granite, sometimes spraying them with droplets of water. Lobster boats out on the bay chug from buoy to buoy, the fishermen hauling their traps. Stan samples all four of her sandwich fillings, polishing off each one in two or three bites. "A feast," he says. "I thank you kindly."

"Thank *you,* for rescuing me the way you did."

He unscrews the cap on a water bottle and swallows a mouthful. "You know, Clara, most folks who come to town are just passing through."

"I suppose that's true," she replies, passing him a baggie of carrot sticks.

Stan takes a few and hands the baggie back to her. "On their way to someplace else. They stop for gas. They might wander into the gift shop across the street." He eats a carrot stick, then another. "They think about buying an old wood lobster trap tricked out as a coffee table. Could be they eat lunch in the Brass Lantern. Once in a while they stay in the motel overnight. Then they move on."

Clara nods.

"But you," he says, "didn't move on."

"No, I didn't. I suppose you're wondering what in heaven's name I'm doing here. A woman of my age all on her own, with no known ties to this place."

"I'm curious, I'm bound to admit."

Does she really want to talk to this man—or anyone—about it? Would he honestly care? They look at each other. Stan's face is weather-beaten, like those fishing gear shacks. But such lovely hazel eyes on the man. Sober. Respectful.

"I'm a widow," she begins. "Henry died almost a year ago. He had tumors in his kidney and liver, and then in his brain, not the way anyone would choose to go. Much better if he'd had a fatal heart attack on the golf course, because for sixteen months he . . . Well, no point in dragging you through all that. Henry was hardly in his grave before my daughters started nagging me about selling my big old house in Concord and moving into a retirement community near one of them. Bloomington, Indiana, or Evanston, Illinois, were my choices."

Stan takes another drink from the water bottle and waits for her to continue.

"The truth is, although I love my girls, I didn't want to go to either place. The very thought of a retirement community gave me the heebie-jeebies. I've always lived on the East Coast, always wanted the sea nearby. But Lynn and Janet kept phoning me up and saying: What if you fall and break your leg and nobody finds you for days? What if you cut yourself and get an infection and die of blood poisoning? What if the house burns down with you in it? Yammer, yammer, yammer. They meant well, but I couldn't stand it. So one morning, a month ago, I just hung up on Lynn in mid-sentence and put some clothes in a suitcase. Two suitcases. I asked the post office to hold my mail, canceled the newspaper delivery. I didn't have to worry about the dog, because he died last summer, a few weeks after Henry went. I locked up the house and got in the car and began to drive north, up Route 1."

She sees on his ruddy, crosshatched face a look of—what? Sympathy? Admiration?

"I didn't tell a single soul where I was going. I didn't know myself. My first night on the road I called my daughters from the motel and said not to worry about me, I was fine."

"I reckon you were, too." He lifts the plastic bottle in a sort of salute.

"The girls had been calling the house for hours, getting Henry's phantom voice on the answering machine . . . *sorry, we can't take your call right now* . . . , and of course they were fit to be tied when they found out I hadn't burned down the house, after all."

"Machine wouldn't have worked if you had."

"No. And my limbs were all intact. I was taking a short vacation, I explained, and they'd hear from me when they heard from me." She takes a deep breath. "Honestly, I felt a little guilty. But at least they weren't going to file a missing person report and have the police on my tail."

"Might've slowed you down some."

"Indeed. So I kept driving north on Route 1, through New Hampshire, up the Maine coast. I'd stay overnight in towns along the way. Just passing through, as you said. And then, right in front of the sign welcoming me to town, I got the flat tire."

"That's where Stan the Fix-It Man came in."

She smiles. "An angel in disguise. By the time you jacked the car up and put on the spare, it was past four in the afternoon. You promised you could have the tire repaired by morning, so I checked into the motel."

Clara takes off her sunhat, lets the salty breeze ruffle her hair. Pixie cut, the young woman in the Clip 'n' Curl called it.

"Well, Stan, I walked around town and felt at home, in the oddest way. Comfortable. The beautiful old Congregational Church could have been the one where I went to Sunday School as a child. I ate supper in the restaurant by the motel, a fried haddock sandwich. I never eat anything fried anymore, but I did it anyway, and it was absolutely delicious. I even ordered a glass of wine. When I was leaving I stopped to look at the table where they display all those tourist brochures. On the table was a stack of photocopied flyers advertising a little furnished house for rent. I'm not sure why—maybe it was the wine—but I took one and folded it and put it in my purse. The next day I called the number on the flyer, and went and saw the house, and fell in love with its quirky coziness and the view across the salt marsh to the bay, and . . . "

"Here you are."

"Here I am."

They eat some chocolate chip cookies that she baked yesterday, letting the gulls do the talking for a while, sitting in easy companionship. Then they begin to pack what's left of the lunch into the cooler. A sudden gust of wind carries off Clara's hat, and as it sails by Stan catches it and claps it on his own head. She wishes she had a camera with her, not just to capture the silly sight, but to preserve this moment—the happiest, she realizes, since Henry fell ill.

They leave the cooler, with her floppy hat wedged under it, and set off down the escarpment. The tiers of pink granite are streaked with basalt. At their foot, where you'd expect to find a pebbly beach, is instead an expanse of smooth boulders the size of round loaves of bread. Boules. Clara and Stan begin to make their way across them, heading in a southerly direction. Broken urchin shells, some with their bristly spines still attached, lie among the piles of stones. Stan tells her that gulls dropped them from the sky to crack them open, so they could get the meat out. Too bad for the poor urchins, Clara thinks. After twenty yards or so she stumbles, and Stan takes her hand. He's sure-footed for a man of his age. He seems to have no trouble moving from stone to stone, without having them slide under him, the way they do to her.

Of course, he was born here. It's like a seaman's familiarity with the roll of a boat.

The tide is low, and beyond the stones, at the base of the granite and basalt cliffs, a tidal pool lies exposed, scooped out of ledge. Gently Stan lets go of her hand. He takes off his shoes and socks, rolls up his pants cuffs, and crouches at the rim of the pool, the water lapping around his ankles. She sees how thin is the hair on the top of his head and hopes the sun won't burn it.

He points out to Clara the creatures that are hiding here, taking refuge. Little whorled dog-whelks and periwinkles in a multitude of colors, some with stripes. Limpets sticking to rock like tiny cones. Blue mussels, with their tough weedy beards.

"Let's see if we can find a hermit crab," he says. "Hermits like to use empty moon snail shells for their houses." He looks around and finally finds one. No snail or crab inside, so he gives it to Clara. The gray moon shell feels lovely in her palm, almost erotic. It gives her a shiver of pleasure. She shakes sand out of the shell's interior and stows it in the pocket of her trousers. Meanwhile, he's come upon a big crab with a rough reddish carapace. "What are you doing here, fella?" he asks.

"Where should he be?"

Stan explains that Jonah crabs are generally denizens of deeper water. He must have been washed here by mistake.

"Will he be all right?"

"He'll leave with the tide, unless a gull finds him."

"Are they named Jonah crabs because they're swallowed by whales?"

"Likely not. A whale will swallow just about anything. What I know is, lobstermen hate the critters. They crowd up the traps so the lobsters can't get in. A nuisance catch."

"Unwelcome aboard then, like passengers who jinx ships. Aren't they called Jonahs?"

He looks up at her and smiles, his hand shading his eyes from the sun. "You're more of an old salt than I thought."

"Hardly. I must have read it somewhere. Have you fished for lobsters yourself?"

"I've done most everything there is to do around here, one time or another. Look, Clara. See that spongy growth clinging to the wall of the tide pool? Crumb-of-bread, it's called. Real old form of life, but a dead-end branch, when you're talking about evolution. It refuses to change into something different or better. No matter how many millions of years go by, crumb-of-bread stays exactly the same."

"Why, do you suppose?"

He thinks a moment. "It's perfect the way it is, I reckon."

Perfect? How disconcerting to think of such a strange creature as perfect. You can't even tell if it's a plant or an animal.

"These shells that look like little volcanoes," he says, "they're acorn barnacles. Kin to lobsters."

"Surely not."

"Looks can fool you." With his thumbnail he pries one off the rock to show her. "See the valve on the top of the shell? He's got it closed now, but at high tide he'll open it up and whip out his arm and grab a bite of algae for his dinner. He may not look like a lobster, but a dog-whelk finds him right tasty."

"How does the dog-whelk get him out of his shell?"

"No trouble at all. He just pries the valve open with his radula and goes chomp."

"What's a radula?"

"A tongue-like thing he has. Lots of teeth on it. Hand, mouth, fork, and weapon all in one. For Mr. Dog-whelk barnacles are easy pickings. Snacks. If he's got a heartier meal in mind, he might fancy a mussel. Mussel's got a lot more meat than a barnacle, but it's a lot harder to get at, too. Now Mister Dog-whelk needs a more patient strategy. Crafty. He'll drill a hole in the mussel's shell with his radula—takes him a couple days—and slowly suck the critter out."

"Good heavens."

"When you come across an empty mussel shell with a neat hole in it, you'll know how the owner met his fate."

Clara is fascinated and horrified at the same time. "I never would have expected such . . . unpleasantness . . . in this pretty little sea garden."

"If it makes you feel better, wrinkles are vegetarians."

She thinks about Stan eating her sandwiches, all that meat and fish, maybe out of politeness. "You're not a vegetarian, are you?"

"Course not." One by one, he's yanking his socks up over damp feet. "How-some-ever, I prefer my mussels cooked."

"How did you learn so much about these creatures?"

"Science teacher I had in school, he brought us here on field trips, here and other places. Woods, swamps, blueberry barrens," he says, lacing up his work boots. "I read books, too. Get 'em out of the library." He's on his feet now. "Tide's turned. We'd better start back, or the stones'll be slippery."

It's chilly, too. When Clara wasn't paying attention the sun ducked behind clouds and the mist crept toward them.

The distance to the relative safety of ledge seems longer on the return trip, the puzzle of navigating from stone to stone without making a false step more complicated. Occupied with his own transit, Stan doesn't take her hand. His bobbing motion reminds her of those drinking-bird toys that were a fad when she was a youngster.

The cooler and her sunhat are right where they left them. So the wind won't seize it, she holds the hat tight against her blue linen blouse and pauses to take a long last look at the dramatically churning sea, the rocks, the gathering mist.

"Do you ever get used to this, Stan?"

"Can't recall when I wasn't used to it."

"But it's so special, so spectacular."

"I reckon it's different for you, being from away." Stan lifts the red plastic cooler containing uneaten sandwiches, cookie crumbs, empty water bottles, and soggy half-full baggies of carrot and cucumber sticks. "Ready to go?"

On their way to the parking area Clara says, "You've told me all about sea creatures, but scarcely a word about yourself. Are you widowed, too?"

"Not me. I never got married."

"You didn't find the right person?"

"Well, Clara, I did, or thought I did, but she wound up marrying somebody else."

"Oh. That must have been painful."

"It happened a long time ago. Forty years or more. I got over it. Most things you get over, if you wait long enough."

"I'm hoping that's true."

"Anyhow, living alone suits me fine."

Earlier, she failed to notice that very near the truck are the charred remains of a driftwood fire. Teenaged partiers? Beer cans and soda-pop bottles are strewn about, a paper bag is caught in a bush, candy and fast food wrappers flutter listlessly, a child's barrette is embedded in the dried mud. It would be a good deed to collect the junk and cart it to a trashcan in town, but Clara feels suddenly tired, much too tired to be picking up someone else's litter. Whoever these careless people were, they weren't tourists. Tourists would never have found the place. She swats at a blackfly that lands on her neck and lets Stan help her up into the cab. The cooler goes under the tarp.

Maybe she and Stan have overdone. He looks weary, too. Still, she learned a great many things today, and it felt good to talk about Henry's death and what transpired afterward. Clara reaches into her pocket and feels the smooth surface of the moon shell Stan gave her. It will be something to remember this day by.

He starts the engine and heads for town.

THE ROCK AS BIG AS THE QUEEN MARY

THERE HADN'T YET been a frost. Inside their wire cages the tomato plants had retracted, though, like little old ladies with bone shrinkage, and the fruit on the vines seemed more exposed. Meg wrested a pair of plum tomatoes from their stem and laid them in the basket that hung from her arm. Nearby, Peter walked through dew-soaked grass, following her. "We don't get vine-ripened tomatoes at home," he said. "We have to grow them under glass."

"I know. It's not even the same vegetable."

She felt acutely the presence of the man behind her. His features had become so much more pronounced since she'd last seen him: the nose larger, the dark eyes more deeply set, the eyebrows untidy graying haymows. Wens had risen on his face and neck. His students must find him forbidding, this distinguished professor of medieval literature. And yet . . .

She turned. He was looking beyond the garden, at the retreating sea, which was leaving a mud flat in its wake. "When is it due back again?" he asked.

Meg began to explain about the tidal system, twice in, twice out, in a roughly twenty-five-hour span, but found herself floundering in the complexities of lunar pull. "Sorry, Peter. You're the one who's good at figuring out things like that, not me." She laughed, shrugging. "It's all a mystery."

"Or a miracle?" He smiled with the same shy but intimate smile that had charmed her all those years ago—intimate not in a sexual sense, precisely, but in a way that said: You and I, Meg, know a joke no one else is privy to.

"That too," she agreed, walking toward the herbs, which grew in a disorderly patch behind the tomato bed. The oregano had sprawled over the parsley and now bloomed with tiny purple flowers. Meg tore off a few branches and laid them across the tomatoes and the second-crop lettuce in the basket, and added a few sprigs of tarragon, whose stems had now become woody.

"Your garden is lovely, Meg."

"Not so lovely at this time of year." He stood so near her now that if she shifted only enough to transfer the basket to her other arm, her shoulder would touch the wool of his herringbone jacket. Fat bees hummed in the oregano. At the top of a spruce a crow cawed.

Slowly she moved away from the herb patch and said, "I don't have enough space to grow everything I'd like to. It's the trees. They don't leave me much sun. I could squeeze in one more raised bed here, I guess."

With the side of his shoe he nudged a flattish stone the size of a dessert plate. "This would be in the way."

"Wherever you dig in Maine you find stones," she said. "It's the number one crop." She started back to the house, conscious of his footsteps following hers across the hillocky lawn, which was really only self-sown weeds and wild grasses that she periodically cut to a stubble with a hand mower.

They entered the house through the kitchen door, and she set the basket on the counter. "Why don't you sit," she said, "and keep me company while I take care of some odds and ends."

He offered to help, but she told him no, just sit. Obediently

Peter pulled a chair away from the table and settled himself while Meg emptied the lettuce and herbs into an enamel pan. She ran water into the pan, then removed a package from the refrigerator. When she'd torn open the paper wrapping she brought it to the table for him to admire the contents, fillets so fresh and thin you could almost see through them. "Lemon sole. Off the boat this morning."

"Splendid."

At the counter she began to lay the fillets onto a square of paper towel. "I'll just sauté them in a little butter, nothing fancy."

He cleared his throat. "I wonder if you'd mind if I poached mine."

Poached? She pictured the delicate flesh disintegrating in an instant, swirling away into boiling water.

"It's my stomach. I can't take butter anymore, anything fried."

He looked embarrassed, and she said quickly, "Of course, Peter. But you don't need to do it yourself, I'm happy to."

Poached. She'd planned for the meal to be artlessly simple, but perfect. Now there'd be a soggy lump squatting gloomily on the white ironstone plate. Oh well, dress it up with a spray of tarragon and a lemon quarter.

Chilling was a bottle of sauterne, the best she'd been able to find in the local market. She took it out and handed it to Peter along with the corkscrew. "You still drink wine, I hope."

"Oh, yes, I still drink wine."

She thought about her twenty-second birthday dinner, the last time she'd seen him, and guessed he was thinking of that, too. Peter had brought two bottles of vintage Bordeaux as his contribution to the occasion. Claret, he called it. Peter not yet married, Meg's firstborn asleep in his crib.

Late that evening, giving in to wine-induced impulse, Meg had brought her son to the table to nurse. She knew that Peter, in the chair next to hers, could not help gazing on the baby's fuzzy head, on her own blue-veined breast swollen with milk. Her last opportunity to provoke a response in the gentle scholar to whom she'd become attached—he'd be on the plane back to Oxford the next day. No one else among the guests at the dinner table noticed a thing, least of all her husband.

The memory of her shamelessness caused Meg some chagrin, and she busied herself rinsing lettuce while he wound the corkscrew into the cork, eased it out, and poured the pale wine into glasses she'd set before him.

She wiped her hands on a dish towel. "Cheers, Peter," she said, touching the rim of her glass to his.

"To absent friends."

"Yes," she replied, "to absent friends." With her glass she returned to the counter.

Peter was Jim's friend before he was hers, of course—Peter Finesilver, the young medievalist on a prestigious one-year grant in the same department where her husband slogged along as a graduate student. Impressed by Peter's mind, Jim began to bring Peter back to the apartment for drinks after the Thursday afternoon seminar, and presently she'd invite him to stay for potluck. By chance she'd have cooked something a little special that day, seminar day. Or maybe not exactly by chance. With a modest smile Peter would produce a bottle of wine from his briefcase. Soon her whole week began and ended with Thursdays, even though she was pregnant with Jim's child, and in the spring semester nursing Jim's son.

After Peter returned to England the men's interests took different turns, Jim's lurching into Tudor drama, where he calculated the jobs were, and Peter's wending into linguistics and theology. Meg was the one who assumed the task of keeping in touch. Except that it wasn't a task. She wrote the offhand, chatty letters responding to Peter's, only once in a while slipping in some small self-revelation, like a wrapped candy tucked as a surprise into a lunch bag. About as often she'd receive something like that from him, a minute confession woven as if by accident into his amusing observations on a concert he'd attended, or some international intrigue, or the commotion among his colleagues when a certain fourteenth-century leechbook inexplicably vanished from the Bodleian. Even after Peter wed, the occasional letters back and forth across the Atlantic continued. Twenty-seven years, and still her heart leapt a little whenever a blue air letter with his curious hooked handwriting on it arrived in the mail.

From the kitchen table Peter said, "You haven't had an easy time of it, Meg."

She would not, she'd already decided, reveal to Peter that the marriage had been as good as dead well before Jim's puzzling symptoms began to manifest themselves. Instead, she sat at the table with her wineglass and talked about the decision to quit her job, sell the house, and move up here, once looking after her husband at home with the help of hired students was no longer a way of life either she or Jim cared to go on with. She'd always dreamed of living near the sea. The inside of a nursing home—as long as it's decent, what difference does it make where it is?

"But will you be all right? Financially, I mean."

She pushed her flyaway hair back from her forehead and explained that money wasn't a problem, Jim's disability pension relatively generous, the kids' educations paid for. They had a nest egg, investments that had done surprisingly well over the years. No fortune, certainly, but enough for Meg to be comfortable, enough to pay for the nursing home until . . .

"Would you like to see him?" Meg asked, still not altogether sure she understood the reason Peter rented a car and drove the three hundred miles north from Boston, where his conference was about to convene.

"Will he know me?"

"Do you mean, does he still have his mind?"

Peter found a crumb on the tablecloth and rolled it between his fingers.

"The sorry part is that he does. He won't be able to talk to you, though. Look, Peter, if you'd rather not . . . I didn't mention to him that you were coming."

He smiled slightly, his eyes cast down on the tablecloth. "That leaves it up to me, then."

"Well, we can play by ear."

Fog, the arthritic gray tabby, padded in from the living room where he'd been napping and wound himself around Meg's legs. She got up and let the cat out the kitchen door, which still had its screen in place. Soon Meg would have to summon the ambition to haul the storm doors and windows out of the cellar, wash and install them. Other maintenance jobs also needed attention. The dripping hot-water tap in the laundry room. A finicky switch in the upstairs hall. Leaves clogging gutters and drainpipes. Maybe Peter . . . But no, not dressed like that. He wouldn't have work clothes in the small carry-on satchel he'd brought with him, which now reposed on the bed in the spare room upstairs.

Neither of them had so far spoken of Enid, the wife he mentioned in his letters only rarely. Because Meg had been rattling on so much about herself, and about Jim, she decided she ought, for politeness' sake, to bring Enid into the conversation. "Your wife. She didn't think of coming with you to the conference?"

Peter smiled. "I'm afraid she's far too busy with her work just at the moment."

"She's a lawyer, right?"

He'd removed his wire-framed eyeglasses and was cleaning them with his pocket handkerchief. They'd left raw-looking dents on the bridge of his nose, as if he'd been pinched in a vice. "She's a partner in a large firm of solicitors. They do mostly corporate work."

"In Oxford?"

"Oh, no," he said, returning the glasses to his face and the handkerchief to his pocket. "In London, in the City."

One by one Meg began to transfer the draining fillets onto a fresh piece of paper towel. "She must find the commute a hassle."

"Enid lives in North London. She has a flat in Hampstead."

"Oh," Meg replied. If he had any feelings one way or the other about this coolly practical arrangement, Meg couldn't tell. Perhaps she was missing a cue that an English person would immediately have picked up on.

"We go on holidays together. We're planning a walking tour of Northumberland next spring."

"That sounds nice."

"You can still find bits of Hadrian's Wall." He paused. "Little heaps of brick, mostly. To see them you have to invade suburban housing estates, go bursting into people's gardens."

She laughed, at the same time wondering whether he was going to reveal more about the situation with Enid. When he didn't continue, she said, "Maybe you'd like a shower before we eat. Would you? Or no, a bath. Englishmen take baths."

While she sliced tomatoes and sectioned a lemon and put the potatoes on to boil, she listened to the bath water running overhead on the second floor. She tried not to think about Peter in the lion-footed porcelain tub, rubbing her clear glycerin soap over his body.

She glanced at the electric wall clock above the refrigerator. Right now they'd be feeding Jim his soft supper, most of which would dribble from his slack jaw and soil his bib. Then they'd lift him onto the bedpan to produce his few smelly pellets. Jim had bedded a goodly number of his female graduate students and at least one untenured faculty member, for years lying in his teeth to Meg and getting away with it. Still, she supposed not even he deserved to end his days this way.

~

After dinner, against the chill that had crept inland from the misty bay, Meg jacked the thermostat up a couple of degrees and built a fire in the fireplace. Her first fire of the season, she told Peter, sweeping up bits of bark and fungus that had fallen from the logs onto the hearth. They sat on the sofa, one cushion's space between them, and drank decaf and port. She talked about her boys, Kevin doing relief work in El Salvador, Mike traipsing around Nepal on a year off between college and graduate school. Maybe Peter found it strange that they'd departed to remote regions of the globe when their father was dying. Actually, it hadn't seemed like defection when, one by one, they took off: Kevin born with a passion for curing the world's ills, perhaps inherited from Meg's missionary great-grandparents; Mike's wandering a kind of family joke, as a child forever going astray in supermarkets and shopping malls. With her thumbnail Meg traced a hairline crack in her demitasse cup. Now that she thought about it, though . . . Perhaps it wasn't such a coincidence that both were so far out of reach now.

To get off that subject she told Peter about joining a church choir in town. For ages she'd been wanting an opportunity to sing choral music. Somehow she hadn't found the time when she was working. The church people were nice, a bit like a family.

Did she miss her job? Peter wanted to know.

Well, writing résumés had its moments. You could think of it as inventing people's lives, like a novelist or a psychotherapist. Or God. But most of the clients would never do justice to the identities she'd conjured for them. Meg set her cup on the tray. Poor souls destined to fail even before they passed through Life Designs, Inc.'s frosted door.

Why? Hard to tell, in an objective way. At one time they'd held responsible positions, successfully applied for mortgages, managed to keep families together. You couldn't miss the doom in their gray faces, though, in the stiff way they held themselves, arms crossed over their chests, fingers clutching their jacket sleeves, dazedly watching the tropical fish swim round the tank. Rubber heels digging into Life Designs' stained carpet.

Sometimes, she told Peter, the ghosts of those clients used to invade her dreams. They'd shake their laser-printed lives in her face, chase her along dark, maze-like corridors, their huge shadows nearly catching up with her. Thankfully, she rarely had those dreams anymore. No, she had to admit she didn't miss her job.

She got up to stoke the fire, and Peter poured a little more golden port into their glasses. He took a cloth handkerchief from his trouser pocket and wiped the stickiness from the neck of the bottle and from his fingers.

The radiator pipes gurgled. Meg began to talk about the weird plumbing in the house, installed in a haphazard way by amateurs half a century ago. She told him how the pipes froze and burst last winter, flooding the downstairs so that she'd had to retreat to the second floor with the cats. She'd felt like Noah's wife, she said, spinning out the yarn, making a joke of her inexperience in managing an antiquated house on her own. Her face was flushed, she knew, with drink and the heat of the fire.

In the silence that now fell over them, the clock on the mantel began to strike the hour of nine. "For me," Peter said, soon after it ceased chiming, "it's two in the morning." At the same moment they set their empty glasses down on the tray, and his knuckles bumped the underside of her wrist. Attentively they gazed at one another, Peter's haymow brows seeming to take on an agitated life of their own. She rose to her feet.

"Peter, I don't want to put you on the spot. I'll just tell you that my bedroom is the one at the far end of the hall, and if you should feel chilly or lonely or anything . . . "

Meg didn't wait for a reply. She crossed the Persian rug and a bare stretch of waxed hardwood and mounted the steps, leaving the port bottle uncorked and a heap of partially burned scraps of log still smoking in the fireplace.

He did come, after she'd decided he wasn't going to, and lifted the quilt so he could climb into bed beside her. "Meg," he said softly, "I don't have . . . I wasn't prepared to . . . "

She'd had her tubes tied the winter she discovered Jim was

spending his evenings in the apartment of a slender assistant professor named, ridiculously, Annunziata Pardoe. "It's been taken care of," Meg whispered.

Now she and Peter began to make love, twenty-seven years and four months after that sweet, urgent farewell kiss in the back stairwell of the Farnum Street apartment building, Meg's breasts leaking painfully through her crushed-velvet dress, her husband at the table holding forth on the *Regularis Concordia*, full of Peter's wine, oblivious. How close she'd come then to running down the steps after the gentle Englishman and folding herself into his luggage, and allowing herself to be transported to an England she knew like the back of her hand from reading Katherine Mansfield and Virginia Woolf. But Kevin's wail dragged her back inside the apartment, and everywhere were perilously stacked dishes to be washed, still encrusted with the remains of coq au vin and cake.

On Peter's back she felt bumps and small scarred depressions, where there must have been minor surgery, and she knew he was feeling the folds on her stomach and the layered flesh that skidded awkwardly under his caressing palms. But how very good it was, this loving. Inside her, his mouth at her breast, he said in a ragged voice, "Such a long time to wait, my Meg."

After he slept she still held him, listening to his slow breathing and to the tide, now high, sucking at marsh grass. *My Meg. My Meg.*

He wheezed a little, drew out of her arms and turned himself over—careful, even in his sleep, not to encroach on her share of the bed—snorted once, fell into a deeper slumber.

Suddenly she remembered rescuing from the trash, that birthday night, the corks from the vintage claret. What had become of them afterward?

~

Meg awoke at first light, pulled on a sweater and pants quietly so as not to wake him, and went downstairs. In the kitchen she found that before coming to bed he'd carried out the tray. She wondered whether he'd been anguishing over what they were about to do as he corked the port, as he rinsed the glasses and demitasse cups and put them upside down in the drainer. Or perhaps he'd been completely calm, with nothing more troubling on his mind than the duty to be a helpful guest, giving her time to change her mind if she wanted to. She let the cats in and fed them and then, filled with an energy she wasn't sure what to do with, went outside.

Over the tough grass she walked down the slope to the water's edge. Tide on its way out again, the rising sun casting an orangey pink shimmer on pools that lingered in wet sand, stippled gray clouds above the horizon like stripes on an animal. How sad that the sunrise was wasted, Peter sleeping through it. In the woods behind her a raven shrieked *quork, quork,* setting off a chain reaction of *quork*s from spruce to spruce.

Her muscles itched to be doing something. She turned and climbed back up the slope, skirted the house, yanked open the shed door. From a box of moldy garden gloves, the finger-ends nothing but fraying holes, she chose a couple at random and took a shovel from among the tangle of tools that leaned against the wall. She'd disturbed a spider web. Just about enough light reached the inside of the shed so that she could watch the disconcerted spider scramble up the planks.

Leaving the door ajar, Meg forced the mud-stiffened gloves onto her hands and toted the shovel around to the vegetable garden. It shouldn't take long to move that flat stone. She could have coffee brewing and muffins in the oven before he came downstairs. With the tip of the shovel she began to lift chunks of turf from the edge of the stone, but as she was doing so she discovered that its diameter was wider than she'd assumed, more like a dinner plate than a dessert plate. Crabgrass and chickweed had matted over the surface several inches all around the circumference. When she had that stripped away, she tried to work the shovel blade down under the stone in order to pry it up, but the blade clanked against rock. Nothing budged; the resistance jarred the bones in her forearms and set her teeth on edge. So the stone must not be flat, after all, but have some depth to it. She moved the blade away from the exposed stone half a foot or so and tried again, forcing the blade down through grass by pressing her heel hard against the shoulder of the blade. This time she was able to move some soil, which, being solid clay, stuck to the blade in clumps.

After four or five more shovelfuls, sweat started to dampen her forehead and her heart was beating faster. Not as young as I used to be, she thought. The rock that had begun to emerge seemed to be granite, coarse-grained in texture, unevenly rounded, a pinkish color. Chips of quartz or mica embedded in the granite glinted in the sunlight. This stone was clearly a lot larger than she'd suspected, even a few minutes ago.

Meg pushed the sleeves of her sweater up to the elbows, then circled the stone and moved another half dozen shovelfuls of the dense gray soil, rested awhile, moved yet another half dozen. She leaned on the handle, her chest heaving. This was going to be some rock.

By the time she had the whole thing exposed, more than an hour later, it sat complacently in a pit maybe a yard deep. Streaks of gray dirt covered her arms and the front of her sweater. Her khakis were filthy, and so were her sneakers. She stripped off the mismatched gloves and tossed them aside.

Peter, dressed in fresh white shirt and herringbone jacket, came strolling over the hillocky lawn toward the garden. "Good morning," he said. "I wondered what happened to you."

"Rats. I was going to have coffee and homemade muffins all ready for you."

"That's a big stone," he said, looking down into the pit. "How are you going to get it out of the hole?"

She thought for a moment and then began to laugh. "Damned if I know."

"What you need is a winch."

"Fresh out of winches, I'm afraid." She picked up the shovel. "Come on back to the house, and I'll give you some breakfast."

~

Water dripped down the nape of her neck. With her left hand she rubbed her hair with a towel, with her right she pulled on a moccasin. Peter was sitting on the edge of the bed, which he must have made before coming downstairs in search of her. "I haven't watched a woman dress in longer than I can remember," he said.

She didn't answer right away. Then, "I'm sorry it couldn't have been a younger and more beautiful woman to break your . . . " Fast? Vow? " . . . whatever it was."

" . . . whatever it was." Without a smile he said, "I liked this woman fine."

She dried her hair some more, threw the towel over the bed rail, combed her fingers through the damp strands. "Every morning I drive into town to see him," she said. "He'll wonder what's wrong if I don't show up."

"You must go, then."

"Are you going to come?"

"Would you like me to?"

She sat next to him on the bed. "It's not a lot of fun, Peter. He can't talk. He tries to, but all that comes out are baby-sounds. *Gaa, gaa.* And that frustrates him terribly, of course. Probably what he's trying to say is: Why the hell don't you just shoot me in the head and get it over with."

Peter took her hand, which was raw and blistered from the digging, and wove his fingers in with hers. She'd stopped wearing her wedding band. The back of Peter's hand bore a couple of liver spots, as well as some spidery graying hairs sprouting from his knuckles. He wasn't wearing a ring, either, but then, she had an idea that wedding bands for men weren't as common in England as they were here.

"And," she went on, "after last night, you might feel uncomfortable, as if you'd taken advantage of him, of his being sick, though you certainly can't be blamed for what we did, it was my idea, and—"

"Blame isn't the issue." He said that gently, almost regretfully.

"Peter, I swore to myself I wasn't going to tell you this, but I have to now."

"What?" She hesitated, and he said again, "What is it, Meg?"

"Jim cheated on me. Quite a bit. Before he got sick."

He looked down at their intertwined hands. "Are you saying that what you want is to even the score?"

She was shocked he'd think that. "No, Peter. What I want is for you to understand the whole situation. Because it feels wrong to keep secrets from you, because . . . " But how could she come right out and tell him that she loved him, without putting a whammy on everything? She withdrew her hand from his grasp and stood. Damned if she'd humiliate herself by weeping in front of him.

"Because Jim and I were friends?"

"Yes, that's it," she said, her throat constricted. "I'd better go."

He followed her downstairs and out to the dooryard. After a moment's confusion, sorting out which was the driver's side of her little compact and which the passenger's, Peter got in and shut the door.

~

At some indefinable time between their entering the kitchen and leaving the house again, the sky had become overcast, threatening rain. The trip to town was about six miles, first on a dirt road along the narrow peninsula, the colorless bay sometimes visible through the trees, then a turn onto a paved numbered route that passed some fields and barns, crossed an iron bridge. Conversation along the way they made deliberately bland: How many people live in the village? How do they earn their living? Meg could bite her tongue for telling Peter about Jim's screwing around, which served no purpose but to make this expedition even more awkward than it would be otherwise. And she wished she'd eaten something, filthy though she'd been, rather than going right upstairs to shower after she'd fixed Peter's breakfast. Her gut felt queasy. She'd developed a headache that was like a narrow-gauge drill bit intermittently entering her skull above her left eye.

Meg pulled into the parking lot in front of the nursing home, and they got out. The home, a white wooden structure with striped awnings, had been a private house in the days when sardine canneries brought moderate prosperity to the town. Now the house looked as defeated as the industry that had funded it, the awnings tattered by winter storms and the house needing a coat of paint. Still, Meg told Peter as they walked up the steps, the aides were kind and competent, and in spite of its age and makeshift repairs, the place was kept pretty clean. You couldn't hope for much more than that.

They found Jim in the day room, in a wheelchair parked near a window that overlooked the marsh. Meg said, "Look who's come to see you, Jim."

She saw him now through Peter's eyes: his hair not exactly gray, but faded and much sparser, the mouth drooping, spittle leaking from one corner. Tall as ever, but the muscles gone as slack as his mouth, so that he had to have a strap buckled around his shrunken torso, as if he were a dummy stuffed with rags, and his neck propped inside a surgical collar. The sweatshirt and jogging pants he wore were easier than regular clothes for the aides to manage when they dressed and undressed him. How the irony in that must rankle, since Jim had prided himself on his fitness. As if it were her own, she felt Jim's shame. She should never have brought Peter here.

He carried two chairs across the scuffed tile floor, which was laid out like a checkerboard, and set them in front of Jim's wheelchair. "Hello, Jim," he said, settling himself into one of them.

Jim did not try to speak. Maybe it was Meg's imagination, but his expression seemed wary—frightened, even.

"It's been a long time," Peter said. The near-echo of what he'd murmured to Meg, his tongue licking at her nipple, made her wince and turn away. She almost would have preferred him to exclaim, "You look grand, Jim," and clap him on his bony shoulder.

She didn't take the chair next to Peter's. Instead she stood at a card table on which lay a jigsaw, half completed. The picture was of a whitewashed cottage, yellow roses climbing a trellis along the left-hand border. Distractedly she chose a puzzle piece and turned it this way and that, trying to fit it into gaps on the trellis. In a far corner of the room an ancient gentleman moaned in his sleep.

"I've solved it, Jim," Peter said. "The Digby *Magdalen*."

She recalled that when he was a graduate student Jim had written a seminar paper on a play about Mary Magdalen, which had given him fits. For some reason he'd expected Peter to help him with the project, and resented it when Peter went on devoting himself to his own research instead. She looked up and saw that Jim's pale eyes had begun to water at the corners. If Peter weren't here, she'd lift an edge of the cloth diaper knotted around Jim's neck and wipe them for him, and the slobber at his mouth. His feet, in their fuzzy bed socks, stirred. A kind of gurgle, impossible to interpret, came from deep in his throat.

. . . indeed a miracle play, Peter was saying *. . . absolutely a coherent whole . . . bridge between medieval and Renaissance . . . Bernardine doctrine . . . by her miracles the Magdalen comes ever closer to divine transformation . . . is not confused with, but* becomes *the mother of God . . .*

Like an egg balanced on end, Jim's head wobbled at the top of his stiff collar. His left hand lifted from the arm of the chair, flopped down again. Meg began to move toward them, diagonally across black and white squares.

Peter leaned forward in the chair. Mysteriously he said, "I did it for you, Jim." His voice seemed to drop a little. "I'm very glad I came." For a horrifying moment Meg thought he was going to confide in Jim what had transpired in the upstairs bedroom. And perhaps he had—with his smile. Gently he touched the sleeve of Jim's sweatshirt and said, "Goodbye, friend."

Out at the car, Meg discovered that she still held the jigsaw piece in her hand. She placed it on the dashboard, thinking she'd return it the following day, and turned the key in the ignition. They didn't speak at all on the way home.

~

Peter laid his chicken sandwich on his plate and said, "Did you ever consider divorcing him?"

"When I found out he'd been sleeping around?" She rose from the table to take from the refrigerator the bowl of fruit salad left from the previous night's dinner. Overnight the cut fruit had released its juice, and the banana turned dark and soggy. She sat and spooned some of the salad onto her plate. "Sure I considered it."

"You could have married again," Peter said, examining his half-eaten sandwich.

"There wasn't anyone around I wanted to marry." Their glances met, then she looked out the window at speckled yellow birch leaves drifting down in a light breeze. Might be going to rain soon.

"Anyway, it would have been so hard, Peter. So painful to drag all those bitter feelings into the open, into a court of law. I figured that having Jim gone for good wouldn't be that much different from the way life had been for me for years. Whether he'd spent his evening in a carrel writing a journal article or in someone's bed, the effect was the same."

Meg ate a spoonful of the fruit salad. "Then, around the time I'd gotten used to the idea of Jim's girlfriend, the odd symptoms began.

The first thing was, he had trouble holding a pen tightly enough to write with it. That hand and arm would twitch, like a cat convinced it has fleas. I suggested his problem might be psychological—maybe he needed a rest from doing so much scholarship. Bullshit, he said. Next he fell down a flight of stairs after a lecture and had to be brought home in an ambulance. Fractured his leg in two places."

"I remember your writing about the broken leg."

"Even then I didn't suspect anything was seriously wrong. People do stumble and fall, even healthy people."

"They do," Peter said.

"So he spent six weeks hobbling around on crutches. During that time he started to have trouble swallowing, would gag or choke on things. Stew meat, vitamin pills, even oatmeal. Finally his doctor made him see a neurologist."

One of the cats was mewing outside the screen door, but Meg ignored it. "And then we knew. After that, there was no question of divorce."

Peter nodded.

She rose from the table and scraped her plate into the compost bucket. "Peter," she said abruptly, "when your wife decided to take a flat in Hampstead, did divorce cross your mind?"

It took him a moment to collect his thoughts. "I understood from the start how important Enid's work was to her. She tried living in Oxford for a year, as we'd agreed, but found it too confining. Her right to a career was part and parcel of our bargain."

Bargain. A strange way to express the concept of marriage, but accurate enough, Meg supposed.

"I felt obligated to honor it."

"And you still do."

"Yes. I still do."

After a silence, during which he attended to his sandwich, she said, "Is your paper really about Mary Magdalen?"

The question seemed to startle him. "Of course. Why do you ask?"

"What did you mean when you told Jim you wrote it for him?"

"Meg," he said, "let's talk about the hole."

"What hole?"

"The hole with the stone in it, where you want to put in another bed."

"Oh, that hole."

He smiled, and his haymow brows lifted. "I was thinking about it on the way back from seeing Jim. Do you happen to have a crowbar?"

She'd inherited a bunch of old tools rusting away in the shed when she'd bought the house. "I think I recall seeing one. Maybe even two."

"Let's have a go."

~

He washed up the lunch dishes, spilling a certain amount of water on the floor in front of the sink, while she rooted around upstairs to find something he could wear. Hanging in Mike's closet was a pair of corduroys he'd worn before he took his great growth spurt—heaven only knew why they'd been preserved, even through the move to Maine—and in the ragbag she found a flannel shirt of Jim's that she'd been saving to rip into dust cloths.

Arrayed in these hand-me-downs, Peter was a comical sight. The threadbare corduroys came only to his shins, and she'd already removed the buttons from the shirt, so she had to safety-pin him into it. The sleeves, way too long, dangled over his hands until he turned them up. She got out the camera, in case she ever needed to blackmail him, she said. But as she watched him trundle the wheelbarrow over hillocks toward the woodpile, she thought there was something indefinably erotic about seeing him in her son's and husband's clothing.

Meg took a picture of him loading logs into the barrow, and then set the camera on a stump, propped on a piece of kindling, so that the time-delay mechanism could capture the two of them together. She came next to him and put her arm around his waist, hugging him to her, feeling the soft, worn flannel under her fingers, and told him to smile. They held still, watching the little red light blink, waiting for the shutter to slide open. If only it never would, if only they could stand that way forever. But the shutter opened, hesitated for a fraction of a second, and slid shut, and the automatic advance whirred. "One more?" she asked. Too late: he'd turned and was heaving a log into the barrow.

After Peter dumped the pile of logs near the hole, he positioned two fat ones, split side down, next to the rim and picked up one of the long crowbars they'd found in the shed. "Right," he said. "With the crowbars we're going to lever up the rock as high as we can, using these logs as fulcrums. Then I'll nudge a log into the hole with my foot, and while you steady the rock, I'll use my crowbar to shove the log under. If we can get enough logs under the rock to raise it to the surface, then all we need to do is roll it off."

"*If*," she said. "Okay, let's give it a try."

Easier said than done. The stone weighed a ton, and it wanted to wobble off the forked end of her crowbar, especially when Peter used his to maneuver the log in the hole. Nevertheless, he eventually succeeded in forcing the first log beneath the stubborn granite. The stone lurched sideways and upward about an inch, and Peter, red in the face, let out a cheer.

"This time, I'll hold the rock, and you do the maneuvering," he said. He repositioned the fulcrum logs, and again they levered the granite upward. Unfortunately, the log she kicked into the hole turned out to be too big, and she had a devil of a time manipulating it. Meanwhile, Peter, struggling to raise the rock higher with his crowbar so her job wouldn't be so hard, became even redder in the face. Please God, let him not burst an artery, she prayed. At last she managed to wedge the log more or less underneath, the granite seemed a little higher, and they both cheered.

"If only we had a third person to work the logs in while we held the crowbars," she said, "it would be a piece of cake. Almost." Both of them, probably, pictured Jim in town in the nursing home, drooling into his bib.

"We can do it," Peter said. "We've made a good start already. We just have to go slow, take rests, spell each other holding up the rock."

Together they developed a knack and a rhythm. Circling the rock with the fulcrums, they jammed the logs one by one under the rock and on top of the ones below it. Little by little the heap of logs Peter had dumped by the hole shrank. There were some setbacks, when the logs under the rock would suddenly shift and catapult it into the clay wall of the hole, and they'd have to ram it toward the center again, Peter grunting and Meg muttering swearwords. Nevertheless, gradually the rock's shoulders, and then middle, emerged.

"It's working, Peter. They ought to give you the Nobel Prize in physics for this."

He smiled as though he'd just finished making his acceptance speech and was modestly acknowledging the crowd's applause. "How long do you think it's been buried?" he asked.

"Oh, roughly since the last ice age."

The higher the rock rose the better they got at weaving the logs in beneath it, outwitting the rough-skinned, clay-encrusted, bullheaded enemy. At last it was entirely out of the hole, squatting on top of what seemed like the best part of a cord of logs, its bottom surface level with the terrain.

Meg flopped down on the grass they'd trampled, feeling the same exhausted euphoria as after the births of her babies. Peter took off his ratty garden gloves and mopped his forehead with the handkerchief he'd stowed in Mike's pocket. His graying hair was stuck to his head, drenched in sweat. He removed his eyeglasses and wiped them, too. "That rock must be the size of a washtub," he said.

"I beg your pardon. That rock is at least the size of a dinghy."

Nearsightedly he blinked at it. "Dory."

"Tugboat."

"That rock," he declared, hooking his eyeglasses over his ears, "is the size of the bloody Queen Mary."

She loved him so much it felt like a disease you could die of, no less hopeless than Jim's. "You're leaving tomorrow, aren't you," she blurted.

He stuffed the handkerchief into a pants pocket and sat beside her on the grass. "Friday is the day I give my paper," he said quietly.

You couldn't get somebody else to deliver it for you? she wanted to ask. You couldn't say what the hell, screw the goddamn paper? But if anything like that were possible for him, he'd have to suggest it himself. She rolled over and pressed her face into the crook of her arm so that if she were to weep he wouldn't see the tears. After a while Peter laid his hand on the back of her work shirt, his fingers light as a leaf falling. "Are you all right?" he asked.

"I'm not having a heart attack, if that's what you mean."

"I don't know what to say, Meg."

"Then don't say anything."

The rain that had been threatening since late morning began as a finely sieved drizzle. Soon Peter stood and brushed mud and dried grass clippings from Mike's corduroys. They returned the crowbars to the shed and went into the house.

~

A week after Peter drove away in the rental car, Meg pulled the tomato plants out of their bed, cut up the stalks with kitchen shears, and added them to the compost.

The following day the minister of the church where she sings in the choir arrived in a pickup, along with two parishioners. With little effort the three men toppled the big rock off the hole. "Which way?" they asked, and when Meg replied that she didn't care, they rolled it toward the seaward side of the lawn, which they chose not for esthetic reasons, but because the land sloped in that direction. The rock came to rest against a knot of skinny stumps belonging to an alder that Meg had sawed down the previous spring, near the edge of the woods.

Her helpers rescued the logs from the hole and restacked them on the woodpile. They shoveled the clumps of clay back into the hole and topped it up with soil from a hill of loam, now nourishing canes of wild raspberry, that had been trucked in the previous year for her first raised beds. Meg could hardly bear to watch the operation, but felt it would be ungracious not to stay outside until they were finished and afterward offer them coffee. To her relief, the men didn't ask who'd helped her lift the rock. Might as well have been done by snapping her fingers and saying abracadabra.

Every time she passes a window on the garden side of the house Meg's eye snags on the rock. It looks naked and forlorn, sitting there on frosty grass. In the spring she'll plant a clump of daylilies next to it, maybe splurge on a mugho pine to nestle up against its rough pink surface.

Before leaving the country Peter wrote her a brief letter on hotel stationery. It was raining in Boston, he said. He'd lost his umbrella somewhere, absentmindedly left it under his chair in the conference room where he read his paper, or perhaps in the taxi afterward. No doubt he'd encounter rain when he landed in London, too. "I expect," he wrote in his tiny, hooked, nearly illegible hand, "it will be a long while until I see the sun again." Since that note she hasn't heard from him.

The snapshots came back from York Photo Labs. The one of Peter at the woodpile is a little blurry and poorly framed—she'd been over-eager. The one of the two of them, shot by time-delay, could be any middle-aged couple on a camping holiday, the woman's hair awry, the man's face mostly in shadow. No details (the safety pins on the flannel shirt, for instance) visible to anyone who didn't know they were there. She'd ordered a double set of prints, but won't be sending the extra pair on to him, probably.

Jim's still hanging on in the nursing home, a little weaker each day. Gradually he seems to be withdrawing to the private place where people go before they die. Yes, she did remember to take the jigsaw piece from the car's dashboard back to the day room. Turned out it wasn't part of the rose trellis, but the feathers of some yellow bird—oriole?—in the upper right-hand corner of the puzzle.

Unaccountably, as the year winds down, Meg finds her spirits lifting. Maybe her disease isn't a fatal one, after all. Yesterday Mike telephoned from Katmandu to say he'll definitely be home by Christmas. She's looking forward to it.

AFTERWORD

Elaine Ford, Writer: A Brief Biography
By Arthur Boatin

Elaine Ford's first three novels, written while she lived in Massachusetts, take place in cities. Cheek-by-jowl triple-decker houses, small rooms, noisy streets, parks with more pavement than plant growth—these are the books' backdrops. Book reviewers noted a cracks-in-the-sidewalk realism and the author's empathy for the residents of ethnic enclaves. What accounts, then, for Elaine's adoption of Maine, especially rural Maine, as the locale for her next novels and for the stories in *This Time Might Be Different*?

Elaine moved to Maine—to puckerbrush Maine, six hours' drive north of Boston—in 1985. An unapologetic realist writer for whom community and physical landscape have always been important, she naturally used the new surroundings in her work. Her success in depicting this different place and milieu in fiction can be measured in reviewers' reactions. *Monkey Bay,* a 1989 novel set Downeast, demonstrates "a wonderful ear and eye, capturing the vernacular of the state's working class and the rhythms of life so close to the sea," as Howard Frank Mosher wrote in *The New York Times Book Review*, and, according to *The Philadelphia Inquirer,* "is accurate about a thousand details of life on the northern coast of New England."

Thus Elaine was able to make the jump from urban novelist

to rural novelist. Or are *urban* and *rural* secondary distinctions in discussing her characters and their often difficult lives? Perhaps for the writer there was no jump, and more ties together her city dwellers and country folk than separates them.

Elaine Palmer Ford was born in White Plains, New York, and grew up in Cresskill, in Bergen County, New Jersey. Her father, John H. Ford, worked as loan officer of a Manhattan savings bank. John was, according to his nephew Richard I. Ford, a frustrated engineer whose inventor father declined to send his sons to college, believing they should make their own way in the world. Her mother, the former Ruth Palmer, was a homemaker active in education causes. John and Ruth met during the 1930s at a socialist convention, Elaine told a Maine interviewer in 1990, but the family in which she was the eldest of three children was "middle middle class."

Elaine excelled as a student at Tenafly High School, where she served as co-editor of the literary magazine. In her senior year a poem of hers won *Seventeen*'s annual competition for high school writers and appeared in that magazine.

Admitted to Radcliffe College, Elaine majored in English, aiming to become a writer. A creative writing course with the avant-garde novelist John Hawkes, she wrote on her website, "taught me the values of significant detail and economy of language." However, she told the 1990 interviewer, "my style [of writing] has always been the same. . . . I'm interested in doing the same things and have more or less the same way of telling the story as I did [in high school]."

In 1958, during her junior year, Elaine dropped out of college to marry a Harvard undergraduate, Gerald Bunker. That marriage would last eighteen years and produce five children, before ending in 1976. "In the '60s, Radcliffe women were supposed to marry Harvard men, produce superior children, and fit into the mold," Elaine told *The Boston Globe* in 1980. "It was the prevailing spirit of the time."

Gerald's academic pursuits and changes of career led to frequent moves. At various times the family lived in New Haven, Cambridge, Demarest (New Jersey), Annapolis, and McLean (Virginia), as well as Kyoto, Japan, and Belfast, Northern Ireland. Elaine became expert in packing and unpacking. In 1959, when their first child, Mark, was an infant, the couple "embarked on what turned out to be a yearlong and in some ways foolhardy adventure," she wrote on her website, "traveling through Western Europe, living in Greece for a few months, then on to Egypt, India, the Soviet Union, and Eastern Europe in a Volkswagen camping bus."

Although "engaged in the business of baby-making," Elaine completed her bachelor's degree, graduating from Harvard in 1964, cum laude.

A turning point for Elaine as a writer came in 1972, when her mother was diagnosed with leukemia. Ruth Ford died in her early sixties. "I had to come to terms with the fact that we're all mortal," Elaine wrote of this development. "If I was going to be a writer I'd better get cracking, children or no." Her family was then living in a working-class, largely Irish-American area of North Cambridge, and the surroundings became the setting of her first novel, *The Playhouse.*

Much of the information about the book's characters was collected firsthand. Elaine took a job advertised in a local newspaper as a door-to-door interviewer for a community schools program, and was able to observe the lives behind the doors of North Cambridge. "I didn't get any characters out of [the interviews]," she told *The Boston Globe* in 1980, "but I did get a feeling for their lives." Many of her interview subjects expect and demand little from life, because "they . . . don't have the money to change their lives in any significant way." *The Playhouse* "is about people making the best lives they can out of what little they've got."

Snatching two hours a day for writing while her youngest child napped, Elaine completed a draft of the novel. But no sooner had she got down to writing seriously than Gerald, who already held a PhD in history, determined to become a physician. At the time, American medical schools did not welcome students over thirty, so he enrolled at a British university, in a six-year program. "So off we went again in 1973," Elaine later wrote, "this time to Northern Ireland. Deprived of geographical context for my infant novel, I found that my writing was stymied. It was at the height of the Troubles. Bombs were going off all over Belfast, rain fell constantly, and my marriage began to disintegrate."

Husband and wife separated in 1976 and divorced after Elaine's return to the United States. There she reconnected with, and subsequently married, the writer of this essay, an old friend. Elaine and I moved to the Boston area, where we would reside nine years, first in Dorchester, while Elaine attended library school, then in Somerville, where she got a job as a reference librarian.

During the 1970s, *The Playhouse* had been represented by a literary agent, but following multiple rejections, Elaine put away the manuscript and gave no thought to writing a second novel. With her permission, I prepared excerpts from the novel and sent them unsolicited to untried publishers. For some time these submissions were rejected, until one day a young McGraw-Hill editor asked to read the complete manuscript. He liked what he saw and made an offer to publish. *The Playhouse* came out in September 1980 to favorable reviews, and already Elaine was at work on her next book.

Somerville provided the budding novelist rich material for

fiction. Her second novel, *Missed Connections* (Random House), is set in the precise area of East Somerville where the Boatins lived from 1979, and draws on local history, including the construction of neighborhood-disrupting Interstate 93 during the 1950s. The protagonist of her third novel, *Ivory Bright* (Viking Penguin), operates a chaotic toy store in Somerville's Union Square, which at the time had yet to experience gentrification.

When Elaine decided, in 1983, to stop working as a librarian and devote herself to fiction writing, we looked to Northern New England as a less crowded, unspoiled, affordable place to live. In January 1985 we became owners of a log home on a tidal bay in Milbridge, Washington County, Maine. Unlike in Somerville, looking out our windows on the Rays Point peninsula we saw trees and water and wildlife but no other house.

Beautiful or not, Milbridge was a poorly informed choice. Washington County, we would learn, is sparsely populated with inexpensive real estate because its soil is poor, its job opportunities limited, and its cultural amenities few. Even Mainers consider the region remote.

The move was poorly timed, as well. After settling in Milbridge, Elaine was hired to teach creative writing and literature at the University of Maine. For this opening the English Department wanted above all a publishing fiction writer, a stroke of luck for Elaine, whose highest degree was a master's in library science. But Orono lies too far from Milbridge for a daily commute, and Elaine wound up renting an apartment in Bangor and spending half the teaching week there during her nineteen years at the university. Had she known of the UM job sooner, we would have moved from Somerville to Orono or Bangor.

Yet this leap of faith, naïve and clumsy though it was, did work out. Elaine found a job that she enjoyed, that utilized her skills and supported the family. As for Milbridge, if life there had disagreed with us, we would not have remained sixteen years.

Elaine joined the town's Congregational church, a denomination familiar from her youth. She sang in the church choir, helped prepare fundraising soup lunches, participated in craft fairs and rummage sales and Christmas pageants, and served two yearlong stints as church moderator. She gardened, as she had not been able to do in Somerville. She served on a committee that helped create a public library in Milbridge. She attended town meetings. She made friends in the community. She observed.

In Orono, Elaine soon found her way in the classroom. That she gave honest criticism leavened with practical advice became a byword among writing students. "She was relentless in her pursuit of the right expression," Marc Grigorov, a former master's candidate in English, has written, "often picking out a single word and reading it out loud like sounding a bell for cracks. . . . She wanted me to write about 'interesting and important things,' as she put it. In order to have something of value to say about my life, I would have to believe, as she did, that my life, as well as all others, contained importance, some piece of a universal reality."

"[Among writing teachers] only Elaine taught me . . . how to live as a writer," Kurtis Scaletta, another former student, said. "She told me it was okay to have written a terrible novel just to have the practice. She prepared me for the reality that publishing a first novel didn't mean the rest of your writing life was a cakewalk. She encouraged me to submit stories and get rejected, because developing a thick skin was part of the process."

In the English Department, Elaine's became a respected deliberative voice, according to a colleague, Harvey Kail, particularly in shaping the creative writing curriculum. Off-campus, by 1990 Elaine had founded a fiction-writers' workshop that met at her Bangor apartment to critique one another's work-in-progress. Elaine submitted her own new work for the group's review, expecting frank criticism.

At home and in Bangor, Elaine wrote. In addition to *Monkey Bay*, published in 1989 and set in a town much like Milbridge, while living in Washington County she wrote at least twenty works of short fiction. Those stories with non-Maine settings appear in *The American Wife*, her story collection published by University of Michigan Press in 2007. Pieces that take place in Maine are included here in *This Time Might Be Different* (Islandport Press). During the 1990s Elaine completed two as-yet unpublished novels set in Maine: *Rampion* and *Through the Fire*. In 1997 her novel *Life Designs* was published by Zoland Books. Its final and longest chapter takes place in Maine.

The one and a half decades in Milbridge were productive for the writer Elaine Ford and for the person Elaine Boatin. Nonetheless, contemplating her coming retirement from teaching, Elaine and I decided to look around. In December 2001 we moved to Harpswell, a town adjacent to Brunswick but more countrified. This location represented compromises: not in town, as Elaine on some level preferred, but only ten minutes' drive from a rich urban center; a beautiful house in a beautiful setting, although without water view; spaces for gardens.

Early in 2005 Elaine became a full professor emerita, free of the commute to Orono, able to write all day, if she chose. At her retirement party, when asked about her plans, she surprised people by answering, "My days of writing fiction are done. The characters don't come to me the way they used to."

What Elaine chose to do instead was genealogical research. A beloved uncle, Dick Ford, had been the family historian. As a high-school girl she accompanied him on a trip to New England to meet cousins on her father's mother's side. Now, using Uncle Dick's notes and hypotheses, Elaine began her own research. But rather than focusing on the well-documented Sayleses of New England, she wanted to learn more about the nineteenth-century Ford family in the antebellum South.

In her pursuit she benefited from the internet and its tools, including Ancestry.com and easy access to National Archives. Through the internet, Elaine wrote on her website, she also "met distant cousins who shared invaluable information and a few precious photographs." Her training and experience as a reference librarian helped. She enjoyed doing research and she relished a challenge, none greater than ferreting out the birthplace and lineage of her great-great-grandfather, Thomas Lawson Ford, who, before moving to Kosciusko, Mississippi, in the 1840s, had been a small cotton planter in Madison County, Alabama, but who had come there from elsewhere.

In 2006 Elaine traveled to Kosciusko, where she consulted courthouse records and met distant kin named Boyd. There she learned of the diary of Judge Jason Niles, which provides a picture of daily life in mid-nineteenth-century Kosciusko and on occasion mentions her great-greats by name. In 2007 she wrote a 15,500-word summary of her findings that was published online in November that year.

What happened next is described by Elaine as follows: Doing this family-history research "I'd collected such an array of good stories that my fiction-writing impulse re-emerged. I felt driven to write a novel about these people." In fact her decision to undertake what would become *God's Red Clay* was arrived at circuitously.

Friends of Elaine, hearing about her Southern ancestors as they emerged in her research, suggested she use what she'd learned as a basis for fiction. Why not make her great-great-grandparents, Tom and Anner Malone Ford, the protagonists of a novel? "Think of all I'd have to learn about the nineteenth century!" she'd reply. "*And* put myself in the mind of a slaveholder?"

Meanwhile, having written up the Fords, Elaine turned her new facility in tracing family history to other ancestors, specifically, my mother's parents, Sol and Fanny Mendelson, 1890s emigrants from the former Russian Empire to Scotland and then, in 1906, to America.

What allowed Elaine finally to overcome her reservations and make fiction out of genealogical research? A chance prompt to the Bangor writers' group was the catalyst. Members were invited to write a story about a character who clings fiercely to something of dubious value. Elaine came up with a tale involving my grandparents when they lived in Rhode Island in 1910. In the story "Providence" the wife clings to her marriage, imperfect as it is, because she cannot imagine herself and her seven children without a husband's provision, however meager.

Elaine now felt as though a door had opened. She began to conceive other biographically based plots about the Mendelsons, their siblings, and their children, taking place in three countries over two generations. But soon another thought registered: if, using period research, she could write about oppressed peoples in Czarist Russia and immigrant Jews crammed into tenements in turn-of-the-century Glasgow and New York, then wasn't she also capable of imagining nineteenth-century Fords, farmers of cotton in Alabama and, later, proprietors of a hotel and a grocery store in Mississippi? In 2011 she shelved my forebears in favor of the Fords and the Malones and all the information about them and their times already accumulated.

A third cousin with an interest in genealogy, Steven Ford Scott, accompanied Elaine on two study trips to Kosciusko that followed her decision to fictionalize her ancestors. According to him, she first planned a short story about Thomas Lawson Ford, which, as she wrote and researched, expanded to a novella, then to several stories in a chain, and finally to a multigenerational novel, *God's Red Clay*. Of his fellow unearther of family history, Steve wrote: "Elaine's research was extensive and copiously documented. . . . [But] her special gift . . . was the fiction-writer's imagination . . . her insight into character, relationships, and the unique dynamics of family that don't always conform to expectation. She had an innate ability to spot clues and follow them. . . . She used others to help gather information, but seemed able to see things there that no one else had ever spotted. The product was a singular insight into people, time, and place [that] coalesced in *God's Red Clay*."

Once that 165,000-word novel was written, Elaine returned to the subject of my relatives in early twentieth-century Europe and America. By 2015 she had completed eleven stories about them, a book's length, spanning the years 1882 to 1933. She titled the collection *Bread and Freedom: Stories of an Immigrant Family's Journey*.

This long-postponed dive into biographically based historical fiction was not the only new undertaking of Elaine's seventies. For Maine Playwrights Festival, an annual competition, Elaine adapted an already-published short story of hers, "Original Brasses, Fine Patina," which, conveniently, takes place in a single scene in a single room, a gallery of the Museum of Fine Arts, Boston. MPF named Elaine's piece a runner-up and gave it a staged reading in Portland in March 2016. The same play received a full production by Gallery Players of Brooklyn, New York, in June 2016.

At her new home in Topsham, Elaine spent the winter of 2016-17 adapting other existing stories into one-act plays. A Maine-set dark comedy called "Elwood's Last Job" received a full production in the 2017 Maine Playwrights Festival. At her death she left six completed one-act plays, four of them yet to be produced.

Industriousness; openness to new forms (historical fiction, plays, light verse for children, newspaper op-eds); willingness to adapt (turning stories into plays, fictionalizing family history, using fact for a story's skeleton when pure invention flags); inextinguishable curiosity. And a sharp eye for telling detail. All these characterize Elaine Ford as a writer. Most are also her personal characteristics.

Looking at her body of work, published and unpublished, a shift in setting from one novel or story to another seems less important than how richly each setting is evoked—rural or urban, domestic or foreign, present day or centuries past. "As the novel progresses," a reviewer wrote in *The Washington Post* about *Monkey Bay*, "the characters become more and more identified with the harsh, craggy landscape in which they live." Similar things might be said of the protagonists of *Missed Connections* and *Ivory Bright*, although their Somerville landscape is hardly craggy. The point is that in all these books, place is important—is used.

More significant are the continuities in Elaine's fiction, whatever the setting. She is a writer with a worldview. "What happens to you largely comes out of who you are," she told an interviewer the year after *Monkey Bay* was published, "and who you are is constrained by the circumstances in which you find yourself." This statement applies to the protagonists in that novel; to those in the Somerville books; to Kori in the story "The Depth of Winter"; to both Lynette Bragg and John Scarano in "Suicide"; and to great-great-grandfather Thomas Lawson Ford, the hard-luck Alabama cotton planter.

"I have always been drawn to write about characters who are

marginalized by class, ethnicity, physical appearance, or geographical location," Elaine wrote on her website, "and about those afflicted by bad luck or devotion to causes doomed to failure."

A reader of *Ivory Bright* once wrote to complain that at the book's conclusion it was "too easy" for the writer "to allow Ivory to accept her [unsatisfactory] life with resignation." Elaine replied in a brief essay titled "Not All Endings Are Happy," published in *The Eloquent Edge: 15 Maine Women Writers* in 1989. "Everybody, including me, yearns for happy endings. The trouble is, life doesn't work that way. People are still sorting out their mistakes and misalliances the day they drop. Most of us do not have the luxury of starting over. . . . It would be lovely if happy endings could be clapped onto lives and novels could honestly reflect that. But it seems to me that the day-to-day living with one's choices is the very essence of life. And for me the whole point of writing is to tell it like it is, not like I wish it were. As long as I'm doing that, I'll have to continue to let my characters struggle on, and on, and finally make the best peace they can."

In February 2017 Elaine was fully functioning, distressed by the election of President Donald Trump but fulfilled and happy in her personal life. She looked forward to a May canal-barge trip in France and to two summer writing projects. She was healthy, so she thought. But the next month suddenly brought her severe neurological symptoms and the diagnosis of an incurable brain tumor. She underwent surgery in April and prescribed radiation in May and June, but these failed to prolong her life or maintain its quality. At the end of June, Elaine chose to abandon treatment and entered a hospice program in her home. She died August 27, 2017.

Sources

Estill, Katie. "Lives of Choice and Chance." *The Washington Post,* July 25, 1989.

Ford, Elaine. "Not All Endings Are Happy." *The Eloquent Edge: 15 Maine Women Writers,* edited by Kathleen Lignell and Margery Wilson. Bar Harbor, Maine: Acadia Publishing, 1989.

Ford, Elaine. "The Lopsided Tree." *Family Chronicle,* November 2014.

Landry, Peter. "Ebb and Flow of Time and Fortune among a Coastal Clan." *The Philadelphia Inquirer*, August 6, 1989.

Machin, Linda. "A Different Story on Cambridge." *The Boston Globe,* November 13, 1980.

Mosher, Howard Frank. "Far from Kennebunkport." *The New York Times Book Review,* August 6, 1989.

Private correspondence with Richard I. Ford, Marc Grigorov, Harvey Kail, Kurtis Scaletta, Steven Ford Scott.

Walker, David. "Out of Order: the Lives of People Who Hang Out in Laundromats." *Preview!,* Ellsworth, Maine, August 24, 1990.

www.elainefordauthor.com/about

An expanded version of this essay appears at www.elainefordauthor.com.

ACKNOWLEDGMENTS

Some of the stories in *This Time Might Be Different* have been previously published, in different form:

"The Depth of Winter." *Passages North.* Winter/Spring 2004.

"Suicide." *North American Review.* May–August 2001.

"In the Marrow." *Night Train.* Spring 2004.

"Bent Reeds." *The Quotable Moose: A Contemporary Maine Reader.* Hanover, New Hampshire, 1994.

"Elwood's Last Job." *Nebraska Review.* Summer 2003. Reprinted in *Contemporary Maine Fiction*. Camden, Maine: Down East Books, 2005.

"Button, Needle, Thread." *Colorado Review.* Spring 2001.

"Fire Escape." *Phantasmagoria.* Winter 2002.

"Dragon Palaces." *Talking River Review.* Winter 2000.

"Why Men Love to Cut Things Down." *Chariton Review.* Fall 2013.

"Junk." *The Eloquent Edge: 15 Maine Women Writers.* Bar Harbor, Maine: Acadia Publishing, 1989.

"Millennium Bug." *The Flexible Persona.* Fall 2016.

"Original Brasses, Fine Patina." *The Marriage Bed.* Wordrunner eChapbooks. November 2015. http://echapbook.com/fiction/ford

"The Rock As Big As the Queen Mary." *Colorado Review.* Fall 1997.